Diamond Jubilee:
Sherlock Holmes, Mark Twain,
and the Peril of the Empire

Paul Schullery

Paperback ISBN 978-1-78705-367-0
ePub ISBN 978-1-78705-368-7
PDF ISBN 978-1-78705-369-4

Published in the UK by MX Publishing
335 Princess Park Manor, Royal Drive,
London, N11 3GX
www.sherlockholmesbooks.com

Cover design by Brian Belanger

Fiction by Paul Schullery

Shupton's Fancy: A Tale of the Fly-Fishing Obsession

The Time Traveler's Tale: Chronicle of a Morlock Captivity

Diamond Jubilee: Sherlock Holmes, Mark Twain, and the Peril of the Empire

for Rick Balkin

Table of Contents

As the Queen was returning to Buckingham Palace yesterday afternoon, she witnessed an accident in St. James Park. Two men had climbed a tree to witness the passage of the Procession along the Mall, and just as the Queen's carriage was opposite the tree the two men fell. The Queen did not stop at the time, and thus delay the Procession, but as soon as she reached the Palace she directed an officer to inquire and report as to the nature of the accident. Her Majesty was subsequently informed, through the medium of Sir Arthur Bigge, that one of the men had been rather badly hurt and had been taken to St. George's Hospital.

The Standard [London], June 23, 1897

Chapter One:
The Other Distinguished Guest

"Watson," Holmes said, looking up from the pile of newspaper cuttings on his lap, "Your fidgeting is unseemly for such a fine day."

I stopped pacing and turned to the window. "I suppose it's the weather," I said nonsensically, looking out on a perfectly splendid June day. The only clouds I could see above the houses down our row were of the least threatening sort, gold-rimmed and glowing in the late afternoon sun.

"Ah, you have enlisted in the legions of worriers, then," he said, and returned to his sorting.

I had, indeed, become one of those vexed souls. Spread in our thousands, if not millions, across the land—but particularly across the city—we intended through sheer force of Christian will to reshape the barometrical isobars of the North Atlantic and ensure that Tuesday next be not merely free of rain, but of such surpassing meteorological glory that jubilation would suffuse the very air. Our Queen deserved no less.

"And in the midst of these meditations have you found the leisure to secure our places?" He asked this through teeth clamped around the stem of a cold and undistinguished clay pipe, his recent favorite.

"My editor has things all arranged. I would have preferred St. Paul's, but he guarantees us the best of vantage points in the Strand. Somewhere near Somerset House, though on the north side. He assures me there is nothing to worry about in the construction of our grandstand."

"It had not occurred to me to worry about that," Holmes said. "Is it too late, or should I begin now?"

"Oh, there's been some stew in the papers over public safety. Throwing up all these rickety wooden stands along the procession route, and stacking hundreds of people on them, you know. Makes the old maids nervous. Temporary workmanship and all that. The prospect of a tier of citizens pitching over into smoking rubble just as the Queen passes by has the alarmists in its grip." Holmes gave me a raised eyebrow, as if to congratulate me on my much more sensible and productive fretting over the weather, but said nothing. "But it appears that the construction of our stand is being overseen by the most prudent of contractors."

I hesitated before continuing, not sure how Holmes would respond to this next. "However, what with all that flammable bunting and raw wood, there is some talk of banning smoking entirely."

"Is there?" He seemed unperturbed. "Well, I suppose heroic measures are called for."

It was a small remark, but along with several other quiet signs over the past fortnight—including his easy sarcasm—it reassured me greatly. Sherlock Holmes had gone into the previous winter with his reserves depleted, and his pace had been grueling ever since. He fancied that he flourished on overwork, but eventually the toll was too great even for his extraordinary constitution. That beastly business in Mullion Cove in March was followed by an unrelenting succession of exhausting and not terribly satisfying little problems. Except for the matter of the Tibetan entomologist, none of his recent cases had done more than annoy him with their tedious hours and transparent solutions. Knowing Holmes' apolitical disposition, I had little hope that the Queen's Jubilee, just now filling the papers and engaging the nation with its anticipatory excitement and impending pageantry, would distract him, so I was delighted to see that he was pulling himself out of his distracted fatigue.

I was about to elaborate on the arrangements for our seats when a hansom separated itself from the thinning flow of traffic and scraped to a stop against the kerb.

"Holmes," I announced, as I watched a most singular figure alight from the cab, "We are about to receive a distinguished guest." I could not keep a bit of thrill from my voice.

"What? Now?" Holmes frowned at the clock in surprise. "She's two hours early."

"It's not a woman, Holmes. It's a man. A very famous man."

"Ah! That explains it, then," he said, setting aside his pipe and newspaper slips and rising to face the door.

I had no time to press Holmes for an explanation of "it" before there was a series of sharp raps on the door. Without a pause, it burst open to reveal Mrs. Hudson attempting to usher an older and very agitated man into the room.

But he was unusherable. Without waiting for Mrs. Hudson's introduction, he rushed across the room, hand extended toward my companion. "Mr. Sherlock Holmes, my name is Sam Clemens, and I need your help."

Chapter Two
Sam Clemens Dithers

"Welcome, Mr. Clemens," said Holmes, extending his own hand. As they shook, their eyes met fully. During my years in close company with the great man, I had learned a little about his incredible capacity for concealing his true feelings; he was a master of what Americans call the "poker face." But just for an instant when their eyes first met, too briefly for even Clemens to notice, Holmes' face involuntarily revealed something very like shock. At first I thought I had seen sorrow, but then realised that it was more like awe. I wondered if perhaps it was the result of belated recognition of our guest, who was at that time the most celebrated writer—indeed, the most beloved person—in the English-speaking world. But I also knew that Holmes was of all people the least impressed with celebrity.

"This is my friend and colleague Dr. Watson," Holmes continued in his most cordial manner, turning Clemens toward me as he released his hand.

"Yes, I expect so. I have read your books," Clemens said as he dutifully shook my hand. He gave the impression right then of someone speaking in great haste, but in fact his words came out rather slowly. His expression as he spoke to me was noncommittal, almost disinterested. His grip was firm and warm, but quite briefly held, as one might expect from someone who must have dispensed many thousands of handshakes to long lines of admirers over the years.

"And I yours, Mr. Clemens," I replied, "It is a great honor to meet you." At this his expression warmed slightly, though I was just then realising that by announcing that he had read my books he was not necessarily intending to compliment me on them.

Holmes, noticing my excitement, directed Clemens toward a chair. "I surmise that Mrs. Hudson was preparing tea when you arrived. Won't you join us?" He nodded reassuringly at the somewhat flustered Mrs. Hudson, who turned to leave.

"Yes, thank you. That would be nice," he said to us. Then, to himself, in a distracted undertone, "Tea," and he fell heavily into the chair. At the sound of the chair's creaking objection to this sudden hostility, Mrs. Hudson's questioning face reappeared for a moment at the door, but then with the slightest shake of her head she hurried off.

As we settled in our own chairs, I had my first moment to study our guest in relative repose (though even sitting still he gave a great impression of anxious, almost strenuous activity). Thanks to my long association with Sherlock Holmes, I have met many of the great men and women of our day, and I long ago recognised the effects that reputation and fame have on first impressions. One is almost irresistibly predisposed in these meetings to be impressed and even intimidated. Whatever belittling things we mortals may say among ourselves about our politicians and social leaders—as we pontificate over our pints and our dinners—it is a heady business, this coming face to face with the world's mighty.

Despite my supposed worldliness in this line, I was quite simply starstruck. Samuel Clemens was, to my mind, possessed of the most remarkable combination of dignity and animation imaginable. Though actually slight, his bearing made him seem somehow robust. But there was no use in studying the physical presence of the man. The effect of that leonine gray mane, and those fierce eyes blazing out from under their luxuriantly cave-like brows, and that likewise bushy moustache, was to bring instantly to mind a parading host of literary images—I felt in the simultaneous presence of every riverboat pilot and cowboy, scoundrel and saint, commoner and king, who had peopled the pages of his books. I was, in short, nearly addled by my boyish glee at meeting the author of so many books of blessed memory. Unlike some of my fellow citizens who took silly offence at this or that historical fantasy of Clemens' pen, I doted on every word.

But Holmes was already getting to business and, knowing that my observations and impressions were often of value to him, I shook off my elation and attended to the conversation.

"How might we help you, Mr. Clemens?" Holmes reached for his pipe and matches.

Clemens' response was somewhat brusque, almost indignant, as if the two of them were already in the midst of a heated argument. "I am sure you can imagine, Mr. Holmes, that I have friends in London, in fact throughout this sweet land of yours."

"That much is plainly obvious." Holmes said encouragingly, lighting his pipe.

"Some of them are of the highest rank. They are very powerful people, Mr. Holmes, and no less the good for it."

"It is a priceless combination of qualities," Holmes responded with all appearances of a most earnest sincerity.

"They have always helped me, not only with my work but with my slightest whim. They pamper me. They spoil me like a willful child. They would do anything to make me happy and content."

"Few of us are so fortunate. Do I take it from your tone of voice that now they have in some way failed you?" Holmes was showing more than usual patience at this oblique approach to whatever subject must eventually come to hand. I thought it nicely deferential of my friend to let the great man get to his story in his own way, though I could see that Clemens himself was struggling—frowning, then sighing with resignation.

"Perhaps they have, though to admit it would pain them even more than it does me."

Holmes' demeanor and voice had lost none of their sympathy as he said, "On the other hand, it is to their enviable advantage that they, at least, must have some slight idea of what you are talking about."

For only an instant, Clemens stared at Holmes as if not comprehending. Then his face, indeed his entire being, turned into one immense smile. Whatever dire circumstance oppressed him, he recognised a wit that was, after all, in some peculiar way much like his own, and it brought him to himself. He visibly relaxed for the first time, easing back into his chair. "Gentlemen," he said, taking in both of us with a glance, "forgive me. I have been dithering, and you have been patient."

Just then Mrs. Hudson reappeared with her tray, and while we fussed over our tea and cakes Clemens continued, becoming suddenly direct and blunt. "I feel certain that I am under some threat of violence. Worse, my family may be unsafe as well. Believe me when I assure you that I have turned to my friends, and they have done all they could, but my fears remain. I am in grave danger."

Clemens paused, seemed to have a thought and turn away from it, then continued. "But you need facts. Here they are. Last year, just a little earlier than this, I was speaking here and there in South Africa."

"This would have been toward the end of your world tour?" Holmes interrupted.

"Yes, of course," Clemens said. "One of my outings in Africa was in Johannesburg. The Standard is a large house, but the manager saw no reason to be inhibited by architecture, and stuffed the place with additional chairs. I even shared the stage with semi-circles of temporary seating, filled with well-fed local merchants and their wives, who paid handsomely to be seen up there with me. Despite the generous revenue, I might have resented our repeated inhalation of each other's atoms of air at such close quarters, but for the knowledge that mine were enriched by the germs of a vile cold I'd been suffering for some days. I confess that this gave me a kind of moral edge that braced me up as the evening wore on. I tried my best to declaim in their direction whenever I could."

Clemens took a bite of cake that raised his eyebrows in appreciation. "I generally talk for an hour and a half or so, and except when I am actually reading from a text my eyes are always on my audience. Their mood and responses are my inspiration. More important, they are my guide, not just to how the evening is going but to how I might redirect it. The audience is a miraculous creature, you know; it sees itself as passive, like a cow, but it rules the stage with a merciless tyranny. My listeners never seem to sense how utterly in command of me they are, bless them.

"Anyway, there with me up front, in the last semicircle of temporary seating, stage left, against a deep burgundy curtain that I suppose must have shielded him from most of the audience, sat a most striking individual. Judging from his seated stature in comparison with those near him, he was of normal height, and I can't tell you a thing about his dress except that if it hadn't been of the best quality I would have noticed it and he would have stuck out in that costly a crowd.

"There were two unforgettable features about him, though. The first was his, well, what in America we call a wall eye. Are you familiar with the term?"

"You refer to a corneal leucoma," I said.

"You're the doctor, and I trust your diagnosis," Clemens said, "but I would call it a magnum. The very shape of his skull seemed altered to accommodate the thing. And it wasn't just a dull white; it had a kind of glow, even in the subdued light of the hall."

"That effect is sometimes noted, but is theorised to be the result of our unfamiliarity with the opalescence of the eye in such an unexpected context," I said.

"What context do you mean?" asked Clemens.

"The face. The eye stands out because it doesn't fit our idea of what a normal eye in a normal face should look like. To some observers the contrast is strong enough to make the eye seem disproportionately large, or even to glow," I said.

"That may be." Clemens seemed unconvinced, but let it go. "The other thing about him was his hair."

"Excuse me, Mr. Clemens," Holmes interrupted. "Which eye was it?"

"The right."

"Thank you. And what about his hair?"

"It was a peculiar straw colour, and of the wildest disorder. Gentlemen, I have some personal acquaintance with unruly hair. Besides my own, I mean." His glance flickered upward toward his brow. "Years ago, in our western mining camps, I saw men who had for years practiced the most perfect abstinence from the comb—from soap and water, for that matter. These were men whose clothes were so thoroughly interwoven with the hair on their trunks and arms that eventually the garments had to be shaved off—true monks of the wilderness, the most devout of their order. But I have not seen anything to match the absolutely anarchic statement that man's hair was making that night in Johannesburg."

"And was it of great length?" Holmes asked.

"No, that's the most memorable thing about it. It could not have been more than a few inches long. It did not cover his ears, though it might have, had it been persuaded in that direction. It looked like the result of some tragic experiment in electrical conduction. There were tight little curls here and there, and a few strangely arcing cowlicks, but mostly it was just a spiky thatch. It brought to mind . . . *agriculture.*

"Was this man alone?"

"If you mean did he seem to be accompanied by anyone else, like a woman, no. In fact, the seat next to his may have been vacant, though considering the circumstances that seems unlikely. I saw him speak to no one, and I noticed that he did not leave his seat during the intermission. Once I noticed him, you can understand, it was hard not to be at least peripherally aware of his presence."

Clemens paused. "I might as well confess that he soon obsessed me, though not because of his distracting appearance. It was because he didn't react to what I said. Worse, he didn't laugh. Some people are slow starters, of course, so for the first few moments I wasn't bothered. But he never weakened." Clemens shook his head, still baffled by the memory.

"I am not accustomed to having my humour fought off so successfully. My best deliveries ran off him like a thin rain. I took that as a challenge, of course, and if the evening was a success with the rest of my audience, it was in part because I worked so hard just to make that stone-faced man laugh. After an hour I would have settled for a chuckle. At the last, a smirk would have thrilled me, even to know that he found humour in my failure to amuse him. But I failed. Not a giggle—not even a twitch that might have suggested the thought of a grin. He was invulnerable to me. It was humiliating.

"Well," Clemens drew back from his subject. "I didn't mean to go on. The point is that you can perhaps imagine my surprise when, a week ago I saw that man again. I had been in to visit my publisher, Chatto and Windus, on St. Martin's Lane just up from the church, you know. My visit was over, and I had just emerged from their building and was walking, let's see, south, down toward the square."

"Trafalgar, you mean?"

"Right."

"Still on St. Martin's?" Holmes asked.

"Yes," Clemens nodded. "I came out and had just barely turned to walk south. I intended to find a cab, but felt a need to stroll a bit. Something, I don't know what, made me look at the passing traffic; the sidewalk's not the widest in through there. Specifically, my attention was drawn to a trade van coming toward me. There was a driver, who I don't recall well, and next to him was that man from the Standard Theatre. I can't tell you the shock I felt to see that big, unforgettable face staring back at me. As soon as our eyes met, he quite literally snarled, obviously in dismay at being seen by me. He turned toward the driver and fled into the van's interior, but by then the van was past and I could see no more. It was one of those vans with the recessed seats, you know; the men were not in the open, and from the side I could barely see them on the seat."

Clemens paused. "I have wondered if when he first saw me he involuntarily exclaimed, and that is what caused me to look in his direction, but I don't actually recall hearing any such sound."

"By 'van' you don't mean 'dray,' do you?" Holmes' interest was high.

"No, just a larger sort of one-horse van, closed top, such as might haul produce."

"More a trade van than a parcel van then. Anything distinctive about it? Lettering? Trim?"

"No, and that is what struck me later as I thought about it. It was the least distinctive, almost as if made to disappear into the traffic. I'm not even sure of its exact colour, though it was dark, probably a slate gray. No trim or lettering, at least that I saw."

"And the horse?"

"Just the one," said Clemens. "Brown, I suppose, or at least dark. I'm afraid I'm not much of a horseman and don't notice their finer points; well, beyond knowing a plug when I see one."

"A good animal?"

"Nothing distinguished."

"Could you identify the driver?"

"No. I don't even recall what he was wearing, except perhaps a floppy cap of some sort. He didn't interest me at that moment."

"Quite understandable. What else do you recall about the Johannesburg man?"

"*His* dress I do remember. It was all gray, an old suit, I think. He was bare-headed.

Holmes said, "Mr. Clemens, I realise that you have already said so, but may I assume that you are absolutely certain it was the same man?"

"Mr. Holmes," Clemens said, leaning forward a bit and speaking in his most intense tone, "you *must* assume that. I have heard of your skills, even besides the doctor's little romances about your work. Certain of my London friends speak of your powers of observation in tones approaching reverence. But I have my own skills in that way—as a writer it is my job, my very passion, to take in my surroundings. I survive only by my capacity to do so. I recognised this man thoroughly and absolutely. Any differences caused by the location or his dress were of no more consequence to my

11

recognition of him than if your mother arrived before your eyes wearing a new coat."

"We will regard the matter as settled then," said Holmes. I was momentarily distracted; though of course I knew something of Holmes' background, the idea of him having a mother still took me by surprise.

Holmes continued. "The likelihood of twins seems ruled out by the damaged eye."

"Twins," said Clemens with a sudden smile. "I had not thought about twins. Funny that it didn't occur to me."

"It *was* the right eye on this man too, was it not?" Holmes' glance narrowed slightly.

Clemens' vision turned inward for a moment as he reviewed his memory. "Yes, no question."

"Mr. Clemens," Holmes said, "I can understand why this sudden and admittedly strange apparition would upset you, especially considering the man's suspicious behavior upon being discovered by you. But I am not sure why it has alarmed you to so great an extent."

"I'm not finished. At first it didn't. It just seemed very, very odd. In fact, it set me thinking about a story in which I might use it. I'm fascinated by coincidence, and this seemed most likely to be just an extreme case—in fact, it seemed the kind of coincidence that would not be tolerated in fiction because it placed too great a strain on probability. Readers experience far greater coincidences in their own lives than they will tolerate in the fiction they read. By the time I returned home it was just a niggling uneasiness in the back of my mind."

"Home is in Chelsea?" Holmes asked.

"Yes, Tedworth Square. We took a place there, let's see, last October, for me to work on my world-tour book. But I have kept it quiet."

Clemens' last statement was along the lines of a question—how could Holmes know where Clemens lived?—but Holmes said nothing except, "And once you returned home?"

"I didn't mention it to Livy—my wife—but later that evening I found myself unaccountably dwelling on that face. I do not loathe or look down on those whose misfortunes are beyond their control, but I found something deeply unsettling about that face, Mr. Holmes. After a while the mood passed, and I went to bed. The next day I felt more easy about it, and about mid-day I went out, just walking down to the tobacconist."

"This would have been last Saturday, then?" Holmes interrupted.

"No, I guess it was Friday. Yes, Friday. It would have been about one o'clock. I was out of the house no more than fifteen minutes. As I was returning and had approached within about three houses of my own, that same van rounded the corner just behind me in a great rush. It rattled past me only to come to a reckless stop directly across from my house! Even from behind the van I could see that the horse almost lost its footing when the driver pulled it up so brutally."

"Did you recognise the . . . " Holmes began, but was cut off by Clemens.

"In a minute, Mr. Holmes, in a minute," Clemens insisted hastily, patting the air toward Holmes with his open hand. "No sooner had the van stopped than the door to my house opened, and a man ran out—it was that wall-eyed fellow, no mistake about it! He sprinted across the street and leapt onto the footstep of the van, which was already underway. Before he was properly in, it raced off, turning the next corner on two wheels, and was then out of sight. The whole shocking episode took less than a minute."

"But your family!" I burst in, causing both men to turn to me.

"Precisely my sentiments at that moment, Doctor," Clemens said. "I won't leave you in the awful suspense I felt during the moment it took me to rush back to the house. They were fine; everyone happened to be upstairs. They saw and heard nothing. They had no idea someone had been in the house; in fact the maid doesn't entirely believe me yet. But he

13

was. I saw him, and I never knew such dread as I felt when he ran from my home."

Holmes, now completely absorbed in this strange episode, said, "You must have gotten a better look at the driver this time."

"I did," Clemens said. "I didn't recognise him, but he looked, well, vaguely like someone I might have known, somewhere. It has bothered me the past few days, trying to place that familiarity."

Noticing Holmes' look of further expectation, Clemens said, "But you want specifics, I suppose. He was slight, in fact he was very thin, body and head both, the literary type of a 'hatchet face.' His suit of clothes was a light brown, no apparent stripe; his face was without doubt that of a white man, but darkly tanned. He drove past me without a glance; he wore gloves. I'm not sure he noticed me."

Holmes looked a little doubtful about this last statement. Samuel Clemens would have been a hard man to miss, even on a quiet street. "Did anything new strike you about the van this time?"

"I barely noticed it, beyond it seeming to be the same one. I got a better look at the horse, though. It was an older chestnut, well groomed I think. Nothing special. Its tail was cropped; you know, the way some are. Not the kindest thing to do to a horse, I always thought."

"Bobbed?"

"No, just cut short, half a foot or so, and rather a ragged job of it."

Holmes considered this, then said, "I assume that it was at this point that you involved the police, or your friends?"

"Immediately, Mr. Holmes."

"Then let us begin our analysis of this alarming situation with them."

Chapter Three
The Doggedness Problem

Clemens shifted in his chair and drained his tea cup. "It is my experience with the authorities that has brought me here, Mr. Holmes. I immediately related this story to my good friend and publisher, Andrew Chatto."

"You did not contact the police yourself?" asked Holmes.

"No," Clemens shook his head, as if baffled by his own answer. He glanced rather blankly around the room—his eyes briefly registering surprised recognition as they came to the portrait of the American divine Henry Ward Beecher—then he returned his attention to us. "You see, due to our recent family tragedy—my daughter Susy, you know, passed away last year—we have been in virtual hiding." Clemens' expression darkened and his voice became flat and quiet as he mentioned this loss. "We simply could not face the stream of well-wishers, to say nothing of the flood of random visitors that have been a part of our lives for so long."

"Apparently the secret was not so well kept as it seemed," allowed Holmes.

"Apparently not," agreed Clemens. "The past few months more and more people have knocked on the door, and it has not helped our state of mind. But we remain as quiet and remote as we can. I . . . we . . . are not prepared for an onslaught of attention yet, Mr. Holmes. Susy was . . . well, I doubt my wife will ever recover entirely, and I am sure I will not."

"Grief is a very devil," said Holmes, whose sympathy for Clemens' suffering brought this surprising observation from a man whom I had never known to grieve.

"Mr. Holmes, it was the shock of my life to have reached such age as mine and still have no idea of the truth of that." Abruptly, Clemens straightened and forcefully shook off this line of conversation. "Here's the thing. The appearance of this new problem, however frightening it might be, and for all that it proved how poorly kept our secret has been, has changed none of that. We still need the utmost privacy. My dropping around to the police station and reporting this prowler to some random desk officer hardly seemed likely to protect those needs. I am sure that the press here, as in America, haunt the precinct offices."

"They do. It is one of their more ghoulish practices, but it serves them well" agreed Holmes. "So instead, you turned to a discreet friend."

Clemens nodded eagerly. "The most discreet. The most time-tested. Perhaps not as formidable socially or politically as some I might have called upon, but without question the most devoted and trustworthy. And as near as I can tell, Andrew—Mr. Chatto—proved as good as my faith in him. I don't know to whom *he* turned with my problem, but it seemed only moments before I was visited by two apparently distinguished inspectors from Scotland Yard, men whom Andrew later informed me were universally regarded as the finest on the force."

"Forgive my interruption; their names?" Holmes asked, and gave me a glance that signified he already guessed the answer.

"Gregson. Lestrade. I will not pretend to have been all that impressed with them myself; neither struck me as the brightest candle in the chandelier. Very businesslike, very thorough, yes, but another descriptive term might be more on the mark—perhaps *plodding*. Yes, that is it; they have about them a doggedness that must serve them well in tracking down your garden variety hatchet murderer or pickpocket but that seems to lack a certain urgency, if you know what I mean."

"We have had some acquaintance with both," said Holmes in a flat voice, but with his customary professional courtesy he refrained from any further comment on their respective abilities.

"Well, their complete failure to turn up any information about this man was at first no surprise to me. London is a huge city. They were good enough to station men near the house, and I must say they were sufficiently discreet about this, and the men have been likewise; it will be some time before the presence of police near the house calls undue attention to us. Our neighbours seem hardly to have noticed. But you will understand that this is only a small comfort. I don't want my family to be in danger. Beyond that, even as constrained as our social outings and my business travel have been, we cannot live under permanent guard. For one thing, I have agreed to cover next week's events—the Jubilee, I mean—for the American press. A ring of bodyguards will just call more attention to me."

"Have the inspectors proposed any theories? Do they seem to be following up any leads, or developing hypotheses?" Holmes asked this in his most emotionless, nonjudgmental tone. I imagine he saw no point in further undermining Clemens' already shaky faith in his appointed officers.

"Gregson . . ." Clemens began, then paused, "or was it Lestrade? They hardly speak directly to one another, so I never have their names reinforced for me while they're in sight. Anyway, it was the one who looks, if you'll pardon me, a little like an aging rat . . ."

"Lestrade," Holmes and I offered in unison.

"Yes. He hasn't said so, but I can tell from his tone of voice that he thinks it's nothing more than an attempt at petty theft on my house, and that my sighting of the wall-eyed man near Trafalgar was just coincidence, or even a problem of mistaken identity on my part."

"And Gregson?" Holmes' impatience with the inspectors was at last beginning to leak through in the slightest hardness in his voice.

Clemens thought for a moment, then said, "Gregson seems the more inventive of the two; he doesn't seem very concerned either, but once or twice he has admitted that there is a remote chance of a plot to kidnap me or a member of my family, presumably for some absurd ransom."

No one spoke for a moment. Holmes relaxed back into his chair and asked the most needed question. "And you, Mr. Clemens? What do you make of this startling chain of events?

Who are these men, and why would they be taking such an interest in you?"

"There's no doubt in it, Mr. Holmes. It's my book. I recently finished it. Well," he started, then paused, then continued, "'finished it' in the sense that it's now more or less sufficiently big for the purpose. My family and friends could probably provide you with several recent dates on which I have announced that it was done. Big, complicated books"— here Clemens gave me a brief, sidelong glance, as if especially concerned that I be aware of the difference between such demanding literary undertakings as his and the little "romances" that I wrote— "can take considerable finishing, as one must often re-read, reconsider, reconstruct, rebalance, all that sort of thing, until the book feels whole."

Then, as if aware of the possibly pretentious sound of this, he gave a slight and possibly chagrined smile and added, "Besides, in my branch of the trade, books are sold like flour— by weight. A successful book has to have just the right raw bulk before the publisher is convinced that it will satisfy the marketplace." He shrugged, smiled almost sheepishly at the air in front of him, and said, "As a literary craftsman, I seem to have the necessary gift for bulk."

As if realising that this was another unnecessary digression, Clemens hurried on. "Anyway, in this new book I take strong positions regarding the unfortunate adventuring of certain members of Her Majesty's government in Africa. Very strong positions. As I am sure you must know, I am by no means alone in holding these views; many people share my outrage at the behavior of Rhodes and his toadies. But if this book sells even half as well as we have every reason to expect it will, my voice—and I am forced to sound immodest here though I am merely stating fact—might add considerable, perhaps unbearable, weight to world opinion against these actions. I believe that someone wants to prevent my voice from being heard on this matter; they want me silenced. Someone, whether connected directly to Rhodes or perhaps only in some kind of twisted commercial sympathy with him, is prepared to go to great and vile lengths to delay, or maybe even prevent, the publication of my book."

"Then the man who broke into your house was looking for the manuscript of this book?" Holmes asked.

"He surely was," said Clemens, now almost as agitated as when he entered our rooms. "His appearance outside my publisher's offices probably had similar motivations. These are not coincidental events. Perhaps he plans to break into those offices as well, to ensure that no copies of the manuscript survive. Maybe when I saw him that first time, he was just driving by for a look at the place."

"But you have no idea who, specifically, might be behind such actions?"

"None whatever." Clemens shook his head. "Or every idea possible; the field is wide open, and my low opinion of Rhodes himself allows me to imagine that even he could be the instigator of it all. But as far as anything concrete, no, I have nothing to go on."

While Holmes thought about this, Clemens looked at each of us in turn, and his expression softened. "My writings have not always been, strictly speaking, well, *courteous* to England, or to Her Majesty and her government. I do not know how either of you gentlemen feel about what I have said." Clemens paused briefly, almost expectantly, as if hoping one of us might reassure him that we held no grudges, and I had a brief thrill of realisation, even of an odd sort of fulfillment: for an instant, the world's greatest writer had reason to hope that I approved of his work.

When neither of us responded, Clemens went on. "But even in my distaste for certain episodes in British history, or certain characters in those episodes, I have never wavered in my admiration for this country and the ideals of its monarchy. After all, I have often been as blunt in my comments on my own government, to say nothing of my treatment of my fellow American citizens. It is what a writer does, commenting on his times." There was almost a pleading tone in these words. My God, I thought, the great man was near to tying himself in knots in his concern that Holmes or I would reject him because his deathless literary works might have in some way distressed us! I was about to object and reassure him when again he continued.

"These recent events, this whole mystery of the wall-eyed man, did not commence in a happy or emotionally sound household. We are, as I have said, a mess. It is only our love for each other that has kept us from complete collapse. The strain of this added crisis—which I was for obvious reasons unable to keep from my family—is enormous. In the past few days, I have watched the thin fabric of sanity that we spent the entire winter weaving begin to unravel again.

"For all I know, your earnest Scotland Yard professionals are, as we speak, trailing these scoundrels in some alleyway, and will arrest them in moments. More likely, however, they are not, and will not, but will continue to slog along for however many weeks or months it takes to exhaust their customary procedures. Mr. Holmes . . . Dr. Watson . . . We do not have that kind of time. Is there anything that you can do?"

Holmes did not hesitate. "I am sure there is, and whatever we can do, Mr. Clemens, we will. We will begin promptly in the morning. Indeed, we would begin now were we not expecting another guest momentarily." Clemens started, whether from fear that our attentions would be divided or from embarrassment that he had intruded on our plans for evening I could not tell, but Holmes hastened to reassure him. "Don't be concerned; this visitor comes on a much simpler matter. I do not anticipate that it will interfere with our investigation of your case." Clemens did not seem especially reassured by Holmes' words, but apparently sensing a kind of dismissal in them, he stood to leave.

"I did not mean that you must hurry off, but yes, perhaps it is best that you do return to your family," said Holmes. "And for the time being, I suggest that you stay as close to home as you can. Give your police guards your fullest cooperation. With any luck we will clear this matter up well before the Jubilee. In the meantime, put your faith in the inspectors, and even more in those constables who are guarding your home. I have known many of the regulars on the police force, and they excel at precisely this work."

As we all rose and Clemens turned to go, Holmes added, "Oh, and leave us the best means of reaching you, if you don't mind; I imagine that more questions will come to mind." Clemens dutifully took a scrap of paper from his coat pocket and scribbled on it, handing it to me. Even in my absorption in the details of this new case, I had the presence of mind to promise myself that this particular little documentary memento would find its way into my own files, rather than into Holmes'.

At the door, Clemens halted and turned back toward us. "That reminds me, Mr. Holmes. My wife and daughters gave me firm instructions to inform you that you were to feel free to come and question them. 'Interrogate' was the word my daughters used, I believe." He allowed himself a small grin as he took in both of us in one glance and said, "They are avid readers of Dr. Watson's books, I sometimes fear even in preference to mine." With that, he closed the door very quietly behind himself, and I could not even make out his soft footsteps as he descended the stairs to the waiting cab.

Chapter Four
The Grief of the World

"Well, Holmes," I said, "I know we've had many distinguished guests, but I must say that was a delightful surprise, having Mark Twain right here at Baker Street!" My exhilaration at meeting the author of so many beloved tales began to bubble up even before the door had closed.

"Who?" said Holmes.

"Mark Twain. The man we just interviewed."

"I am at a disadvantage, Watson. I am certain that he introduced himself as Sam Clemens."

"Yes, yes, of course, that's his real name, but he writes under the pen name of Mark Twain. Surely, you . . ." Holmes' expression was blank. The appalling truth suddenly dawned on me. "Holmes, you don't mean to say that you have not heard of Mark Twain?"

"You seem to think I should have. I gather that his books are well known?"

"Well known?! Holmes, he is the world's most famous story teller—*Adventures of Huckleberry Finn? A Yankee at the Court of King Arthur? Adventures of Tom Sawyer?*" To my astonishment, no light of recognition appeared in Holmes' eyes at the mention of these titles. "Can it really be that you have not read . . . ." My question fizzled out and I stood staring dumbly at my friend.

"Perhaps I should. Do you think they would help us with his case?"

This proposal stirred me from my mute surprise, at least to the point of—to use Clemens' word—*dithering*. "But you knew all about him. You were aware of his world tour, of his political connections, where he lived . . . . You seemed as familiar with his career and reputation as I!"

"You know my methods, Watson. It was a simple matter to deduce those few details of his life from his words and his appearance. If you thought of it a moment, I am sure you would realise that determining his address was even

simpler. You must have observed that his left knee . . . ."
Holmes was interrupted by a light ringing of our bell, and he
said, "Ah! That must be our other guest."

It is only as I write this that I remember that I never
did remember to ask Holmes how Samuel Clemens' left knee
could have revealed a Chelsea address. However, my inability
to hold that question in my mind at the time still seems quite
understandable to me, because only seconds later, Mrs.
Hudson tapped on the door, then ushered into our presence
one of our age's most dazzling beauties, a woman whose
renown in the musical arts matched Clemens' fame in the
literary world (unlike our previous guest, she arrived most
graciously, even regally). But as her case was indeed as slight a
matter as Holmes had claimed moments earlier, and as it bore
an obligation of the utmost discretion and has no bearing on
the Clemens situation, I need say no more of it here.

I did remember to ask another question after this
second guest left, as we were retiring. "Holmes, when Mark, er,
Clemens first arrived and you rose to shake his hand, I would
swear I saw you give the slightest indication of surprise, or
some similar shock, when you first met his eyes. It was that
recognition, for such I took it to be, that led me to assume that
you were familiar with the man and his work."

"You saw that, did you?" Holmes said with a frown.
"Did he?"

"From my angle of view, it would be impossible to say
for certain, but I saw no sign that he noticed anything. He was
distraught, and I don't think he was concentrating on such
small things right then. He was anxious to get to business."

"Yes," he said, relieved. "Still, you are correct. I did
react as you say. But it wasn't out of recognition. At least it
wasn't out of recognition of the man. It was what I saw in those
eyes, Watson. It took every ounce of discipline I had to restore
my composure, and I suppose I must congratulate you on your
perceptiveness in having me out over my momentary loss of
it."

"I meant no criticism, Holmes."

"But your observation is the best kind of criticism, Watson; it exposed a weakness."

"But what happened, Holmes? What did you see?"

Holmes did not answer immediately, but seemed to think back on the moment in question. "I saw an immeasurable sorrow, Watson. The man says he is carrying the grief of a lost child, and that is, I am sure, a devastating burden, but in those eyes I saw a greater, deeper grief than I knew any man bore. I tell you, Watson, that from that instant, I was already decided to do whatever I could to help him."

Holmes stood thinking another moment, his eyes focused distantly. "It is as if Mr. Clemens carries the grief not merely of a bereaved parent, but of the whole world. Not only am I frankly amazed that he can function under such a weight, I am also terribly curious why he has obliged himself to take it on."

Next morning, Holmes was up long before I, and when I joined him at the cooling ruins of his breakfast, he was, as promised, already fully engaged in our new inquiry. Though the shops could hardly have opened yet, a stack of books by Mark Twain spilled from a tall, partially unwrapped brown paper parcel there among the toast crumbs. *The Stolen White Elephant* lay open across his napkin, and Holmes was leafing through *The New Pilgrim's Progress*, and frowning slightly.

Not troubling to wish me a good morning, he said, "Our friend Mr. Clemens goes to great and often brilliant lengths to play the clown, but he is, I think, a very subtle man."

Picking a copy of *The Prince and the Pauper* from the top of the pile and fanning its pages, I agreed. "It is part of his magic, Holmes. You may read him with no more attention than you would give to the cheapest railway literature, or you may address yourself to the same pages with all the penetration and acuity at your command. He will readily meet you on your terms."

Holmes grunted in apparent agreement, pausing here and there to scan a page. I poured a coffee and asked, "Have his books helped you at all with this little mystery?"

"Not directly, I am sure. But if I had any doubts about the rigor of his observations or the keenness of his mind they are dispelled by all this," he said, indicating with his glance the books in front of him. "I think we had best take Mr. Clemens at his word."

I located a plate of toast under the brown paper. "Where shall we begin?"

"On several fronts, Watson," Holmes said, decisively closing the book and moving the stack to the sideboard. I have called in our troops to pursue Mr. Clemens' housebreaker. I have sent Barber to the shipping offices, to see what he might find about the arrival of this curious, unfortunately afflicted South African man." Barber was a recent addition to Holmes' highly fluid set of informal associates, a personally repulsive but consistently effective man when it came to certain narrow investigative tasks. I had no idea where, or even how, Holmes had found him.

"It seems a faint chance, considering how long an interval there might be since his arrival from South Africa and how many ports were open to him," I said. "But yes, Barber has the sort of"—again I found myself borrowing from Clemens' vocabulary—"*doggedness* that might prevail."

Holmes nodded. "And I have sent word to the Irregulars to join us. I expect them presently."

Holmes' little *agency*, as he liked to characterise them, had been reconstituted countless times since first organised almost twenty years earlier. Indeed, it now contained at least two youngsters whose fathers were once among the original band of street boys he gathered to carry out sensitive reconnaissance among the less approachable elements of London society. The current captain of this force, Anthony Wiggins, looked to be about eleven years of age. An older brother had held the position for some years, but had recently moved on to other more mature pursuits. It was Anthony who led the troop noisily up the stairs as I finished the last of my coffee. By no means either the oldest or the largest of the group, his authority seemed a combination of family inheritance and confidence, no doubt buttressed by occasional episodes of strategically administered pugilism.

For some years, Holmes had insisted that only Wiggins come to our rooms; the disruption caused by any larger invasion invariably discommoded Mrs. Hudson's temperament for the rest of the day. But finally recognising that dealing with him directly was part of the fun—and thus of the incentive—for these boys, he relented and allowed the lot of them to visit, dedicating himself to intensified diplomacy with Mrs. Hudson after each visit.

As always, Holmes handled the little corps of ragamuffins with the most appealing mixture of respect and commanding authority. Towering over them in both height and dignity, he treated the soiled and fidgeting little band as the professionals they truly were. Describing their mission and their quarry with almost scientific precision, he avoided that self-important tone of voice that most adults conversing with children slip into—and that all children hear with resentment. And yet he played fully to the urgency of their interest in money and to the absolute delight they took in these little adventures. With the parting promise of a generous additional cash reward to the one who found their man, he sent them thumping back down the steps and out into the great tributary system of London's human river. It was hard not to share their excitement; the hunt was up.

"And what of us?" I asked.

"I believe that we should pay a visit to Tedworth Square, where no doubt your literary fame will ensure our hearty welcome. I have notified Mr. Clemens of our intentions, and ordered a cab; there it is now." At this he rose and moved toward the door. "It promises to be a pleasant day, but depending upon what we learn from the Clemens household, we may be out long into the evening," he said, tossing his dressing gown across the back of a chair and laying his frock-coat over his arm. Grabbing my coat from the closet, I did likewise, and followed him downstairs to the street.

As the cab jerked into motion I asked him what he thought of Clemens' theory about the unpublished book being at the heart of the problem. "It is much too soon for me to form a theory of my own, Watson. But I will admit this much; I do not think that we are concerned with—how did you put it?—a 'little mystery.' Something more is at stake here than mere coincidence or a minor case of trespass."

"You mean to say that Gregson may be on track with his theory about the threat to Clemens' family?"

"I could not say, beyond my earnest conviction that a Gregson 'on track' is a Gregson going in the right direction by fortuitous chance. What I mean is that my every instinct cries out that, though our Mr. Clemens may or may not be utterly incorrect about any criminal interest in stealing his book manuscript, or about the possibility of a threat to his family, he is without question correct in the magnitude of his alarm. This is a serious, if not a grave, matter. For now I prefer to let it go at that."

Later, as we turned into Tedworth Square, Holmes scanned the houses with curiosity. "Watson," he said, "I would have expected the world's most famous and honored writer, as you say he is, to live in a much finer part of the city than this. These are not in any sense poor homes, but I suspect that none of Clemens' neighbours travel in his social circles."

"For once your lack of familiarity with a man cannot be easily compensated for by your observations of his person, Holmes," I said. "Remember that the Clemenses are grieving. They may have chosen Tedworth Square because of its near invisibility as much as for its modesty. I have occasional dealings with London's literary scene, you know, but until he stepped from his cab in Baker Street, I had heard not the vaguest hint of rumor that he was in London at all this year, when he seems to have been here continually since last autumn. As he told us, his family members have not wished to share their grief, and are essentially in hiding. A nondescript neighbourhood of this sort may serve them best.

"But, as you suggest," I continued, "it is also possible that this choice of residence was dictated by the realities of his finances. It is no secret that in recent years Clemens has suffered disastrous financial reversals, apparently to do with poorly placed investments. It is well known that his world speaking tour was undertaken wholly in an attempt to raise sufficient funds to liquidate an immense personal debt."

"Is that so?" Holmes said. "He seems to have a highly developed sense of honor. And how has this noble effort of his turned out?"

"There have been no announcements for some time, but the general impression is that the tour was an enormous success, and the debts have been nearly if not completely met and will be left far behind by the eventual receipts of this new book. What I have seen in the press suggests that the entire tour was something of a triumphal global procession for him, further solidifying world affection. But, yes, it was also a financial success, and has freed him from a debt that would have crushed most men half his age."

The cab came to a halt in front of the designated address just as Holmes said, "But this does not suggest that he would be in a position to pay a substantial ransom if a member of his family were kidnapped."

"I suppose not. At best, his efforts so far may have restored him to zero in any accounting of his personal wealth." I waited for Holmes to step down, then followed him. "Perhaps these scoundrels assume that his many admirers, or his wealthy friends, would hastily provide ransom money, if need be."

"If need be—precisely, Watson," said Holmes, mentally following some line of thought that I did not grasp.

Chapter Five
Tedworth Square

The moderately ornate house occupied the corner of a red-brick block of residences facing the small square of a woody park. Along its open side, there was a second entrance near the back of the house and half below the level of Tite Street. Clemens met us at the front door and led us into a spacious if severely decorated sitting room, where a surprising number of people were gathered. Clemens introduced us to them. His wife Olivia and daughter Clara occupied a couch. His wife was a gracious woman of middle age whose face showed the strain not only of her grief but of extended frail health; had I only a few minutes to speak with her alone I imagine I could have confirmed my suspicions that she had a weak heart and perhaps additional complications. Clara, a thin but elegantly postured young woman in her early twenties, exuded a protectiveness of her nearby mother that overwhelmed any other impression I might have gained. Jean, Clemens' other surviving daughter, was perched on a straight wooden chair; she appeared to be in her mid-teens, and there was something about her expression, particularly when she was most guilelessly absorbed in the conversation of others, that spoke of some medical problem or nervous frailty of her own. In all, it was clear to me and (as I was later to learn) equally clear to Holmes, that we wanted great caution in further disturbing or unnecessarily intruding upon these women in our pursuit of this case. Clemens had not overstated their fragility.

The Clemenses were just then entertaining houseguests from America—a sister of Olivia's and a niece— but these two had been out touring London the entire day of the episode in question, and though they lingered in the room out of a combination of courtesy and curiosity, they naturally had nothing to add. I think they were as eager as the Clemens women to meet the great detective and see him at work.

Only one servant had been in the house at the time of the break-in; the others had gone off to market or on other errands as soon as luncheon (apparently this was seen as "breakfast" by the family) had been concluded. Clemens had not thought it necessary to have them present for this gathering in any case, though Holmes said he might wish to speak with them at some point. The only servant who had been in the house when the intruder was there was Katy Leary, a long-time companion of the Clemens family who functioned variously as lady's maid and housemaid. To Clara's ardent protectiveness of Olivia Clemens, Miss Leary added a worshipfulness of the entire Clemens family that was somehow both quiet and aggressive. A short and rather broad-faced woman in her thirties, Katy had a knowing air, and listened to the proceedings with unusual intensity. Several times she seemed on the verge of adding a comment of her own to the proceedings, but always refrained from doing so. Holmes noticed her vital interest in the conversation, but did not encourage it, beyond a few routine questions.

Despite Holmes' most careful questioning and the most avid desire on the part of this group of bright and obviously concerned females to assist us, we added nothing of substance to our inquiry. The Clemens women had all been upstairs, engaged in some extended conversation to do with their dress for the upcoming Jubilee. Katy divided her time between attending to their discussion and her housemaid chores, which just then occupied her in the third floor rear of the house. None of them recalled hearing any noise to suggest that someone had entered the house, either before Clemens left for the tobacconist or in the few moments that passed between his departure and his return. Indeed, they had not even heard his return until he climbed the stairs and breathlessly burst into the sewing room to determine that they were unharmed.

Clemens was accustomed to writing in a comfortable study on the first floor, which he showed us upon Holmes' request. There was a large table, a kind of portmanteau, two wall shelves, and some extra chairs. Every level surface was stacked with books, maps, letters, and smaller documents.

Heavily draped windows prevented any sunlight from entering the room. "I have not disturbed anything since then," Clemens said. "Clara reminded me that the doctor's books emphasise the need not to disturb the scene of the crime. Of course I was unable to prevent the inspectors from rooting around here and there, but they spent very little time in this room."

"Have you noticed anything missing?" Holmes said. He stood in the doorway, slowly studying the room from there.

"Not a thing."

"Anything moved? A drape awry, a door or window ajar, perhaps one of those stacks of books moved?" Holmes pointed at the cluttered work table, where a scatter of large books, an unruly pile of handwritten sheets, and various pens and pencils suggested that perhaps Clemens was even yet not really finished with his manuscript.

"No, Mr. Holmes, and that is a great puzzle to me. I have spent at least an hour standing in different places in this room, looking for anything that was not as I left it before the intruder's visit. I have seen nothing. I have even stood on a chair in that corner," he indicated a narrow space by a book shelf; "you know—for a fresh angle on things."

Holmes abruptly stopped his visual wandering of the room at this remark, and turned to Clemens. "What a novel idea. Whatever made you think of it?"

Clemens smiled in return, pleased to have surprised the detective. "An artist friend, an engraver by trade, tells me that when a drawing or painting is partially complete but he isn't quite sure that it's going well enough to continue, he finds it helpful to place it on the floor beside a chair, then stand on the chair and look down on it, to get a fresh perspective. He claims that looking at the whole thing from a greater distance, or even from an angle, brings it into some kind of clearer view. I suppose he is visually testing its accuracy. I don't know what brought that to mind here, but it seemed worth a try. Not that it gained me anything, though I did relocate some cigars I'd misplaced last week."

Holmes gave the room a much less exhaustive examination than I would have expected, but did spend a few minutes quietly walking about, looking most intently at the things on the work table and at the carpet and the room's corners, where bare wood floor was exposed beyond the carpet's edge. He paid especial attention to the door to the hallway, kneeling to run his fingers along the underside of the door on both sides. Then he stood and said, "I can only agree with your assessment, Mr. Clemens: little has been disturbed in this room. Where do you keep your manuscript?"

"That's the clincher, Mr. Holmes; it's not even here, not the whole thing, anyway. The most recently finished portions of it are at the typewriter's, and the rest of the final typed version is at Chatto's office, where it is under lock and key. I sometimes think he has a larger stockpile of my manuscripts than I do. Oh, there are large sections of earlier drafts of the thing, handwritten, scattered here and there," he waved vaguely at the room. "But those are undisturbed as well. Frankly, I don't see how a thief could have figured out what to take."

I could see why. Thick sheaves of manuscript, some tied with string, protruded here and there from the general confusion of books, newspapers, clippings, and other documents. "If it were me," Clemens continued, "I would have hauled off every likely looking bunch of papers and sorted it out later. Or just burned it all, to be sure I got the job done right." I flinched at the thought—every writer's nightmare—of an entire manuscript so cruelly consigned to flames.

"You have checked on the manuscripts at these other addresses?" Holmes asked.

"I immediately telephoned the typewriter, but she had nothing to report. I assume that our housebreaker was unfamiliar with the process of writing a book, and just assumed that there would be a nice pile of pages stacked neatly in the middle of the desk. When that wasn't the case, he left."

"So it would seem," said Holmes, though from his expression I doubted that to him it seemed anything like that. "And the manuscript at Chatto's?"

"It's safe and undisturbed."

Toward the rear of the house, Holmes took a quick look down the stairs at the side door that was half below street level, and at a few of the ground-floor windows, then said, "I believe we have occupied enough of your time for now, Mr. Clemens. You have been most helpful, and this case grows in interest by the minute. We shall continue our inquiries, and let you know the results." Seeing Clemens' questioning expression, Holmes added, "Expect to hear from us this evening, or tomorrow morning. By then we may have news, and may also require your further assistance. Until then, please continue your vigilance, and stay close to home; if it is not too great an inconvenience, you might ask your houseguests to do the same."

"By all means, Mr. Holmes. Have you made progress? I mean, do you see something more than I have?"

"Perhaps, Mr. Clemens, but for now I prefer to hold my interpretations close until I can clarify or confirm them. I can assure you, however, that it seems highly unlikely to me that you will be the victim of a further intrusion by this man. Though he may have disturbed nothing, it is my suspicion that he got what he came for."

Clemens looked baffled. "What could that have been, Mr. Holmes, when nothing is missing?"

"Without knowing better what he sought, we cannot be sure he did not find it," said Holmes, more than a little mysteriously, but he would add no more. Instead, he asked, "Have you informed Gregson and Lestrade of my involvement in your case?"

"No. Would you prefer that I had? I wasn't sure if I would offend them by doing so."

"No, that's fine. Let me take care of that when the time comes. So far there is no real need to trouble them. We have nothing substantial to report, at least nothing that *they* would regard as substantial."

Clara and Jean were waiting by the door—Clara earnestly acting in her mother's stead as the hostess to see us out and wish us well, Jean with copies of all four of my books, which I was flattered to sign. Even Holmes was persuaded to add a good-natured inscription to each book; I had never known him to do this before. I suppose that among bibliophiles of some remote future, his signature will increase the value of those copies even more than mine might. But considering the enthusiasm with which young Jean clutched the books I doubt that they will drift into the open market for many years.

Our hansom was poorly sprung and somewhat aged, and the ride home in the heavy mid-day traffic was a weary one. Our inquiries at the Clemens' home had seemed unpromising to me. Perhaps Holmes felt the same, and that is why he decided we should return to Baker Street and fortify ourselves with a meal before settling on our next step. Still, though I had seen and heard nothing to inspire new thoughts, Holmes was meditative, hardly seeming to notice the irksome suspension of our cab or the halting progress we made toward home.

Finally, we rounded the corner from Oxford Street, crept along Orchard Street and onto Baker Street, then made our way through what still seemed to me to be an oppressively heavy flow of cabs and carts. "Holmes, you have told me that there are upwards of fifteen hundred omnibuses in London, have you not?"

"And at least five times that number of cabs, Watson. And wagons, drays, vans, and other conveyances beyond counting."

"I believe they are all out today, and they seem to have it in for us, the way they pack themselves into every lane and intersection along our route."

"This suggests a conspiracy of colossal dimensions, Watson; why would so many diligent tradesmen, presumably unaware of our existence, to say nothing of our character, go to all this trouble against us? Could they possibly find so much satisfaction in delaying our lunch?"

I grinned. "It could just be spite on their part, I suppose, but I . . . something seems to be going on up there." As we entered our own block, my attention was suddenly drawn to a slight jumble in the flow of vehicles ahead of us. Both northbound lanes seemed to slow momentarily, then the curbside lane ceased to move at all, while the traffic going the opposite direction continued to pass us smoothly on our right. I could not see what caused the problem, but by leaning out the right side of our cab and peering across the traffic directly in front of us, I could see that the obstacle must be a vehicle stopped in the lane of traffic.

"Someone has stopped, I think; they must be nearly in front of our door, but they have not pulled to the kerb. Maybe we are missing callers."

"I was expecting no one; it's probably a delivery," Holmes said, but rising from his seat and steadying himself with a grip on the roof frame of our hansom, he swayed back and forth, looking for an opening through the intervening traffic. Our respective contortions set the little cab to swaying and wobbling uncomfortably. Holmes, dodging the reins that swung by his head, ignored the protests of the driver, and said, "Yes, it does seem to be near our door; wait, I can't get a clear . . . Good Heavens, Watson, I've seen him! And he's into the van. It must be the one!"

"Seen who, Holmes? Which van? You can't mean the one Clemens described, surely! What would it be doing up here?" Traffic flow was now fully and noisily restored, but Holmes continued in his half-crouch, dodging and straining for a look ahead through the tangle of the traffic.

"Quickly, Watson! You must exchange seats with me, and when we reach 221, prepare to jump out. You'll have to chance the other lane; be careful. I am certain that I have seen that strange man Clemens described. He has just emerged at a run from our door. This is our chance; he can't possibly know we are this close. I will continue after him in the cab, but you

35

must see that he has done no harm. Make sure that Mrs. Hudson and the boarder are unharmed!"

Holmes continued to lean precariously forward from the hansom. Switching seats behind him, I slid to his side and lowered a foot to the step, prepared to jump down. Holmes instructed the driver, who was still grumbling about our gymnastics, not to stop for me, but to follow the van.

Our velocity was slow enough that I was in no danger from our wheel. The jump was an awkward one, though, and I momentarily lost my footing in the grit and soil on the pavement. I was up from my knees in an instant, brushing my hands as I leapt between a carriage and a coal trolley onto the walk.

As I reached the door, I turned hastily back toward the street. Holmes leaned out of the near side of the hansom toward me, and over the clatter and rumble of the traffic he cried, "Alert Lestrade and Gregson! Tell them I think Clemens is onto something!" He may have said more, but he and his voice were both lost behind a rattling furniture van, and I could see him no more.

Chapter Six
Gregson Condescends

It was a matter of a few seconds to rap on Mrs. Hudson's door and determine that she was preparing a lunch that Holmes, at least, would miss entirely. "No, I heard nothing, Doctor. You say the man ran from the door? I usually hear the door close, but as you know, if I am rustling about in the pantry I don't always even hear the bell."

After finding the boarder not at home and her door securely locked, I hurried upstairs. The door to 221B was slightly ajar, but that was the only evidence I found of any untoward activity. Disturbing the room as little as possible, I decided that I too had best forego lunch and follow Holmes' shouted instructions to visit Gregson and Lestrade.

I found a more comfortable hansom this time, with a driver who knew his business. As we moved through the traffic, it finally penetrated my consciousness that the presence of novel costumes, uniforms, and obviously foreign faces that I had been aware of for some weeks had greatly intensified; our slow progress through the city these days was no doubt the result of the enormous number of people flooding into the city, not only from around the country but from around the world. I saw at least a dozen types of military uniform, and many more styles of dress that I could not identify, before we reached Westminster and I stepped to the kerb in front of the imposing granite pile of New Scotland Yard.

Not having Holmes' imperturbable sense of independence in such matters, I was uneasy about the nettlesome diplomatic necessities involved in dealing with Gregson and Lestrade together on the same case. Ever since my first experiences with Holmes, we had watched these two ambitious investigators clash. "Jealous as a pair of professional beauties," Holmes had often said of them. So it was with considerable relief that I discovered that the first of their offices I reached, Lestrade's, was unoccupied. Not that I preferred Gregson, but I did not wish to have to choose one over the other if they were both in; the one I neglected would most assuredly take the choice as a slight, and the pouting could go on for days.

Gregson was apparently thriving, either professionally or socially. He had a spacious, handsomely furnished office overlooking the river, and to my further relief he was in it. It appeared that he must spend most of his time there; his usually fair complexion was now nearly pallid, and if it were not for his otherwise energetic and even athletic movements I would have wondered about his health. After a few pleasantries, I told him that Clemens had brought us in on the case.

To my even greater relief, rather than show any signs of disappointment at this news, Gregson seemed genuinely pleased. "Though I have my doubts that there is anything much to Mr. Clemens' worries, I don't mind telling you that I welcome the interest of you and Holmes. Oh, I realise that it might suggest a lack of faith in Scotland Yard on the part of Mr. Clemens, and for that reason may not reflect well on me or my colleagues here," he said offhandedly, continuing his longstanding habit of alluding to Lestrade without actually making himself say the name. "But you may not appreciate just how big a fish Samuel Clemens, or I should say Mark Twain, is in this city. You may not be familiar with his work," Gregson said, with an almost idiotic air of presumption that he was among the few well-read individuals in London, "but I find it necessary to keep up on these things."

"I know of his books," I said, but did not elaborate. Gregson seemed to want to feel knowledgeable on this matter, and I saw no advantage in challenging him, as desperately as I wanted to deflate his arrogant puffery.

He continued, "I personally have always found his little tales rather rude and shallow. I'm not at all sure what the fuss is about. But he has somehow won the hearts of many prominent people—*very* prominent people." With one eyebrow raised, he gave me his most knowing look, to indicate the extent to which he was intimate with such rarefied social circles, and, I suppose, also to emphasise the extent to which I was not.

"I daresay," he said, "that in that way, Clemens is not unlike your Mr. Holmes, who likewise has quite a following in high circles." Gregson's tone did not quite indicate disapproval of this situation, but it implied certain professional reservations, as if to suggest that celebrity was all right for the amateurs but was of no interest to the genuine experts. I had not remembered Gregson being so consistently insufferable; prosperity apparently agreed with him.

"So if we are correct that this is merely a slight or even trivial matter that Clemens has fallen into," Gregson continued, now almost seeming to imply that it was somehow Clemens' own fault that his house was broken into, "then our ability to settle it quietly, and to persuade Clemens' important friends that there is no problem, will be made much easier if our opinion is shared by a independent consultant, particularly one of such, ah, *renown* among these people as Holmes."

This startling series of pomposities only increased my relief that I was not dealing with both inspectors at once. It seemed not to have occurred to the inspector that Holmes might come to a different conclusion regarding the Clemens case, so I set about as politely as I could to disabuse him of his misunderstanding.

"Mr. Clemens suggested to us that you, at least, might have some sympathy for his concerns, particularly about the possibility of some kind of threat to him or his family."

Gregson nodded. "That is correct. I am not as inclined as some to disregard the less likely hypotheses until all the evidence is in. Though it seems improbable in the extreme, the possibility of some kind of conspiracy against Clemens cannot wholly be ruled out."

Seeking to put the most affirmative cast on this admission of his, I said, "Well then, you may be encouraged in your thinking by a recent development. Holmes sent me directly to you," I left it for Gregson to presume that "you" meant him alone, "the very moment it arose."

"Indeed." He was gratified. "Tell me."

"About an hour ago, as we were returning from a relatively unproductive visit to the Clemens household, we unquestionably saw this same odd fellow."

"The one Clemens refers to as a 'walleye?'" Gregson interrupted with surprise.

"The same." I related our experience in Baker Street, concluding with Holmes very words—that he was now certain that "Clemens is onto something."

"It certainly is a singular turn of events, but I am not sure why it should lead Holmes to such a certainty. There seem to be any number of other possible explanations, but yes, it is a most intriguing coincidence."

"Coincidence?" I asked, baffled. "How could there be a coincidence in it?"

"Simply that both Clemens and you should happen to see such similar-appearing characters in such a short period of time? It seems obvious."

"Similar-appearing?" I cried. "You think it's just a matter of chance, and there's no connection? That this is not the same man, jumping in and out of the same van?"

"Oh, I suppose that is possible too. But we don't really know yet, do we? After all, you did not see Clemens' man, and he did not see yours. We cannot be sure, can we?" His calm dismissal of the certainty of the situation was stunning. "It is rather a shame that Holmes did not simply abandon his hansom and run up to the van. Surely the traffic was not moving very fast. He could have confronted the fellow right then and there and settled all this."

"I think that he preferred the chance to gain more information by discretely following the van to its destination."

"Yes, quite. Well, we shall just have to wait and see if that works, won't we?"

Not wishing to do either Clemens or Holmes a disservice by annoying Scotland Yard so early in the case, I decided not to argue the point, and, having already fulfilled my purpose, I rose to go. "Well, now you have our report. Presumably, if Holmes manages to trail his man successfully, we will have more to say, and will of course keep you informed."

"That would be just splendid, Doctor," Gregson said, with just a hint of patronizing in his voice. But as I turned from him, he suddenly added, "Oh, you know, it may be nothing, but I could perhaps return your kindness."

"Eh? How is that?"

"Our early inquiries have not been without effect. Constable Marston, one of the men we've assigned to the Clemens home, has, uh, struck up an acquaintance with their help."

"With whom?"

"The maid, a Miss Leary, I believe it is." He consulted a notebook on his desk, but apparently found nothing there and set it down still open to the unhelpful page. "I remember her, an impertinent little woman, full of silly questions until I quieted her down." I wondered what the Clemens family had thought of this, if they saw it, and if the "quieting down" of Miss Leary explained her reticence to contribute to our conversation that morning at the house. I made a mental note to tell Holmes that Miss Leary might deserve encouragement.

"Yes, we met her," I said.

"Marston was assigned directly from other duties. He has a certain polish, socially, that made him an ideal candidate for this delicate assignment. He was straight away put to guard the house. Apparently someone neglected to give him the full background on the case, but he learned from this maid about the, uh, walleyed man."

He paused, with a look of amusement on his face, then said, "You know, it *is* an apt term, if somewhat crude. Anyway, Marston sent me a message, a note, I have it here somewhere." Again he rummaged through his notes and papers without success. "It said that he might know something of use about the identity of this disfigured man. Meant to have him in to talk about it, but what with the rush of my own schedule I haven't had the time. The Jubilee, you know." He added this last as if to hint that he was working closely with Her Majesty on all the arrangements. "Perhaps you and Holmes would like to speak with him when next you visit Mr. Clemens."

"This man Marston has seen the fellow too?" This was surprising news, however casually Gregson might regard it. Had the man completely lost his investigative interests, or was he really so overworked that he was unable to concentrate on any one matter?

"Not sure," Gregson said with a mildly annoyed frown, again sifting for the note. "He might just have heard something. Can't recall offhand. You'll have to check with him." His tone made it plain that he wished to move on to his next duty, though I doubted he had yet decided what it was.

"We will do that, Inspector, and my thanks to you for the assistance. I am sure Holmes will share my appreciation." With that I hurried from the office and made my way home.

Chapter Seven
Deductions of Little Consequence

It was late afternoon when I arrived, and Holmes was already there. When I opened the door he was standing pensively on a sturdy chair by the fireplace, pipe alight and fuming.

"Worst of luck, Watson," he said without greeting me otherwise. "I lost them." As he climbed down from the chair, I thought of how Gregson would lord it over him if he heard this. "We kept a nice distance until Regent's Park. My driver proved more resourceful than I might have hoped, once he understood my intent and was tempted by a modest cash incentive. But when the van took toward the park, we turned to follow and there was a violent ratcheting along the axle and the whole affair buckled up in a heap. Thankfully, rather than panic, the horse simply stopped as if he'd been expecting something like this; he didn't even start when the right wheel rolled past him as if it intended to follow the van on its own. The cab rolled to the ground on its side. I jumped free, but the driver was pitched off and hit the ground at a dreadful angle. He occupied my entire attention, of course, so I lost sight of the van almost immediately."

"Badly hurt?"

"Just stunned, thank heavens. He was older than he looked, and at first I feared that he'd broken his neck. Hit the ground like a sack of coal; took a moment for him to get his breath back, then he was full of apologies—and lamentations over the state of his cab. Fortunately, a constable saw the whole thing from a distance, and the two of us were able to get the man out of the traffic and into some shade. Once he had his breath and the constable was seeing to clearing the wreckage, I whistled down a crawler and came back."

"Wretched timing," I said, "but that hansom was well overdue. It was a miserable wreck even before it broke down."

"Quite. Mrs. Hudson tells me you went to Scotland Yard?"

"Yes, but I had hoped to return first, to warn you—that man was in our rooms, Holmes, right here!" I was conscious of a sense of violation I had not imagined possible. I hadn't realised the extent to which I cherished our humble apartment's sanctity, and I felt a chilling sympathy for Clemens when he likewise saw this villainous fellow fleeing his home. "But I stayed only seconds, and I didn't disturb anything."

"Nor did the intruder, it seems. I have been examining the room since I returned, and except for a few obvious trivialities, it is almost as if he never even set foot on Baker Street, much less entered here." He glanced to the chair he had just vacated. "Even Mr. Clemens' clever approach didn't yield much, though I did find that pipette I was unable to locate last week." Holmes twirled the fine glass tube between thumb and forefinger.

"But why would this man enter our homes if he didn't want something? Could he have come here—or to Clemens' house, for that matter—intending to harm us, only to discover we weren't in?"

"It seems unlikely in the extreme, Watson. The man's movements and timing are more those of a sneak thief, and a very timid one at that. He flees even without opposition."

"What, then? And what are these 'obvious trivialities' you mentioned?" I knew his ways, and his preference for marshaling his facts until his own good time, but I also knew that he was aware that his reticence often exasperated not only the police and his clients, but me as well. "Perhaps this is not a time for you to hold your interpretations too close, Holmes."

Holmes looked at me doubtfully. "You may be right, Watson. But I fear that this time, at least, my deductions are of such a scattered and inconsequential nature as to make them all but irrelevant."

Sensing that he weakened and might well divulge his findings, I pressed him. "Then you have little to lose by sharing them."

"Well reasoned, my friend." He sighed. "All right. As far as what I know—and I will keep what I merely *suspect* to myself—here it is:

"First, as to our strange break-in artist. This man has other afflictions besides his eye and his unruly hair. He is without question somewhat slow in his mental faculties, though his training and experience in the service of the more refined social circles is surprising, even formidable, probably because he entered the domestic service and is only recently discharged from some respectable if somewhat bohemian household where he was, I assume, a footman."

"Holmes!" I said, in amazement, "How . . . ."

"Oh, and he came here directly from the docks," Holmes added, as an afterthought that seemed even less significant to him. "I suspect he spends a fair amount of time there. Perhaps at least that information will be of use to us, but considering how many people inhabit the docks, I doubt it."

"Holmes, you must explain yourself. I might have followed your reasoning if you had actually met the man, but you did not. These are not conclusions you could have drawn by direct observation of a person, like some abraded cuff on a clerk's sleeve or the mud on a man's Hessians."

"You disappoint me, Watson. Surely you have noticed that not all of the information I gather from my surroundings is visual, or requires examination of the man in question." He paused, then began again, more in the tone of a lecture. "Imagine, if you will, the passage of a man as a kind of three-dimensional trail he leaves, not merely in footprints but in the very air. Now, now," he added, as I began to object, "I admit that a man walking through a room often does not leave tracks like a beast in the wild; only soiled shoes leave a trace on a hard floor, and only the most freshly cleaned carpet could be counted on to take identifiable impressions. But think of our visits to rural areas, Watson; your wise gamekeeper, whether he seeks the otter, the hare, or the stoat, knows how to read the evidence. A daintily nibbled branch here, a disarranged tuft of weed there, a discreetly deposited pile of feces on a riverside rock—your wild animal can not pass by without leaving its calling cards, and, indeed, often does so quite intentionally, for its colleagues and competitors to read."

Again I made to object to the improbable comparison of wild beasts with the crafty and foresightful human burglar of modern London, but Holmes cut me off. "Let me start with my last observation. The man came from the docks. Think back, Watson. On our many rounds of this grand, tumultuous city have we not inhaled a thousand subtle variations on the very air we breathe?"

"We have," I said, "and some not so subtle." I said, remembering some of the city's more sordidly aromatic quarters.

"True," Holmes nodded. "But while you, like most people, have been reacting only with approval or distaste to these momentary immersions in the city's diverse fumes, I have created in my mind a map of them, an olfactory cartography of London. It is most helpful.

"You see, Watson, odor makes us uneasy; we are suspicious of it, perhaps because it is invisible. If it is unpleasant we wish to escape it and the embarrassment it might cause. If it is pleasant, or wonderful, we may be a bit suspicious of its power over us. Scent seems to us a more personal invasion of our inner being than does sight. Most people prefer not to attend to odor, and thus they treat the odors they encounter quite passively, wishing only that they would go away.

"And what a shame they are so unreceptive! When they enter a chapel, they do not anticipate the calming scents of hot beeswax and warm sacramental wine, but are immediately caught by the recognition and familiarity. Those scents become an unconscious element, indeed even an invitation, in their devotional exercises. Afterward, when they enter a favorite restaurant, they are literally swept to their table on savory currents of gustatory aroma, their hunger awakened, their very consciousness heightened."

"Holmes, I admit that what you say has merit, but the world of scent is all so fleeting and momentary," I said.

"So it seems, Watson, and so we treat it. Unlike the other senses, the stimulants of our sense of smell are peculiarly ephemeral; it is the poor sister of sensations, the least honored and the soonest forgotten. We may reminisce endlessly about a favorite symphony performance, or the taste of a fine dinner, or the sight of a vivid dawn. We do not indulge in similar nostalgia over a wilted bouquet; we just throw it out."

"May I assume from this lecture that such olfaction has served you in this case?"

"Most exceptionally. Beyond most prior experiences."

"And . . . ," I said.

"You have been with me on many a visit to the docks, Watson. You know the ground, and what covers it. The aromas may vary as you move, but nowhere else will you find that peculiar mixture of powerful, even overwhelming, fulminations as are routinely generated there. Let me name just a few.

"One expects the fragrance of coffees and spices, and though they may rise in a thousand subtly different combinations, they are of a type, and are of course singularly durable.

"On top of them, almost seeming to struggle against them, is a pungent barnyard rankness. The source is all those animal hides, not quite rotting but forcefully sharp in their very number.

"Then there is wood. Oh, Watson, you must admire the sweet scent of new-cut wood! I know a cabinetryman in this very city who can identify twenty-three species of wood merely by the aroma they release when milled; I confess that I can manage only sixteen, but I am working on it. The softwoods are particularly vexing in that regard. Traces of freshly milled cork, mahogany, and other raw lumber permeate the dockside yards; they almost shout their presence.

47

"There are chemicals of many sorts, of course, but you may recall that the sulfur bins are a signature of the docks, and who ever forgets their peculiarly sharp foulness? Once identified as a constituent of any odorous combination, you are almost assured that it originated dockside.

"And if you long for a finisher to this banquet, wait but a moment and the faintest hints of tobacco and rum will waft by. In fact, they may literally walk by, exhaled by the thousands of men who labour at handling all these commodities as they come and go.

"Except perhaps for the many strong odors emanating from very specific places of business—the bakeries, the dust yards, the cabyards, the dining establishments—I find no district in the city as easy to identify for the general content of its airs as the docks. It is all so assured; once one is disciplined to detect its character it is impossible to miss."

Holmes seemed momentarily lost in exotically scented memories, then his gaze changed from mild rapture to puzzlement as he added, "Oddly enough, though most of these items on the docks have just been transported across some vast expanse of sea, the unmistakable tang of salt air seems to expire from the brew most quickly. I wonder why.

"In any event, Watson, perhaps not all of these odors, or the many others I could name, will present themselves to you on a given occasion. No matter; the recipe's fundamental recognisability persists despite variations. I tell you Watson, that once the docks' unique atmospheric soup of aromas, fragrances, and outright stinks has been introduced into a room, however briefly, it will remain in some faint trace for days, waiting to be registered by the attentive nostril.

"When we entered Mr. Clemens' study, even though much time had passed and several others had been in and out of the room, I twice caught the faintest hint of that rich tangle of dockside olfactory signals. There was a corner by the portmanteau—somewhat out of the line of traffic, I suppose, and its little airs therefore less disturbed and more easily attached to the fabric of the curtain—where I finally identified it without a shadow of a doubt."

I shook my head. "I remember you crouched there; I thought you were examining the floorboards."

"My eyes were, Watson, but my nose was otherwise employed. Of course I had no way of knowing if the bearer of the dockside signal was also our strange intruder. Anyone who entered the room in the previous week could have brought the dock with them. It wasn't until I entered our own apartments that I could confirm this. There by the table," he nodded toward it, "and here by the mantle, the scent lingered most clearly, much more distinctly than in Clemens' study. And those two locations led me to the *visual* clues our visitor also left."

"I thought you said he left no trace."

"None of consequence, Watson, by which I mean none that lead me to any clear course of action. In my investigations, I often notice other traces, but just as often must discard them as irrelevancies."

"So what are these 'irrelevancies,' if you will share them before discarding them?"

"They are similar to one or two at the Clemens' house. Do you not notice anything peculiar about the table where we breakfasted?"

I studied it for a moment. Mrs. Hudson had carried away all trace of our breakfast, and all that remained on the table were Holmes' scissors (left from his newspaper clipping exercise of the previous evening), a pencil, his small pen-knife, and, of course the lamp. The table was otherwise empty. "It seems quite in order to me, Holmes. Were there other items there that now are missing?"

"No, Watson. Mrs. Hudson left everything but the breakfast things. But your choice of words is appropriate. Look again; does it not seem *unusually* 'in order,' to use your words? Have you or I, or Mrs. Hudson for that matter, the habit of placing things on the table quite that way?"

I looked again, and was taken with the chill, creeping sensation one experiences when the seemingly familiar reveals itself to be utterly alien. The pencil, the pen-knife, and scissors were not placed at random; someone had lined them up neatly, parallel to and equidistant from one another. A moment's study revealed that they were also in parallel with a dominant line of inlay in the table's worn parquetry. The lamp had been shifted too, from one edge of the table to the exact centre. "Holmes, what does this mean?"

"I've told you already, Watson: a mind of considerable regimentation has entered the room. As its host body stood in that spot, facing the table, doing whatever it was here to do, the hands became busy, perhaps even without the conscious attention of the mind, at what could only be a deeply entrenched mental habit of ordering things. Inasmuch as a practiced housebreaker would neither waste time on such an enterprise nor desire to leave any unnecessary additional evidence of his presence, I surmise that this mind is somewhat dim in that regard.

"But there is more, Watson. Here on the mantle, if you bend low so that the angle of the light allows you to see the very thin film of dust that has briefly eluded Mrs. Hudson's vigilant patrols, you will notice more." I came to his side and bent slightly to imitate his stance. "The entire surface has been the scene of tiny movements. The slipper, these two bottles, the magnifier . . . well, practically everything that is not fastened down has been touched—just lightly, not even with great curiosity, merely for the sake of touching, or, I might better say, the *need* of touching."

"My word, Holmes, whatever for?" Involuntarily, I glanced around the room for other such subtle changes.

"Children do this, of course; they learn through their fingertips as much as through their eyes and ears. There was a childlike intellect at work here, but I sense much more. Things have not been picked up and placed back without thought. They have been adjusted, re-arranged—*managed*. The magnifier's handle now runs exactly parallel with the front

50

edge of the mantle; from the dust I can see that I laid it down with the handle pointing slightly away from the wall. The bottles are now likewise placed in linear perfection along the back of the mantle. Everything has been *straightened*. But straightened *up* would be a better term, for this could only be the work of a mind trained, or somehow indoctrinated, in the improvements to be had by tidying. Few butlers would be this particularly attentive, but someone in a lower station who had a chance to observe an admired butler at work, especially if such a person were of somewhat limited mental faculties, might readily enough develop this habit out of admiration, or from some striving ambition to 'perfect' a room."

"That is fully plausible Holmes," I admitted, "and I see how this might lead to your assumption of a domestic career, but it seems to me not the only possible explanation. As you know, there are troubled souls of all ages who do these things out of some mild or even desperate and uncontrollable necessity. Such behavior does not seem to me to constitute proof of a service career."

"Not by itself, true. But I think you will agree that the evidence on that chair is conclusive," he said, indicating the chair by the door. I looked. There, across the heavily brocade of the chair, lay his dressing gown, just where he had tossed it aside when we left that morning, but a moment's examination brought from me a small cry of surprise. "Look! It has been . . . it has been . . ."

"Attended to," Holmes nodded. "It has been picked up, the shoulders and sleeves properly squared and aligned, the collar straightened, and the whole thing neatly replaced across the chair back. I wager that it hangs as low behind the chair's back as it does onto the front."

From my angle I could see that it did, and told him so.

"Our visitor is quite strange, but I must admit that he is also rather charming," Holmes said with a smile. "When before have we encountered a burglar who so thoughtfully tidied up as he burgled?"

"You may be amused by this, Holmes, but I find it quite disturbing. There is something almost, well, *monstrous* in this kind of behavior. It is unnatural in the extreme."

"Quite the opposite, Watson. I find it natural in the extreme. Someone once, for some reason, perhaps out of nothing but simple affection, took this. . . what did you say, 'troubled soul?' . . . into their care and directed his limited attention into what must have seemed the worthiest of pursuits for such a person: orderliness and service. He surely would not have had a chance of employment in most households with domestic staffs. In your average home, nothing outside of strict orthodoxy would be tolerated by either the family or the hiring agencies. Thus I assume that he was taken by some less straight-laced household. Perhaps he was the butler's relative, and was given simple tasks in a footman's role. No matter. Now, wherever he is and whatever he might be doing—right or wrong, criminal or not—he reflexively continues those pursuits. I genuinely doubt if he would recall completing all these little attentions he gave our belongings. He does them as *naturally* as he breathes. And he does them quickly.

"Besides, Watson, he did them in Clemens' study. The manuscripts and other papers were still in complete disarray—I suppose they seemed overwhelming for him to take on in the few seconds he spent in the room—but the pens and pencils on the work table were placed in a similarly perfect row, their butts aligned and perpendicular to the forward edge of the table. At the time, I didn't know but that Clemens himself had this habit, though I doubted it considering the formidable disarray of everything else in that room. But because, as you pointed out, in its extreme form this sort of orderliness is seen as something of a mental malady, I hesitated to call attention to it for fear of embarrassing him, especially when he insisted that nothing had been disturbed. Now I see it was not his habit, though I am a bit surprised that he did not notice the change."

"Astounding," I said, and sat down.

Chapter Eight
Wiggins Delivers His Ketch

Over our dinner, I explained to Holmes the results of my visit to Scotland Yard, none of which seemed to surprise him except the news that Constable Marston might have information about our "tidy burglar," as Holmes had now begun to call him. "It seems a particularly fortuitous development," I said, "in a case that otherwise has not been going our way. Quite a fine coincidence, in fact, that this constable may have information about this strange fellow."

"Quite," said Holmes, with a curious but unreadable expression.

Then, setting aside whatever thought had occupied him, he said, "We had best visit this constable first thing tomorrow. But now," he said, pushing back his chair, "I must leave you for the evening. I have a few inquiries of my own to make, and must prepare."

With that he disappeared into his room, emerging transmuted into one of his disreputable back-street characters. In a matter of a few minutes he had gone from his normally fastidious appearance to that of a wretch who had seen neither a bath nor a change of clothing for many months.

It was not an outfit I had seen before, and bears describing for what it illustrates of Holmes' gift for camouflaging his true appearance, to say nothing of his dignified bearing. It consisted of a filthy and ragged coat that might have begun life on the back of a flamboyant cabby, but was now down to one thin cloak torn almost loose; equally disreputable breeches of no definable colour; ancient gaiters whose laces were largely replaced by finely twisted rags; and a pair of long-deceased Wellingtons whose opened sides seemed to bid welcome to whatever passing air or moisture might approach. Holmes' lean, sharp facial features had been replaced by a countenance of bloated indolence, and, most amazing of all, he seemed to have lost a good foot of his normal stature. How he managed such a transformation was beyond my imagining, but he was now for all purposes a bleary, greasy, and unspeakably foul little vagrant.

He seemed so much the product of abject, desperate impoverishment, that I could not help saying, "If you intend to carry on conversations with anyone who shares your appearance, my medical advice is that you stay upwind of them."

"There are few winds of any kind where I will be, Watson, but I appreciate your concern." With that he slumped out the door, already practicing the unsteady gait that would see him through whatever grim pit of despair was his destination for the evening. Comfortably left behind, I turned to the stack of Mark Twain books still resting on the sideboard, and spent the evening in enchanted wanderings through far more pleasant and stirring settings among less inscrutable heroes than my companion.

Though I did not hear him return during the night, Holmes—fully re-civilised in his dressing gown—had already finished his breakfast when I emerged from my room. I was in a buoyant mood, refreshed by dreams of American riverscapes that I doubted would be more vivid were I to stand next to Samuel Clemens himself as he piloted some grand old sternwheeler up the muddy current. As I made my way down to the sitting room, I was surprised to find Holmes standing on the little landing at the turning of the stairs, looking out the small window. He was frowning off into the distance at the roof line of the houses behind ours. I was about to accuse him of having joined the masses of Englishmen who, like me, were just then fretting over the weather for the impending Jubilee when he turned and greeted me. "Good morning, Watson!" he said energetically."

"I trust your evening was fruitful?" I asked cheerily, full of certainty that my own had been.

"Not especially," he said, "unless the accumulation of additional authentic grime on my costume can be judged as an achievement. But I share your obviously elevated spirits,

Watson. My hopes are higher for today, and I am anxious to speak to our constable as soon as possible. However, we must wait a while here."

"I take it there is no word from Barber?

"Not yet, but his methods are somewhat sluggish, which is why they are so fruitful. But I am expecting young Wiggins momentarily. The Irregulars move through the city like an over-ripe scandal, and I am sure that their captain will have an interesting report, even if he has no news."

He had both. About an hour later, as I was reaching for the last of the bacon, the bell—followed by the familiar rumble on the stairs—announced the arrival of our boy.

At first his report did not sound promising. Their search had been excessively successful. London's coarser social elements might well have been suffering an epidemic of corneal leucomas, so many did the Irregulars identify. But working from Holmes' other details about our quarry, especially his unique hair and his relatively recent arrival from South Africa, they were able to narrow the field. From a tragic array of unfortunates, Wiggins had sorted a most likely candidate. "'e's the one, gov'nor, hain't a doubt."

"How are you so certain?" Holmes asked, with a collegial tone he might have adopted in speaking to the neighbourhood chemist about the finer points of a complicated formula.

"Hain't my own ketch, you know. Hit's my *hinformant!*" Wiggins pronounced this word with obvious pride in his terminological sophistication, pausing briefly for effect, then continuing. "Ol' Funny Herc, what was penny-gaff clown at the Albion, as has never led me wrong, is now, uh, some'at *reduced*, and gets by on a little screeving in a bit of a lane off Wapping High Street." Holmes' glance met mine at the mention of this address in the heart of the London Docks. "But mostly he jist watches. Don't seem to eat nor drink as I could see. But he watches good, an' he seed this man o' yers reg'lar since Easter Day. Tol' me 'bout the dotty 'air you mentioned afore I asked, 'e did."

Further inquiry revealed helpful specifics. Wiggins' informant usually saw the man about dusk, striding purposefully (rather than strolling) in any of several directions, always alone. Wiggins seemed justified in his confidence in "Ol' Herc." However hard the times that were fallen on the aged thespian, he "jist watched" with the discrimination of one whose entire subsistence depended upon his ability to "read" passersby.

Holmes handed Wiggins his earnings. He had yet, in my hearing, to remind Wiggins or any of his predecessors that the money was to be fairly shared among his little platoon, nor had it ever reached our ears that the distribution had gone awry. As he gave Wiggins his extra share for finding the needed information, he asked the boy, "I daresay your 'informant' placed some demand on your resources in exchange for his assistance?"

"Not as such, sir. We 'ave an understandin'. . . ." The boy was not quite willing to ask for more than had been agreed to, but at the same time his expression made it plain that he had incurred some obligation to the old man in the complex economics of the streets.

"Well, then, this should keep the record clean between you," said Holmes, adding a bit more silver to the pile in Wiggins' grubby paw. Wiggins nodded in restrained professional approval.

"Now I have a simpler mission for you and your associates, if you don't mind," said Holmes. Wiggins brightened. "I am looking for a particular cabyard. It will probably be somewhat run down, and it will house not only cabs but small vans. We are looking for the plain gray van that this man you have been seeking sometimes rides in: cab-over, no trim whatsoever, all the gray of roof slate. But I doubt it will be there often, so concern yourself with finding the yard, van or no." Wiggins cocked an eyebrow at this last command, as did I; without the van, how to know the yard? Holmes continued. "The manager of the yard will almost certainly be an older man, perhaps even elderly, but—and this just may be the most important thing, Wiggins—he will keep a goat or two on the premises, and they too will likely be quite old." Wiggins' eyebrows rose again in curiosity at this, as I suppose mine also did, but he made no comment and was off, thundering down the steps and out to distribute the earnings among the Irregulars who, I was sure, were waiting nearby.

As Holmes closed the door, he said, almost to himself, "It would not seem possible that such a small creature could generate such shocking impacts merely through use of his bare feet."

As he reached for his coat, he turned to me. "This news increases the urgency of our visit with the constable, Watson. I fear we must trouble the Clemens' household with an unannounced call."

It was late morning when we arrived at Tedworth Square. Clara received us with manifest delight, and seemed disappointed that we did not need to interrogate her further.

When asked about Constable Marston, she said, "The constable has been stationed in the back. Our Katy is probably with him." She added this last with a slightest trace of a smile, then said, "If you will wait in the sitting room, I will bring him."

"That would be splendid," said Holmes. "And I am sure that before we leave, if your father can spare a moment, he would be glad to hear a report of our progress."

"Oh, I am afraid you've missed him," she said. "He had some business with Mr. Chatto. He will be so sorry not to have seen you."

"Don't be concerned. We will see him soon."

As we waited, I remembered to apprise Holmes of Gregson's condescending attitude toward Miss Leary. "Thank you for mentioning that, Watson. It seemed to me that on our last visit she was behaving rather shyly for someone who, I might say, is clearly both bright and very much a member of this family. We must find time to have her impressions of the situation," he added, "but not, I think, while we talk with the constable."

The constable was not in the least what I would have expected. I believe even Holmes was somewhat set back by his appearance and personality. Richard Marston was a robust, energetic man who, as I think back on him now, was quite similar in build and demeanor to the later American president, Theodore Roosevelt. His barrel-chested frame supported a large square head with an open, clean-shaven, and frequently grinning face. It was no wonder that Miss Leary found him appealing. His uniform, if not tailored to his powerful frame, was at the very least worn with considerably more *elan* than even the most fastidious police officers I had yet seen.

But his speech was the biggest shock. There was no trace of the lower classes in his grammar, none of the predictable constabulary brogue in his inflections. He spoke like a man of considerable education, and had the eye and bearing of a man of wide experience in the world.

And he knew us, both by reputation and by way of my books. "Dr. Watson, I have enjoyed your stories immensely! I was a devoted reader from the first page of *A Study in Scarlet*, where I learned of your wounding at Maiwand. How could I not follow the career of one so near a comrade at arms?"

"You were at Maiwand?" I asked with surprise at meeting a fellow veteran of the disastrous Afghanistan campaign. Almost half of our force had been lost in the battle that day or in the subsequent miseries. I rarely encountered a fellow survivor, nor did many of us who had been there even want to. It was not the sort of experience that made one an enthusiastic nostalgist.

"No, no, I am sorry not to have served with you at that awful place. My lot was a better one. It was my honor to be in at the righteous calling to accounts. I was with Roberts," he enthused, "all the way from Kabul to Kandahar! I was among the first into the camp of that butcher Ayub Khan when we overran his artillery." He paused, swept away in his own memories, and clearly proud to imagine himself the agent of my avenging.

"I cherish my Roberts' Star as I do my own good name," he said, suddenly solemn, and I was deeply touched by his sympathy and his powerful sense of comradeship. Many from those campaigns came home embittered by the futility of it all. I admit to having harbored doubts about the entire enterprise many times, and avoided speaking of it even in response to well-meaning inquiries from the best-intentioned acquaintances. Holmes had sensed this early in our acquaintance and never pressed me about it. But to my surprise I found that I welcomed this fervent affirmation of the worth of the suffering so many of us had endured. I was about to ask the first of a hundred questions old military men must ask at such a time, when I noticed Holmes looking my way with raised brows.

"Oh," I said. "At some later time, Mr. Marston, perhaps you and I might reminisce a while, but we are confronted with pressing matters here. Holmes?" I turned the conversation back to my companion, who nodded appreciation for my restraint.

But Holmes did not immediately launch into his investigation. Through a series of quick inquiries he established that Marston was, as he seemed, an anomaly on the police force. His family had provided him substantial education before being ruined both financially and socially (we did not ask for the gruesome details of what was obviously a painful personal episode). He took to the military, it seemed, out of pure ebullience. The man loved action, and motion, and anything that would satisfy his craving for the new and different. Upon his return from Afghanistan some fifteen years ago, following an extended period during which, as he said, "I dined off my medal," he experimented with a variety of callings here and abroad, finally settling just within the past two years on the constabulary. His peculiar combination of military distinction, utter lack of financial resources, and reasonably good education led him to believe that he could work his way up through the ranks. He wanted to be a detective, which explained his reading not only my accounts of Holmes' cases, but tales of every other real or even fictional criminal investigator.

I did not know quite what to make of Holmes' line of inquiry. It did not seem necessary, as it so often did in these matters, to put the person under questioning at ease. Marston was already warmed to us and had been directed by Gregson to assist us in any way possible. I could only assume—and it would soon turn out to be so—that Holmes wanted as good an understanding as possible of the qualities of this man with whom we might have extended contact, or even find ourselves side by side in a tight situation.

Finally the conversation turned to the case. Holmes asked Marston how it was that he learned of our odd burglar. "Upon my arrival at this duty station," Marston said, suddenly turning formal and sounding for all the world as if he were reading from a prepared statement, "my eyes were caught by Miss Leary, the Clemens' girl. Without in any way shirking my official duties, I have found a few moments these past days to get to know her." Here he paused, as if deciding how long an aside were needed on the point. "I have looked for the right woman for many years, gentlemen, and my situation long ago broke me of any foolish concerns about social standing. I seek the person, not the station. My eye is not untrained. Miss Leary is an exceptional individual. True, she is deeply attached to the Clemens' family, and I may find myself at odds with them if our, uh, *romance* should advance to the point where she must choose between this lovely family and me. But to this point we have not spoken of such things, though I do not flatter myself when I say that they are on her mind as much as on mine."

Marston's guileless manner was contagious. Remembering Clara's smile when she mentioned Marston and Katy, I said, "The family seems to be pleased that Miss Leary has found agreeable company."

"Yes, I have hoped so. But to set that aside, the reason I mention it at all is that it has enabled me, through Miss Leary's explanations, to learn of the precise nature of the case you are engaged in, and to hear of the man who the whole Clemens family now refer to as the walleye. It is for that reason that I got word to Inspector Gregson that I might be able to help in this matter—help, I mean, beyond my guard duties.

"You see, my brother-in-law, that is to say my younger sister's husband, is something of a gamesman. Oh, he doesn't let it interfere with his family duties. They have been married for upwards of ten years and it has never developed into a problem, and he has always resisted the worst sorts of things. But he has what I might call a contained passion for some of the cruder sports."

"What is this man's occupation?" Holmes asked.

"His circumstance is a most happy one," Marston said congenially, plainly glad to talk about how well-situated his sister was. "He rather plays, as he himself puts it, at being a tailor." He glanced happily down at his own uniform, and my suspicions about its quality were confirmed. "Indeed, his rounds do include some distinguished citizens, and if he were to apply himself he could thrive on that trade alone. But his comfort, and his capacity for gaming, come from a substantial family annuity. Unlike those scoundrels one reads of so often in the shilling shockers, he disciplines himself most admirably, conscientiously budgeting his expenditures for his recreational pursuits much more tightly than he does my sister's household interests. My own fate in life may remain uncertain, but it has been a blessing all these years to know that Adelaide is secure."

Holmes and I listened to this with a mixture of entertainment at the man's pleasant volubility and wonderment at his way of drifting from the subject at hand. He noticed our somewhat blank expressions and said, "Ah, I have lost the track again, haven't I? Here's the point. Tom, my brother-in-law that is, was telling me after dinner just the other night about a peculiarly lively ratting match he'd attended, and he dwelt upon the most singular character, a man who fits our culprit to the 'T,' who he said had become something of a regular at the matches lately. Tom said the man put on an awful show; 'ungodly,' I think he called it. Must have been quite a sight."

"What sort of show?" Holmes asked.

"Oh, acting the fool, jumping about, apparently all but interfering with the dog on several occasions. Tom said this fellow would growl and yip in response to every kill, and though he didn't explain exactly what he meant, he made a sour face and said the man also took the most sordid interest in the dead rats after the match. Tom didn't pursue it, and I didn't have a chance to ask more, as our conversation was ended when Adelaide joined us in the parlor. In fact, I must admit I was just as glad to see the subject dropped. The fellow sounded the worst proof of old Darwin's beastly throwbacks, you know. Some kind of lost soul, like a savage. Tom said his blank eye and mop of wild hair made the fellow's behavior genuinely monstrous."

"I see. Did your brother-in-law give you the name of this establishment?"

"Not at the time, but I have since spoken with him and acquired it. I also spoke with the inspector, and he gave me leave to accompany you there. I am sure—from the doctor's writings, you know—that you gentlemen are accustomed to the perils of the city's rougher quarters, but I dare say it could be to your advantage to have an officer with you, and I would be honored to show the way."

"Yes," said Holmes, "we would be pleased to accept your invitation. Could we plan on it for this evening?"

"That was my hope as well," the constable said, rising. "Gentlemen, I am at your service. I propose that I come to your rooms—Baker Street, isn't it?" he added with a smile at me, "about 9 this evening. That should allow us plenty of time to make the matches."

"And where are they?" Holmes asked.

"Oh, right. Off Tench Street, at the London Docks." By now mention of the docks was so predictable that Holmes and I did not even trouble to glance at one another. "Tom gave me the most detailed instructions. We will be entering through an establishment known as Black's, a popular beer shop, but Tom tells me it's a somewhat winding course from there, so it's not entirely clear upon whose business premises the match occurs. No doubt that is the intention of the proprietors."

"No doubt," Holmes said. Marston now having nearly dismissed himself, Holmes accommodated him, asking him to send Miss Leary along our way if he saw her.

Concern fleeted across Marston's expressive face, then he relaxed and smiled. "Of course, of course." He gave us another of his bright grins. "I just happen to know where she is."

"What a jovial fellow," I said to Holmes when we were alone. "I would enjoy some time with him when this affair has been concluded. I wonder if Gregson or Lestrade have any notion of his unusual qualities."

"No," said Holmes. "I am certain they do not."

Chapter Nine
Miss Leary's Pardon

It is remarkable how an individual, even a physically striking and personally forceful one, can enjoy near-concealment in the smallest crowd and yet be instantly revealed when encountered alone. Through all the interviews in which I had assisted my illustrious companion over the many years of our association, I had never been as aware of the contrast of impression that arises from this circumstance as I now was. When Miss Leary entered the room, I was instantly aware that my earlier impression of her, when all the occupants of the house gathered in this same room, had been sadly inadequate. Here was a character Mark Twain himself would have found daunting to portray. Temporarily released from the passionate solicitousness that consumed her when any family member was in sight, Katy Leary's own presence asserted itself.

Stout but not corpulent, perfectly tidy except where a few small bundles of her dense black tresses escaped the confinement of a large bun, her large black eyes shining from under heavy dark brows, she seated herself opposite us with a straight-backed air that the less perceptive might have mistaken for defiance, but that I suspected was just a splendid independence. In Holmes' eyes I saw a dawning of interest in this self-assured and obviously beloved member of the Clemens' household.

"Miss Leary," he began in his most circumspect tone, "it has come to our attention that the police inspector may not have had sufficient opportunity to benefit from your insights." At the mention of Gregson, her broad face darkened for an instant—confirming my suspicion that he had indeed treated her poorly if not rudely—before her eyes brightened at Holmes' judicious way of dispensing with past discourtesies. "Dr. Watson and I are now in a position to take up this inquiry with you. We are sure that you share our concern for the well-being of the Clemens family, and our desire to clear up this troubling situation."

"I most certainly do, Mr. Holmes. This is *my* family, you must understand. My life." Her voice was a higher pitch than I had anticipated based on her physique, but sharp and strong, even harsh at times. The slightly halting cadence of her speech suggested someone who had come to polished conversation rather later in life than is customary. Perhaps lacking in proper schooling, she had educated herself in grammar and syntax through attention to the extraordinary conversations she must have routinely overheard among the members of this household and their parade of distinguished guests.

Holmes asked her how long she had been with the family, a question she answered directly by explaining that she had come to their house in late girlhood, and at the same time evaded discreetly by giving no hint of how many years had passed since that stage of her life. Trained in the dressmaker's trade as a child in Elmira, New York, she served the Clemens' family in many ways and was proud that her sewing skills were still called upon almost daily. She was, in fact, sewing Clara's Jubilee dress when Clemens burst in upon his family following the break-in.

"I seem to recall," Holmes said to her, "that during our first visit to this house, when we met the whole family in this room and enjoyed a genial conversation with them, there were times when you seemed near to speaking on this or that matter under discussion. We are most eager for any impressions you may have to offer."

Still, despite such firm encouragement, she hesitated—Gregson must have been deucedly awful to her in some way—so I said, "In our first interview with Mr. Clemens, he indicated that you seemed unconvinced there had even been a break-in here."

This was sufficient provocation to open the floodgates.

"Oh, not at all, Dr. Watson, not at all." She seemed agitated at the very idea that she could doubt anything Sam Clemens told her. "I remember the very moment you refer to, however. Mr. Clemens had just rushed in with his news of the intruder, and I suppose he just misunderstood the expression on my face. I did not doubt him. I was merely annoyed and perhaps a little hurt that he should seem so fearful for the well-being of our family. *I* was there, after all. I would allow nothing to harm them."

She uttered this last statement with the surety of a veteran officer with a crack regiment poised behind him, sabers drawn. Had most men made such a statement, I would have been inclined to disregard it as delusion at best and cheap bravado at worst. But coming from this singularly confident woman, who said it so matter-of-factly with not the least hint of *braggadocio*, it was so persuasive that I found myself silently admitting that were I a housebreaker I would not like to test her resolve.

I was about to ask her how she would have gone about protecting the family from an assailant who, for all she knew, might have been armed, but she gave me no time. Now that she was talking, she intended to hold the floor.

"The intruder entered the house through the kitchen, Mr. Holmes. I do not know what he sought, but I do not think he was a thief. In fact, I do not think he was an . . . ordinary man. It does not surprise me that his appearance was irregular. In fact, I imagine that he was irregular through and through."

She took a breath to continue, but Holmes was too quick for her, and said, "Miss Leary, you give us more information in one breath than the police have uncovered in days of investigation. How do you know these things?"

"Which things do you mean?"

"Let's start with the kitchen. How do you know he entered that way?"

"I mean no disrespect, Mr. Holmes. You are a famous detective and no doubt you have your reasons, but you and the others barely looked in the back of the house, so you wouldn't have noticed things there."

Holmes' eyebrows rose. "Things?"

"Jean often shares her books with me. I know that you are. . . *adept* at seeing little things that others miss. But you had no reason to notice certain things that someone more familiar with the situation might." Holmes' eyebrows could rise no higher, and I could see that though he was surprised by the sudden turn in the conversation, he was enjoying the unfamiliar situation of having this woman as much as offer him her pardon for his failure to measure up to his reputation.

"Please, Miss Leary, what did I miss?"

"Things were . . . *touched*, Mr. Holmes. Things were *changed*. The man treated the kitchen, well, almost like a gentleman's dressing room. Or he did so at least along the line of his travel."

"Perhaps it would be better, Miss Leary," Holmes said, abruptly rising from his seat, "if you showed us these 'things.'" He indicated that she should lead us from the room, down the long hallway, and into the kitchen at the rear of the house. She bustled eagerly from the room and we followed.

The kitchen was somewhat larger than average for a house this size, stretching most of the way across the building's rear; a pantry door led off to additional space. The stairway down to a short interior hallway that led to the street door was centred along the wall on the street side. Two large tables with a scattering of chairs pulled up to them dominated the floor. Most of the walls were covered with cupboards, under which spread commodious counter space.

Holmes and I paused just inside the door. Katy moved directly to the stairs down to the door on the Tite Street side of the house, turned, and announced, as if conducting a student tour, "The intruder entered through this door." So saying, she walked briskly between the tables, adding, "Then he came this way, and along that counter," she pointed to the counter along the wall behind us, "and through the door into the hallway," she concluded, passing to our right and pausing at the door.

Seeing our puzzled expressions, she explained. "Everything is changed now; the staff has been at work. But immediately following Mr. Clemens' sudden return and his telling us of the intruder, I came to the kitchen for some water for Mrs. Clemens." She indicated the wet sink opposite the pantry door. "The cook, Mary, had left her apron on this chair." She indicated a chair under the right-hand table, on the side nearest the other table. "When she and the housemaid had left on errands, I saw her toss it over the chair, like so." She made a casual gesture. "I am not usually attentive to such things, but a few weeks ago I had made her this very apron as a gift for all her kindnesses to me; I remember thinking how pretty it was as it hung over the chair back." She glanced round the kitchen. "It's here somewhere, I suppose, but I can just tell you that I was especially proud of the border smocking."

She straightened and gave us her most direct gaze, as if to strengthen her next statement. "When I came here for water, I was the first person to enter the kitchen after Mr. Clemens returned and, well, under the circumstances, it was impossible for me not to notice that the apron had been moved. It was still over the same chair, but now it was . . . . draped neatly and evenly. I remember noticing that the smocking, which I had seen so clearly earlier, was now hidden."

Katy again glanced around the kitchen, as if seeing it then instead of now. "There was a good deal of clutter in the kitchen. The Clemens family maintains somewhat . . . unusual hours, especially for dining, and even after all these months the staff are still adjusting. Cooking pots, quite a bit of dinner ware, some produce, and other things were out on both tables and most of the counters. The silver polish was sitting right there, with a tray of silver waiting.

"This may seem unlikely to you gentlemen, but through this one part of the kitchen," she indicated the path between the tables with a wave of her arm, "things had been tidied up. Several pots had been stacked in each other, by size. On that counter behind you, jars of spices had been placed in a straight row. It took no time at all to notice, and, once noticed, to follow the path of the intruder from the back door to the hallway. No one else could have done it. For the life of me I can't imagine why someone would sneak into a home for such a reason, so I can only assume it was not done for . . . for a reason we would understand. This intruder was not normal. But I am not a detective, so perhaps there are things that burglars do that I do not understand. Can you explain this, Mr. Holmes?"

"I cannot, Miss Leary," Holmes said. "But I congratulate you on your perceptiveness. We noticed similar disturbances, or should I say attentions to neatness, in Mr. Clemens' study. Our mysterious intruder does seem to have some very odd habits." Katy Leary showed both pleasure and relief to hear her theories so readily and fully endorsed. "Did you notice any other changes?" he asked.

"The hallway carpet is loose and is constantly being shifted by the passage of the staff. I think he may have straightened it as he went through, but then it was just rumpled and moved again by the next people to go that way. It needs tacking, but somehow we all forget."

Holmes studied her thoughtfully for a moment, then asked, "Has anything else peculiar about this affair come to your notice, Miss Leary?" I saw something of a common awareness pass between them. She seemed a little startled.

"Nothing else as . . . *certain* as what I have told you, Mr. Holmes," though it was clear there was more on her mind and she had not expected Holmes to realise it.

"Anything at all might help, Miss Leary. Anything at all."

"Well, Mr. Holmes, I mean no offence, but it's about the police." She grimaced, obviously hesitant to continue.

"Scotland Yard is a splendid institution, Miss Leary, but Dr. Watson and I are among those few with abundant opportunities to witness our finest law-enforcement professionals in their, let us say, less illustrious moments. You need not worry, either that you will offend us—or surprise us."

She smiled slightly at this admission, and suddenly barged ahead with her opinions. "This Inspector Gregson is a ninny, of course. I am more annoyed at myself than at him that I let his . . . *pretensions* have such an effect on me. But it's not just him. Because of the . . . quality of some of our guests, as few as they have been, I have had chances to meet your bobbies. They are a handsome lot in their fine uniforms and shiny buttons, but they are . . . too full of themselves, and they are without exception shameless flirts. Sarah, the housemaid, attracts them like moths to a lantern; she's a pretty young thing. And even Mary occasionally has to warn one off, though she says they only want her scones." Katy Leary entirely passed over any dealings she might personally have had with these troublesome officers, and continued with her inventory of their offences. "There is always beer in the kitchen, and they help themselves to it on the slightest pretence of needing to enter the house. Beer is cheap, of course. It's not the expense, it's the . . . *presumption*."

"Some, or at least one, of them, is, I understand, rather more welcome than the others?" Holmes tried to lead the subject toward her own growing romance with our new constable friend. At first Katy seemed to miss his inference, and said only, "Yes, Constable Marston at least had the good grace to approach Mary in a respectful manner." Then, with a start and perhaps even a slight blush, she understood what Holmes meant.

"Oh," she said. "You have been talking to Clara, haven't you?" Without waiting even for a nod of assent from us, she continued. "My family," — she used the word as a matriarch might, surveying her brood from above— "do not always . . . *comprehend* what is going on around them. From the morning of Mr. Marston's first arrival, I identified him as a much different man from the run-of-the-muck bobbies. And when he aimed his very obvious charm at Sarah, I felt compelled to step in. You may regard this as meddlesome on my part, but I could not stand by and watch that child be . . . *victimised* by his type. I took my first opportunity to give her a talking-to, and simply made myself more available for his conversational convenience. I am sure that Clara has seen me talking with him now and then, and assumes that an . . . *understanding* has been reached." She frowned. "I should have been more alert to this .

.. *eventuality*." She seemed especially pleased to have come up with just this word.

"Miss Leary," said Holmes in his most solicitous manner, "We have no right to pry into your private life. This entire matter is beyond our business here, and solely your concern. But I must admit to a great curiosity over how you are so certain that the constable's interest in you is not sincere? Just this morning he expressed to us a great fondness and admiration for you." Holmes, perhaps because he was treading on such unfamiliar grounds of romantic etiquette, looked at me, seeking either affirmation of his statement, or reassurance that such a question dared be asked by a comparative stranger. I nodded my head and said, "He was most emphatic in his statements in that regard." I wondered, again, about Holmes' wide-ranging interest in Marston.

"Was he, now?" Katy seemed only mildly surprised and not at all persuaded. "Mr. Holmes, I would never claim great worldliness, or any special gift for penetrating the . . . *motivations* of other people. And you are correct, I suppose, that this is none of your affair. But I can tell you that as sure as I am standing before you, Mr. Marston has no serious interest in me." She gave this statement some additional thought, no doubt never having heard it said aloud before by her or anyone else. "In fact, now that I am confronted with the question of Mr. Marston so directly, I ask myself if he, too, is all he seems to be?"

"The question has entered my mind as well, Miss O'Leary," Holmes admitted, to my utter surprise. "I would be grateful if you would keep your eyes and ears open, and perhaps later we might reconvene and discuss these matters, *all* these matters, in light of additional evidence?"

"I would be delighted by that opportunity, Mr. Holmes," she said, without the least hesitation.

Chapter Ten
Temple of the Dog

We were barely underway in the cab before Holmes lit his pipe and visibly withdrew into himself. The man had a singular gift for making himself seem unapproachable merely through posture, though it was a gift he only exercised under the most pressing of circumstances. I dearly wished to ask him about Marston, whom both he and Miss Leary plainly saw in a different light than I did, but it was obviously not the time to do so. Upon reflection, I decided to play the bystander and wait for further events to provide illumination.

Holmes maintained his air of concentration and distraction through an early dinner. He smoked continuously, pacing our rooms with a slow gait, coming to a stop facing a wall, then turning to face the window or the door but showing not the least interest in whatever his eyes rested upon. I had rarely seen him so utterly, almost helplessly, absorbed in a problem, though at this stage in our investigation I could not imagine what had so suddenly captured his attention.

Just as suddenly, as he paused by the fireplace in yet another distracted circumambulation of the room, he shook himself like a man emerging from a trance, glanced at the clock on the mantel, and announced, "Watson, our constable will be here within the hour. We must make a few preparations."

"A few preparations" included my first personal acquaintance with Holmes' art of disguise. "Not much is necessary, you understand; we won't be expected there, and the light will be poor, but this is still a needful precaution." He quickly fitted me with a short dark gray beard and a rather tight old hat of a rounded style unlike anything I'd seen before.

"The beard itches, Holmes."

"I expect it does, Watson, but take comfort in knowing that it is inhabited only by you, which, I fear, is more than I can say for this frock." He completed his own transformation from natty consulting detective to nondescript sporting man with a misshapen cap. "It is not so much a matter of us not looking like ourselves, you understand. It is a matter of not looking like anyone—of achieving that high state of ordinariness that, at its most artful, will cause us simply to vanish from notice."

"I would hope for no less, were any of my acquaintances to encounter us along the way," I said, barely resisting the urge to claw at my face through the irritating beard. "But then I suppose that any friends of mine who are where we are going would be just as eager that I not notice them, either."

"One other precaution is especially important tonight, Watson. I anticipate the likelihood, almost certainty, of danger, indeed a peril beyond what we might expect even in such a hostile quarter."

"I already extracted one of my revolvers from the cabinet, Holmes. What about you?" I asked.

"Yes, certainly." With his hand he vaguely indicated the back of his coat, suggesting either a weapon on the back of his belt or somehow ensconced in the lining of the shabby garment itself. "Ah, I believe that is Marston's cab; let us not wait for him." He hurried for the door. We were soon on our way through the late dusk.

It was a clear night, and even along the river there was little mist to mute the illumination from the street lamps. But the moment we stepped from the cab into Black's we might as well have passed from the planet we knew into some parallel plane of existence in which things clean, and easily seen, and worth seeing, did not exist.

The barroom was distinguished from countless others of its kind only by its immense size, and by the peculiar nature of its ornamentation. It was a huge, low-ceilinged room, and whenever one wandered near a wall or any of its furnishings, one was grateful for the bleary smoke that prevented any sharper examination of the place.

At its most artfully honest, the English tavern is as fine an institution, as solid an expression of humble yet wholesome human society, as might welcome a weary soul anywhere along the world's byways. Black's establishment struck precisely the opposite note. Every fixture was a ruin, every surface was begrimed, every eye suspicious or openly belligerent.

And yet as we walked the length of the room I could almost feel us merging with the crowd. Marston had, like us, "dressed down" for the occasion. His brisk manner and grand physique had been so well concealed, partly under a faded travel cloak and partly through a change in posture, that the three of us were to all outward appearances just a few more undistinguished bits of refuse on the heap. I fancy that our shuffled passage to a quiet corner table was achieved without undue notice.

Our successful camouflage was reinforced by the remarkable variety of our fellow patrons. Lingering here and there, or holding court at this or that table, was a cross-section of London's male population. Two or three silk-scarved barristers of obvious distinction sat quietly at a table directly opposite several sailors already well along toward inebrial oblivion and delighted to display their state to one and all. I was startled to identify at least two distant acquaintances who were well known in the city for places of honor on the Medical Register. Throughout the room I saw the intermixture of faces of refinement with others marred by common toil and yet others deprived of all but the coarsest of human impulses. I had expected to see many dogs, but only a handful of the men carried small, furry bundles that in the excessive smokiness I could not further identify.

Holmes was scanning the room like a gourmand studying the menu at a beloved and generous trough. It occurred to me to wonder just how many of these faces were familiar to him, and how many would pale if they knew his eyes were on them.

"Is your brother-in-law coming tonight?" I asked Marston through my beard. I had already discovered that whenever I sat down, the change in posture caused the false whiskers to rise and half-smother me.

"No, I warned him off, just to keep things simple for us if there is any trouble." Apparently Marston shared Holmes' anticipations. Marston turned to me and asked, "I am concerned for your safety, Doctor. Are you armed?"

I reassured him on that matter, and he was visibly pleased to hear it.

As my eyes adjusted to the shadows and smoke, I was struck by the decorations. Where a typical gin palace of this class would feature the most ghastly pictorial offences against both art and nature—specializing most often in obscene affronts to everything moral and chaste in the world of daylight—this establishment featured nothing but dogs: paintings of dogs, mezzotints of dogs, photographs of dogs, dogs mounted whole in dingy glass cases, and head mounts of dogs holding rats in their mouths, every bloody fang and bulging eye accentuated. In a gruesome way, this dark place was a temple to the dog—not as man's companion, but as a killer.

I am not naive about London's underworld. I have seen much of it, and read enough of Mayhew and other *voyeur*-travellers in London's grimmest underways not to be easily surprised. But for all that, I was still morbidly engaged by the incredible flexibility of human passion, and freshly shocked that it could find an outlet for the recreational urge in such vile pursuits. The rat, the loathesome adversary of my profession, the purveyor of everything filthy and corrupt, was at the very centre of a tradition—I could not bring myself to call it a "sport," though its enthusiasts proudly did so—that in this city was no less robust and eagerly pursued than were the manly field sports of the rural counties, or the time-honored cricket rivalries of Eton and Oxford.

It was more than a tradition; it was a kind of industry. Many a wretch, and a few less wretched, made entire livings capturing rats by the hundreds—from rural farmsteads, from ditches, from public parks, from the hideous architectural warrens of the city's ruined sections—not for the sake of cleanliness and safety, but merely to sell to the followers of the "fancy," as they proudly called their bloody obsession.

On the walls around us were memorials to the legendary figures of that pursuit. Had I the stomach for it, somewhere here I no doubt could find a portrait of the famous "Billy," a near-mythic rat-killer who, decades ago in a "pit" very like the one we were about to visit, was said to have killed 500 rats in less than six minutes. I never will mourn the death of a rat, or a thousand rats; but no creature, even the foulest sewer rat, should be compelled to die in such a pointless display of canine torment and human degradation as was and is routine in the pit.

Holmes roused me from my angry reverie. Marston had beckoned us to move toward the rear of the room, as indeed others were already doing. Though there had been no discernible signal or announcement, the hundred or so men in the bar were thinning gradually as some here, some there, drifted that way and through a dim passageway.

The vast wormholes of London's dock district are known fully by none. Centuries of construction, rebuilding, and renovation have resulted in labyrinthine mazes, more like artificial downs made of wood than like normal buildings. No sub-basement is immune to further delving. Our passageway, about the width of two men's shoulders, was walled with the crudest brickwork, roofed by rough, raw planks encrusted with the vapors of generations of dogs, their fanciers, and no doubt other nameless horrors. Weakly lit by intermittent lamplight, the route seemed to follow the rectangular contours of some ancient building foundation. Once a wall of immense, crudely hewn stone blocks was exposed along one wall and then replaced by equally monumental timbers. The stone brought to mind Roman times.

Twice we passed through large rooms, one completely vacant and almost too dark for walking, the other just another low-ceilinged barroom thinly populated along one end, apparently by patrons with no interest in dogs or rats. Were it not for the general flow of the others ahead of us, we might not have found our way, though the entire winding route could not have been more than 400 yards and may have been between two points less than half that far apart in a straight line.

At last we descended narrow stone steps—the walls were barely head-high, and of roughly planed board—and emerged into a brightly lit chamber perhaps 100 feet on a side, whose floor sloped unevenly to the centre. A bulky man took our half-crown each, and we were free to find a place. There were benches scattered here and there, but most of us were expected to stand. Along one side of the room, against the wall, were three small railed-off spaces, like feeble parodies of opera-house boxes. Apparently even the "fancy" had its quality enthusiasts who required separation from the *hoi-polloi*.

Holmes saw me observing the boxes, and leaned over to mumble, "The status of rank required to enjoy those seats of honor is not based on the sorts of distinction familiar among some of the guests." He nodded toward a small unlikely claque of finely dressed gentlemen, possibly financiers. "A radically different class structure and political system prevails." I wondered if Holmes had been in this very room before.

From two other doorways in the corners of the room additional enthusiasts filed in. A few were carrying or leading dogs of various kinds. Though many of the beasts were without doubt mongrels, I was surprised to see several Skye Terriers and others of recognizable breed. Some of the dogs were quite agitated, and while the rumble of human voices was surprisingly subdued, the piercing yaps and barks of the animals were at times nearly painful, and made conversation in a normal tone of voice difficult.

As with so many of the men, the dog's eyes were naturally drawn to the most brightly lit portion of the room, a small circular depression at the lowest middle of the floor. This was the notorious pit, surrounded by a chest-high wall that sloped slightly outward—enough to facilitate the view of spectators but not enough to enable the rats to climb out. The floor of the pit must have been about eight feet across. The floor and inside of the pit were freshly whitewashed, and they shone brightly under the numerous branches of a decrepit but fantastically ornate gas lamp. Only in the very back of the room, if too many heads intervened between the viewer and the pit, was the view of the pit's floor completely obscured.

Following Marston's lead, we seated ourselves on a tottering backless bench toward the rear, Holmes in the middle. I noticed with satisfaction that Marston had positioned us at the best possible angle to observe all three entrances to the room, and wondered if perhaps he, too, had been here before. Though we all surreptitiously glanced around the room, we saw no sign of our quarry. For the first time it occurred to me that this entire evening might be a waste of time. We were, after all, depending upon the appearance of a person whose mental makeup, much less his motivations, suggested an inscrutability perhaps beyond even the unique perceptual range of my famous companion.

Chapter Eleven
The Pit, and Worse

Just as the room began to feel crowded and close, and at least 250 men were standing, sitting, tending to dogs, and otherwise milling about, a murmur swept from one doorway across the crowd and we all became quiet. Then, with all the pomp of a palace ball, a last small party entered the room and moved through the parting crowd to the central, and largest, of the three boxes. There was a man and a woman in front, and another man towered over them behind.

"This is the proprietor," Marston whispered to us. "Name's Wakefield, or so they say. He directs the show, and if there's any argument over a wager, he settles it." He paused. "Or his assistant does."

The proprietor was an extravagantly dressed slender man of about fifty. His clothes were a garishly hued parody of a gentleman's evening dress, but for all his self-conscious pretence of bearing it was impossible to study him for any length of time, because of his "assistant," a giant nearly seven feet tall, almost grotesquely broad-shouldered and thick-limbed. His strength must have been enormous. He was conservatively and (it must be admitted) handsomely dressed, and extremely pale of face—as if he never left this subterranean empire. A stern expression upon his broad, heavy-jawed face, he walked immediately behind the left shoulder of his employer, indeed crowded directly against his employer's back as if such intimate contact was required to shepherd the smaller man to his box.

Beside these two, the woman seemed all out of place. Even in the lurid shadows and flickering light, her beauty was stunning. Her hair was that most striking black that is so lustrous it seems almost blue. Her face was a breathtaking combination of Caucasian and Asian features. She was dressed in a surprising and yet somehow appropriate combination of dinner dress and ball gown in shades of palest yellow, which had a magnificent effect against her dark skin and hair. With her flashing eyes directed strictly forward, she moved with regal ease through this foul den.

"Wakefield's wife," Marston whispered to us, then added, "More or less, anyway; near's the same. They say he bought her as a child in the Far East, Singapore or some godless such place, but now she runs many of his enterprises. She is quite gifted." Then, probably because he saw the awe in my face as I gawked at this exquisite creature, he added, "And the meanest of the three."

Holmes frowned a bit, as if this may not have agreed with some knowledge he had obtained elsewhere.

The hush of the crowd even quieted the dogs, though sharp whacks here and there indicated that some required their masters' reminders to stay quiet. The audience was making only the softest rustle as the Wakefields took their seats—the only chairs in the middle box—and the giant assumed his apparently customary protective position, standing immediately behind them.

All eyes were now upon Wakefield, who, without a word or a hint of acknowledgment of his audience's attention, nodded to two men standing by the pit directly down from his box. These were dressed so like professional mourners as to leave no difference, presumably some quirk of formality favored by Wakefield, whose obvious personal flair for the preposterously flamboyant may have demanded the somber contrast.

The high theatre of this little procession had entirely knocked any thought of our quarry from my mind until Holmes' elbow and a slight nod of his head brought me to myself and directed my attention to a singular figure now peering over the far wall of the pit—and I had my first glimpse of the strange man who had been our constant concern these past days. Dressed in a plain but well-cared-for brown suit, his ragged hair living up to all Sam Clemens' superlatives, his half-sighted attention riveted to the two black-clad men, and his very posture speaking of an intense and ill-controlled agitation of mind, he gripped the top of the pit wall with thin, wiry hands, his one good eye rolling frantically from the men to Wakefield and back again. He seemed himself like one of these hatefully perverted dogs, awaiting the order to kill.

Marston's brother-in-law had not exaggerated. Had this poor soul been openly slavering, the effect of soul-twisting ecstasy could not have been more pronounced.

Then the proceedings were underway. One of the attendants at the pit easily leapt the wall. As he landed in the pit, I noticed that his pant legs were tightly laced against his shins just above his boots, and Marston whispered, "You don't want three or four of those little devils making their way up your trouser legs. Never know *what* they'll find."

As soon as the pit-man's feet hit the floor, the calm evaporated and the crowd roared. The other attendant crouched low among the benches, where no doubt some pens were located, then raised the night's first contestant, a small rough-haired terrier of about ten pounds, which he showed to the crowd in all directions, announcing a wager of twenty-five pounds on a match between this animal (whose name was given as "Benjamin," to a hearty laugh from the crowd) and forty of the best sewer rats in eight minutes. The dog strained toward the pit, though no rats were visible from our viewpoint, and several other animals set up an ungodly chorus of howls, barks, and bays. Even from this distance the little dog's numerous scars, even a couple still-raw wounds, were easily visible.

The audience was now engaged in large, argumentative wagering among themselves. Exactly how or where the announced twenty-five pound wager was to operate in this chaos of shouted bets remained unclear to me. A few yells expressed indignation that the odds were too short—there were too few rats for so much time, they objected—but others disagreed, sewer rats evidently having the highest reputation as fighters.

Marston leaned across in front of Holmes and told us that we too must now appear to be discussing our wagers. Taking a stub of a pencil and a tablet from his pocket, he added that there would be no need for money to change hands among us after each match, because he would pretend to be keeping a tally.

While the buzz of wagering continued, a small boy hurried down one of the open aisles carrying a large, flat cage about two feet square and jammed full of squirming rats. This he placed on top of the pit wall, holding it steady while the attendant in the pit opened a small trap on the top and, with considerable ceremony, reached inside barehanded, stirring around for a choice rat. "It's a matter of pride among some of these fellows that they do this without gloves," Marston said. "There's no end of misery in the bites and scratches from those rotten things."

As he found rats that met his needs—these seemed to be the largest ones—he casually tossed them into the pit, one after another.

The dog now writhed madly in the arms of the other pit-man. The cage was less than half empty when the man closed the trap and called for another, which was promptly delivered by another boy. In moments, forty huge rats were scattered about the pit floor, some quietly grooming themselves or squabbling with their fellows, others mounding up in a corner, their tails snaking across the backs of each other as they sought a way out.

The pit-man gave a clap of his hands and vaulted back over the wall. His companion abruptly released his grip and the dog rocketed from his arms into the pit. Rushing from rat to rat, he grabbed each by the back or neck, shook it furiously two or three times, and then let it loose at the end of the last swing of his head so that the limp corpse often smacked hard against the pit walls, leaving dark smudges of blood. This efficient, systematic slaughter seemed what the crowd most wanted; their bellows, cries, and whistles of encouragement seemed to feed the little animal's frenzy.

But one rat, perhaps the tenth and the largest yet, was a tougher character. The crowd quieted as the rat rose upon its hind legs with all the ferocity of a cornered bear and faced the dog with an audible hiss. It somehow evaded the quick jaws, which got only a partial grip on a hind leg. The furious rat latched itself to the dog's snout, claws digging into the tender nose flesh while the teeth snapped within a whisker's breadth of the dog's eyes. Then the noise of the crowd was suddenly deafening, many of the men seeming to favor the rat who, for all his vile nature, was showing a valor that could only be admired in this hideous setting.

But at that moment my eyes were distracted from the pit by a second disturbance. Our South African housebreaker seemed in a nervous fit of epic proportions, shrieking hysterically, then suddenly cooing like a happy mother to its babe, then wildly wringing his hands above his head, all the while sort of dancing in place, slamming his knees against the outside of the pit wall. Looking about, I could see that many in the audience were now watching him instead of the match, and indeed some of the catcalls and yells were clearly directed towards him. Wakefield seemed to be watching him with a mild, almost fond amusement, though his wife's expression was not as easily read. Marston's brother-in-law was not the only person to have noticed this strange soul's tortured ways. It seemed likely that he had even become a casually advertised part of the entertainment here.

When I looked back at the dog, he had somehow disposed of the big rat and was burying his nose in the squirming pile of rats gathered in the corner, pulling one after another to its death. He finished his killing in five minutes, and it took only two more for the pit-man to gather the carcasses with a coal-shovel and dump them in a sack, which another small boy lugged away.

The next two hours were the most disgust-filled of my life. Match after match the death and revulsion went on, until brutalised rats and debased dogs merged in my mind into one horrendous mass of blood and torment. The raging bloodlust of the audience only heightened with each new spectacle, and there seemed no end to the supply of rats and small boys to deliver them. The only marginally useful thought I carried away from the nightmarish performance, which dawned on me some weeks later, was that the magnitude of London's rodent infestation must be far worse than ever I or my medical colleagues had imagined, if they could be so readily obtained in such tremendous numbers by the ratters who supported this grotesque parody of sport on a nightly basis—and in who knew how many venues besides this one?

Toward midnight, as the pit-man introduced a visiting champion, "the king of all Birmingham ratters," to the earnest applause of the crowd, the subject of our surveillance took the course of the evening into his own hands. He had been growing more and more extreme in his actions as his madness overcame him. I could see that even Wakefield's big assistant was now watching him with concern. I was unaccountably reminded of the impatient expression I had seen on the face of an attendant at the British Museum as he stepped over to admonish a patron for whistling in the galleries.

The madman's progressive deterioration into bestiality had reached the point where, though he never tried to interfere with the dogs, his gleeful attention to the dead rats had passed all bounds. As rats died, he raved directly at the little carcasses here and there on the floor of the pit; the words, if indeed they were real words at all, were unrecognizable over the din, but his tone of voice seemed at times sympathetic, then admonitory, then gentle. The pit-man was still scooping up the last of the previous match's dead, and passed directly in front of this distracted soul, shoveling up a rat at which the walleye was directing a stern, incoherent lecture. As if angry that the rat was removed before he finished with it, the madman nimbly leapt over the wall and grabbed the dead rat from the pit-man's shovel. As the entire crowd let loose a huge cheer and the pit-man gaped at him in surprise, he held the bloody little animal against his cheek with an expression of maniacal joy.

Several things then happened more or less simultaneously. The pit-man turned questioningly toward Wakefield. Wakefield's wife, whose voice was drowned out by the crowd, clearly spoke the word "No!" as she shook her head toward the men in the pit. Wakefield, annoyance and amusement mixed on his face, with a flick of his hand sent his assistant toward the pit, presumably to remove this disturbance. And the crazed focus of all this attention, still dreamily cuddling the dead rat against his cheek, by chance glanced our way, took in the three of us with a wide-eyed start, tossed the rat aside, and fled from the pit and up the aisle toward the door along the far wall.

"Great Heavens, Holmes, he saw us!" I cried, even as Marston and Holmes rose and began shouldering their way through the crowd, which was still half cheering the lunatic and half booing the assistant who, to my surprise, continued to pursue him even though he had left the pit.

Marston's powerful frame and free-ranging elbows ploughed a comfortable passage through the cheering men, and we were soon across the room. We reached the door directly after Wakefield's assistant, who seemed not to notice us in the turmoil of the crowd and lumbered into a long, poorly lit passageway. As low as its ceiling was, it seemed not to slow his slouching figure, which was soon lost around one of the corners that were an exasperating feature of these ugly hallways. We rounded the corner to find ourselves facing adjacent entries to equally dim hallways, one turning abruptly to the left and the other continuing straight on. We could see the giant in neither.

We hardly paused long enough for me to pull the irksome false beard from my face and discard it when Marston shouted over his shoulder, "Take that one!" waving to the straight hallway as he dashed into the other.

Holmes glanced back at me. At first I thought he was checking to see if I had kept up, but he said, "Now you must be ready, Watson!" I groped my revolver from my pocket.

As he hurried on in the direction that Marston had indicated, Holmes reached into his coat and drew not the revolver I expected, but a *cosh* of the most extraordinary size and length. Gripping it just below the knobbed end and trailing a handle longer than a riding crop, he ran along the rough floor of the passage, through a stretch that was almost lightless, and to an entry into a larger chamber. He slowed as he approached this opening, and I caught him up so that we entered the room as might a man and his shadow.

Holmes, being first to emerge from the narrow tunnel, suddenly let out a bark of alarm that sounded like "Down, Watson," and folded himself over, rather to the right than straight ahead, in time to avoid the sweep of an enormous wooden club that swung from the left side of the doorway. I was just far enough back from Holmes that the club, aimed for his chest, caught me a hard but glancing blow on the left shoulder and sent me spinning back against the door frame with such force that I not only lost my breath, my footing, and my revolver, but was momentarily stunned. As I slipped to the floor, I was only vaguely capable of watching as Wakefield's giant, recovering from the momentum of his blow, began to turn back toward Holmes. I recall thinking it curious that Holmes had not risen to his feet, but remained rather in a half squat, extended laterally with his head away from our assailant. But pivoting slightly on his right foot, Holmes quickly drew his left knee up against his chest, then with all the force he could muster, straightened that leg and drove the heel of his booted foot against the rigid, forward-leaning kneecap of the big man. There was a sharp, crunching snap, and the man crashed down with a scream of agony, releasing his club and clutching at the shattered joint. Holmes was up in an instant, and when the enraged giant, still roaring with pain and rage, released his knee and pawed under his coat for another weapon, Holmes' hands slid to the base of the long cosh, and in a whistling swing that would have done full credit to the hardiest Rocky Mountain lumberjack, dealt the giant a skull blow that resounded even more loudly than had the broken knee.

In an instant, Holmes assisted me to my feet. "We have no time to waste, Watson. Are you able to move on? Their plans have gone awry, and we may settle more than we could have hoped for!"

I tottered slightly as I collected my revolver from the floor, but despite a shoulder that hurt like fire I felt my strength returning. "*Whose* plans, Holmes?"

But his only answer was, "The cosh is hardly sporting, but even under a proper referee I would not want to face that man in the ring." He jogged to the centre of the room, stood gazing about for a moment, then said, "This way, Watson!"

But no sooner had he uttered those words when Marston came thundering from the very door Holmes had indicated. He took in the rumpled pile of the unconscious giant with a quick approving glance, and said, "Well then, at least he's out of our way. I wondered where he'd got to. Are you all right?" He glanced anxiously back and forth between us.

"Watson took a shock, but I think he's fit to continue now. You have not caught our housebreaker?"

"No. I got turned around back there. My sense of direction is quite good, but the bloody halls of this godforsaken hive are a mystery."

"Unless I have lost my orientation," Holmes said, as if there were in fact no chance of such a development, "I believe our chances are best back the way you've just come. There are additional passageways branching from the one you took to get here?"

"Several," said Marston, "and having gone wrong this time, I think I've figured out the right one. Come on." He spun back toward the door, and then we were again twisting our way through more tunnels.

"I don't mind admitting," I panted at Holmes' shoulders in front of me, "that I don't have the faintest notion of where we are. Why are all these passages even here? Why are they lit? Surely the people attending the ratting match didn't need this many entries."

Holmes, who hurried along while visually absorbed in every foot of the floor beneath him, rather absently said, "North is to our left, or a little forward of that. We have returned, I imagine, to within about 100 yards of Black's barroom," he pointed to our right, and rather at an upward angle, "though of course I cannot assure you that it can be attained without great sidelong excursions from this point. As far as why the lights are maintained, that has puzzled me too."

"Do not assume that ratting is the only enterprise underway in this vicinity of an evening," Marston offered in puffing breaths, "though I didn't expect to see so little traffic besides us. Right after we separated, I did pass a few. There were two men with a woman, no doubt on their way to conduct some business of their own. But the emptiness of these passages sets my nerves on edge. We must be watchful, especially at turnings." Then, with some pleasure, he suddenly announced, "Aha! Here we are!"

"Here" turned out to be the nearly vacant barroom we had passed through earlier in the evening on our way to the ratting match. This time we entered it from a doorway farther along the wall from the one we'd exited it earlier. "Egad, Holmes," I said, "this whole place is like a hideous nightmare of Lewis Carroll's!"

"And the Cheshire Cats carry clubs," Holmes said as we stopped to get our bearings.

A long wooden bar stretched the entire length of one wall, and about half its stools were occupied by still, hulking figures. The rest of the large squarish room was nearly vacant except for a few tables and an irregular forest of wooden pillars that faded into a dusky gloom along the wall opposite the bar.

It was as I was rubbing my aching shoulder and trying to imagine how this establishment could possibly have a door giving on any public street that the night's adventures were suddenly wrenched to a momentous peak.

It has often struck me as odd, in the many years since I received my wound in Afghanistan, how terribly brief are the most telling incidents of our lives. We identify them later when, looking back, we can see great stretches of time dragging toward a lightning flash of fate, followed by another interminable string of inconsequentialities. Had I been asked as we stood there, I would have pointed confidently to the attack upon us by Wakefield's giant as the obvious lightning flash this night, but suddenly, from the deepest shadows came a *real* flash and the rapid, high-pitched crack of pistol fire. Twin bursts of recurring muzzle flame seared my vision, but reflexively, calling upon who knows what aging reflexes and long-neglected training, my revolver was again drawn from my pocket and returning the fire as rapidly and precisely as possible at the narrow space between the flashes. I was remotely aware of a tug at my right sleeve, where I later found a few singed threads—the only evidence any of us had of the assailant's marksmanship—and then I heard the thud of a body striking the boards of the floor somewhere out there in the shadows. The entire deadly crisis could not have taken more than four or five seconds.

In the almost oppressive silence that followed the exchange of fire, I came to my wits enough to dimly perceive men crouched along the bar, or peering timidly from behind it. There was a whimper, and then a belch, which brought a tension-relieving round of laughter from the drinkers.

No doubt the firing had been shockingly loud, but as so often happens in actual combat, the participants barely heard the shots. My empty revolver was hot proof of the fight, but though my vision still sparkled with the fading muzzle blast I heard no ringing in my ears from the concussions that had resounded in that closed place. Finally thinking of my companions, I looked over and saw that Marston, rising from a half-crouch, had evidently fired too. His right hand was coming free of his coat, where I suppose he had just reholstered his own pistol. Holmes, his hands at his sides, was standing at his full height and squinting into the darkness as he said, "He's down, but we must approach carefully. Barman!" he shouted, "Raise your lights, please!"

The lights went up a modest amount to a slightly less dark brown. I hastily reloaded from my pocket, then moved slowly forward, Marston arriving first to announce, "By God, it's the walleye! I would never have taken him for a shooter!"

Even in the poor light it was easy to see that Marston seemed shaken. He bent to check for a pulse, then removed a brace of small revolvers still clutched in the man's delicate hands. "I had better get some assistance here," he said, and rushed out another door that he apparently had reason to believe would take him to the street. I envied him the fresh air; the emotional weight of what had just occurred began to settle above my heart.

Perhaps I am not in any way the distinguished physician I once enjoyed imagining myself to be, but a physician I am, clear to my soul. Though I have never shrunk from gunplay in dire situations, I have always been haunted by the dread of a result precisely such as this. How many human lives must a dedicated medical man ease in some minor way, or even rescue from mortal danger, to balance the deliberate and violent taking of one life? At that moment my soul's accounting seemed desperately short of any such balance.

Exhausted as much by these realisations as by my injury, my shoulder suddenly a burning knife-point of agony, I sagged heavily onto an old bench just behind the body. I could see a narrow doorway to one side of the pillar our assailant had apparently stood in front of as he fired upon us. I guessed that he must have come in that way and waited there in the murk until we were most exposed. In my suddenly drained state, I still had the presence of mind to wonder how he had known we would come this way at all.

Then Holmes' hand settled lightly on my other shoulder. "Buck up, old man. You had no choice."

"I know, Holmes, I know. But the wicked waste. . . . " My voice and my thoughts both trailed off, and we were silent a moment as the bar emptied of all the patrons who—no doubt for a substantial variety of personal and professional reasons—did not wish to be in attendance when the police arrived. Holmes knelt beside the body and bent over for a closer look, seeming to concentrate most on the several bullet wounds but occasionally glancing my way as if to reassure himself that I was resting comfortably.

Presently, just to make conversation and assure my friend that I was not without remaining mental resources, I said, "Oh well, at least Sam and his family will have nothing to worry about now. We may remain ignorant of this poor soul's story, whatever it might have been, but the matter is settled, for better or worse."

Holmes sat back on his haunches and looked off vacantly into the room's dingy spaces as he said, "Oh, no, Watson. The matter is most decidedly not settled—and I am hard pressed to imagine how things could be much worse."

Chapter Twelve
The Art of Lying

Marston soon returned, trailing a small blue flock of officers. Explaining that he had convinced his superiors to send along a few uniformed men to watch the known exits to the building during our attendance at the ratting match, he directed a pair of bobbies to the corpse. While they carried the poor wretch's body back the way they'd come in, Marston and two or three others made a hasty job of examining the room, especially the door the dead man had probably come through into the barroom.

I was clearly done in, so Holmes helped me to the street—which to my great surprise was only a few yards down the hallway—and into a cab that Marston had thoughtfully hailed from somewhere. I remember little about the ride back to Baker Street, except that my shoulder throbbed with each bump and jostling turn.

Once home, Holmes helped me determine that I suffered no broken bones under the massive purple bruise that was blossoming as I watched. I knew the shoulder would hurt like blazes by morning, so I took something for the pain and eased myself down on my bed.

Despite the drug and my extreme fatigue, I did not fall immediately to sleep. My thoughts lurched haphazardly through the evening's events, and in my dazed state I couldn't muster a continuous chain of inquiry in any particular direction. For awhile I found myself wondering about all those anonymous souls who so efficiently and promptly vacated the bar as soon as the shooting stopped. Without a word of introduction or even an inadvertent comment that might identify themselves, Marston and Holmes, and perhaps even I, probably gave such keenly practiced observers all the indication they needed that the victors in the gunfight, if not themselves police officers, were so near to it that the real thing would be along shortly, possibly in good numbers and almost certainly with an eye out for familiar faces.

From that brief rumination on the power of simple physical presence and posture, I for the first time found myself joining Miss Leary and Holmes in wondering about Marston, who now seemed to justify Miss Leary's question if he was all he seemed to be. In fact, he seemed to be considerably more than that. The ease with which he directed the other bobbies— and the unquestioning haste with which they followed his directions—cast him in light for me.

But before I could consider the question further, my mind—which was now drifting at large among various other half-addled memories—moved along. For the first time it occurred to me that none of us, including Holmes, gave any thought to Wakefield's giant, whom we had left semi-conscious and groaning only moments before the shooting began, and who, for all we knew, was still there and in need of both medical attention and a stern round of interrogation. But with the startling thought of this apparent omission of responsibilities on our part, I faded and neither thought nor dreamed until late the following morning.

By the time I arose, Holmes had been out and returned. He greeted me as I emerged from my room, solicitously pulled back a chair from the breakfast table for me, then poured me a coffee. As soon as I was settled, he gave me his report.

His first stop was the morgue, where a second examination of the body of our strange quarry revealed little more than had his hasty first look the night before. In one of those acts of kindness that remind me of the great humanity that broods under his intensely logical surface, he spoke to my distress over having been compelled to kill a man. "You and Marston shot not only with fine precision but in lavish abundance. The centre of your man's torso was considerably torn up. As the two of you were firing very similar weapons, and as several of the rounds passed clear through him and into that pillar just behind him, I am confident that even the most accomplished forensic specialist would have no chance of pronouncing a specific bullet as the fatal one." As trivial a bit of evidence as this information provided, I found it comforting to learn that, at worst, I had not killed our assailant alone and that, at best, I could always nurture a private sliver of hope that perhaps I had not killed him at all.

Holmes also returned to the scene of the gunfight, where, after persuading the proprietor to again turn up the lights, he found a puzzle that was obviously still gnawing at him. "Whatever the man's mental or physical limitations may have been, it is difficult to reconcile his abysmal marksmanship with the straightforward conditions of the moment. As you and Marston so amply demonstrated, the distances involved were not of the sort that would prohibit fatal accuracy, and yet the bullet that grazed your sleeve was the only one that came anywhere near any of us. Having noticed a distinct lack of holes in the wall behind where we stood, I devoted the better part of an hour to discovering what became of the rest of his shots. They were generously scattered in a quarter circle from us in all directions. One hit the floor about halfway between us and him, and another was embedded in the ceiling over above the bar; those fellows were wise to take cover. Most of the other shots came to rest in the walls well off to either side of the three of us."

I said, "He seems to have approached firing his weapons with the same passionate disregard for reason with which he immersed himself in the ratting match." Even as I spoke, I suddenly wondered if his behavior could mean something. "It would have taken a good deal of very rapid flailing around for even a skilled shooter to accomplish such a distribution." I raised my arms to imitate the motions required, then gave an involuntary yelp as my swollen shoulder reminded me to be more careful. "Good Lord, Holmes, you don't suppose he was *trying* to miss us, do you? Just to frighten us, or fulfill some daft urge for excitement? I must tell you that nothing seems beyond him, in my professional opinion. In all my years, even in the heat of extended battle, I've never seen a human being so frenzied as that poor soul was when he rushed from the pit."

"I suppose nothing about this man, Watson," said Holmes, "but your questions are important. Dead he may be, but we are far from done with him." Then, tapping an envelope that I had not noticed on the table in front of me, he said, "But we have more immediate business. Clemens is on his way over, and would like to hear what results we have to report. I am sure he will be interested in last evening's events."

Distracted by Holmes' report, I had hardly done justice to my breakfast when we heard Mrs. Hudson bringing Clemens up the stairs. Though less agitated than on his first visit, it was plain that he was not in an easy state of mind. I was a bit surprised at how little comfort he seemed to take from our news about the death of his mysterious persecutor.

"I suppose I should feel some vindication, what with all that you have been through," he said. "At least our friends at Scotland Yard may take my case a little more seriously now that one of their officers has been involved in gunplay over it. But I find your news very disturbing, especially for you, doctor." His concern was touching. "It was selfish of me not even to consider that by seeking your help I might be placing you in some danger too." Though Holmes and I both downplayed my injury, my gingerly movements and clear discomfort would have been difficult for a much less observant man than Sam Clemens to miss. Holmes and I both opened our mouths to reassure him but we were interrupted by a commotion at the foot of the stairs.

Mrs. Hudson's most commanding tones reached us first, but were almost immediately drowned out by the familiar thumping of sturdy bare feet on the stairs. Holmes smiled and said to our guest, "I believe that we are to receive additional news about your case."

Clemens' eyebrows were still lifting in interest at this news when the door flew partway open, then abruptly stopped as a boy made his way hastily and awkwardly around it. Apparently Mrs. Hudson, judging that the main pack of Irregulars was simply beyond the capacity of our rooms, had decided to corral them at the door and send Wiggins on alone.

Wiggins, upon whom the finer points of indoor etiquette were as pearls, was probably obeying a poorly understood order from Mrs. Hudson as he knocked rapidly on the outside of the door even while opening it and coming in, finally giving even the inside of the door a couple of sharp raps before hurrying to fidget at attention by my chair, facing Holmes, who had risen for the occasion.

Clemens had taken in this performance with unbridled joy, as if all his worries had for the moment evaporated. As he beamed at our new guest it occurred to me that here, just by the whimsy of chance, the world's most authoritative chronicler of boyhood met and instantly recognised as pure and unspoiled a specimen of the form as could be found anywhere. During Wiggins' brief visit, he and Clemens exchanged hardly a glance, much less a word, but I sensed that Clemens found greater satisfaction in the company of this young fellow—who was in his way a veritable Huckleberry Finn of the streets—than in ours.

Wiggins' report was terse, notably the opposite of his effusive narrative last time, perhaps because one of his lieutenants was the successful investigator this time and thus Wiggins had less personal stake in celebrating the "ketch." Individual triumph aside, Wiggins was still proud to announce that they had located the cabyard Holmes sent them to find.

It was a search conducted and refined by stages. Holmes' marching orders to the Irregulars could hardly have seemed more hopelessly vague. Locating a plain gray van in a cabyard distinguished only by such mundane characteristics as a run-down appearance, the presence of both cabs and vans, and the advanced age of the manager, would have daunted the most determined members of the constabulary. It was Holmes' apparent afterthought in his instructions—that the yard would also house a goat or two—that was, in Wiggins' words, "the topper." Having discovered that there were, indeed, quite a few yards that met the general terms; that aging cabyard managers seemed to be as common in the metropolis as the victims of the corneal leucomas whom they sought on their previous outing; and even that goats were not unique to any single cabyard, the Irregulars proceeded to discreetly monitor activities at the several locations that met all of these terms, on the assumption that either the desired van would show up or it wouldn't. Wiggins found it necessary to recruit additional forces for this comprehensive a campaign, and no doubt it was this enlargement of the ranks that caused Mrs. Hudson to draw the line and deny them admission when they all showed up at our door.

It was only yesterday that their vigilance was rewarded. They had seen more than enough gray vans and gray-haired cabyard managers by that point, but finally, late in the afternoon, all the long-desired things appeared at once at a small cabyard by Paddington Station, when the gray van drove in with the "dotty cove his very self" seated next to the driver. Luckily, the boy assigned to this yard was one of the Irregulars who had been in on the earlier search for this very man, so he immediately knew he had the right place and rushed to inform Wiggins. Wiggins, his own arcane procedural protocols firmly in place, chose first to spread the word throughout the city for all his troops to withdraw before informing us of this discovery, which explained why it was only this morning that he was able to assemble them at our door.

Holmes and Wiggins, in their usually quick and businesslike manner, agreed upon a considerably enlarged financial compensation that would cover the additional manpower that Wiggins had to recruit for such an expansive campaign. This amount changing hands, Wiggins ran out, pausing only an instant to look at the door he'd left unclosed upon his arrival, as if wondering if Mrs. Hudson's admonition about knocking was also to apply upon departure. Apparently deciding not, but perhaps a little shaken in his confidence about the door generally, he carefully eased through the narrow space again, touching neither door nor jamb. There was a brief fuss at the bottom of the steps as he led the troops away, and all was quiet. Holmes took his seat. I sipped a bit more coffee. Clemens continued to beam.

After a moment, Clemens said, "Holmes, I must congratulate you on your innovative use of the city's resources. There are few people of our age who would imagine the potential of a crew like that, and fewer still, I daresay, who could bring them sufficiently to heel to get such remarkable results. And that boy—what a prize!" Clemens glanced around the room in apparent puzzlement as he said, "Wherever did you find him?"

Holmes, seeming not to notice that Clemens had grouped the three of us into one "age," briefly explained the genesis of the Irregulars. "As for Wiggins, he is the second of his family to assume command of the 'crew,' as you put it. There are leadership skills there that would daunt many in Parliament, were they fostered properly. I hope at least that his little endeavors on my behalf may nudge him into some more productive line than he might otherwise have been destined for."

"By all means, by all means," agreed Clemens. "He is certainly earning whatever opportunities you can put in his way. Remarkable child." Then he added, as if unnecessarily pointing out the obvious, "He was lying, of course. What is his given name?"

I began to wonder if Clemens was already plotting a new novel—*Wiggins of London*—in his mind when his statement belatedly registered in my mind. Holmes and I simultaneously said, "Lying?!"

Clemens seemed as surprised at our reaction as we were at his comment. "Well, yes. You must have noticed. It's what boys do, you know, especially, uh, *independent* ones like that."

"What was he lying *about?*" Holmes asked.

"Oh, I'm sure I couldn't tell you. But the signs were all there." Despite my own surprise, I enjoyed this rare instance of Holmes being unexpectedly exposed to someone else, for once, apparently having analytical skills that were as mysterious to him as his were to the rest of humanity. The effect could not have been more satisfying to watch if Clemens had actually said, "You know my methods, Holmes."

Holmes, on the other hand, seemed torn between wanting to know more about Clemens' methods and wanting to know just what the lie might have been. "I wonder that you take it so calmly, that this boy might have been lying about a matter of importance to your case."

"Ah, I see the problem here," Clemens said. "I have not been clear. I apologise." He paused, seeming to gather and organise himself for a serious disquisition. "You are not appreciating the full breadth of dishonesty. Surely in your many interviews with various witnesses to crimes, and with the criminals themselves, you have noticed that in their communications with you they are managing many personal interests at once. They may, for example, answer your questions truthfully, but leave out unpleasant or inconvenient details. Often those details have little bearing on your concerns at the moment; perhaps they are sheltering a beloved family member who has an embarrassing or scandalous secret. And perhaps, in fact it is probable, that you don't need to know that detail anyway. But the effect of their decision to tell you less than everything will be a kind of dissimulation nonetheless."

"I appreciate the distinction you are making," Holmes said, as attentive as an earnest student.

"Well," Clemens continued, now plainly enjoying himself, "from such a simple case we move into a host of progressively more ambiguous instances in which the lie may do more than merely exclude marginal information of dubious potential value. Here, lying becomes more artful and nuanced, a matter, let's say for example, of special emphasis on a favored point, or an unnecessarily vivid portrayal of a person in order to suggest, if only to the listener's subconscious, that this person is deserving of special credibility or skepticism. The examples are legion, Mr. Holmes, and I imagine you also are familiar with many such."

"I am."

"Then I am sure you are also aware that sometimes we lie without even knowing it. For whatever combination of reasons, perhaps love, perhaps politics, perhaps greed, perhaps any other urge to which we are especially susceptible, we get our story wrong without being conscious of doing so."

"But that's not really lying, is it?" I objected. "It's merely being in error."

"That, Dr. Watson, is the comment of a kind man, one who is generous in his assessment of human nature. I applaud you for it. But if I as writer were that gentle in my characterizations my books would all be dismal flops. No, being in error is no excuse; virtually all people have, what shall I call it, the basic mental equipment required to reason clearly, and to distinguish right from wrong, or truth from lie. When through whatever combination of self-interest and sloth their mental equipment is allowed to grow so rusty that it no longer prevents them from foolish thinking and lapses of logic, they are not merely in error. Their lazier or more selfish nature is tyrannizing their own good sense in the interest of a stupid preference for the illogical and the foolish." Clemens shook his head and said, "No, we are not helpless in this. We all can decide not to behave stupidly. Thus, if you stand far enough back from the individual to appreciate the full array of choices with which life presents him, there is no room for equivocation on this question. All his actions are the result of his own decisions, even if today's actions are the result of poor decisions made long ago, and even if he is in fact lying to himself." Clemens paused, perhaps a little embarrassed that his answer had turned didactic, but still with the confidence to conclude, "In short, we can all decide not to lie."

"While I have considerable sympathy for that argument," said Holmes, "and while it is doubtless progressive in our times, I'd prefer to focus specifically on your assessment of Wiggins and his honesty."

"But that was my point," said Clemens. "Wiggins is, I am sure, well-practiced at the various arts of street survival, and that would necessarily include many of the finer points of lying. I, on the other hand, am equally well-practiced, in fact, I fancy myself something of an authority, in the study of boys, especially wild ones. But as I have just now suggested, lying is a fine and ancient art, with as many causes and effects as there are people who lie—which, I guess, is all of us. So in the case of Wiggins, I am only putting my art up against his, and the results on the best of days will only reach so far. I know he is lying, but I can barely guess what he is lying about, or why, or if it matters to our interests today."

After a moment's gloomy reflection on this shortcoming of his working knowledge of boys, Clemens brightened a bit and added, "I have just realised what made me notice that he was lying in the first place, and perhaps this suggests something to us. Perhaps not. What I noticed, and what I found troubling, was not that he was lying; as I say, that's what boys do. What worried me was that he very clearly was not enjoying himself as he did so."

What with Wiggins' discovery of the hard-sought cabyard, we were keen to set out for Paddington. As we concluded our conversation, Clemens urged us to take great care. Now that his case had led to actual physical violence, his anxiety over the whole affair was even greater. I even sensed that his faith in his theory that his forthcoming book was behind things was a little shaken. We tried to reassure him that we would indeed be careful, but we may have been less convincing because Holmes also emphasized the importance of Clemens and his family staying close to home and attending faithfully to the instructions of the constables who continued to watch the house. "I must tell you that I am a little less certain than I was a day ago that you will have no more trouble there at Tedworth Square," Holmes said, "though the presence of the constables makes it seem unlikely in the extreme that any associates of our late housebreaker will come near the place."

"So you believe there are others involved?" Clemens asked.

"Yes, I do," Holmes said. "The mere existence of the van's driver proves that. The real question—the one we are little nearer to answering even after the alarming events of last evening—is just what all they might be involved *in*. Until we have a better idea of that, caution is advised for all of us."

As Clemens rose to go, he paused, suddenly remembering something from Wiggins' report. "By the way, Holmes, what was that business about the goat? I gather that the presence of a goat at the cabyard was somehow significant?" As this same question had been on my mind, I also turned in rising to hear Holmes' explanation.

"The thought came to me from your account of the gray van's visit to your home in Chelsea. You will recall that you said that the horse's tail had been trimmed, but not very carefully."

Clemens thought a moment and said, "Yes, that's true; I'd almost forgotten."

"You have a livestock disease in America known as glanders, I believe?"

This abrupt turn in the conversation set Clemens back for a moment, but he thought about it. "Glanders. Yes, I know of it. People call it farcy. Dreadful thing. I knew a man in Missouri, a groom at a perfectly respectable stable, who came down with it and suffered hideously."

"Yes, that is its other name here, too. For reasons that I cannot explain, there was for many years a widely prevalent bit of country wisdom to the effect that this disease could be kept from infecting the animals at a stable or farmyard if a goat or two was allowed to roam freely with the most vulnerable stock. No one I have spoken with about this has been able to explain how the goat protected the other animals from infection, but there it is."

I resisted the urge to ask "There *what* is?" but Holmes did not need to be asked. He continued, "As I'm sure you're aware, goats are notorious opportunistic feeders, and one invariable side effect of housing a goat with horses is that he will in short order eat down their tails as high as he can reach. It was an easy intuitive leap for me from your account of the raggedly trimmed tail to the presence of a goat in whatever cabyard that horse routinely inhabited. Modern veterinary medicine and—even more important, I suppose—improved enforcement of regulations about the handling of infected animals, has led to important strides toward a more scientific containment of glanders. But as with so many other traditional beliefs, this one about the goat lingers, and still has its adherents. It seemed that someone in authority at the cabyard we sought was still devoted to this folklore, which suggested to me an elderly ostler who stubbornly clung to older ways. As Wiggins and his compatriots have so ably demonstrated, these little hypotheses of mine were correct enough to lead to the discovery of the yard and van we seek."

"Remarkable." Clemens turned to me. "Doctor, this may not be the ideal time to mention it, but I don't mind telling you that in my reading of some of your stories about Mr. Holmes I was quite skeptical about his famous deductions. I have even entertained the thought of writing a parody of your adventures together. But I will tell you right now that I sympathise with those occasions in your books when you, after having been completely baffled by this man's declarations," here he indicated Holmes with a smile and a wave of his hand, "wonder how you could have failed to reach such obvious conclusions once he has described them to you. It is somewhat unsettling to realise that I may now be inhabiting such a tale myself." He paused, then added, "My daughters, on the other hand, seem to think it's more fun than anything that ever happens to us at home." With that he bid us good day and was gone.

As we set out on our drive to Paddington, Holmes said, "Well, Watson, I hope you retrieved the compliment from Clemens' admission of skepticism about your little accounts of my cases.

"How do you mean, Holmes? If he hadn't added that about sympathizing with me, his statement could have been taken as a great insult to you."

"Oh, not at all; if there was an insult there, it was inadvertent, I am sure. Besides, the insult would have been much more to you as the writer than to me as a character in your chronicles. No, I thought that the real point you should take from his remark was an enormous compliment. I mean, how many writers the world over could say that their work came so urgently to the attention of Mr. Mark Twain that he felt compelled to write a story, any kind of story, complimentary or not, in response to it? There is quite a distinction in that, I think."

"Yes, I see your point, though I suspect that many writers would say that the distinction lies not in the attention but in having produced such an egregious literary abomination that Mr. Mark Twain himself could not let it pass unlampooned. That seems a less desirable achievement."

"Perhaps. Still, I hope he writes his parody."

Uncomfortable with this line of conversation, I asked Holmes what he hoped to find at the cabyard. He answered, "What would *you* look for there?"

"There must always be the hope that the driver of the gray van will be in attendance. If so I can think of several questions I would have for him. I would start by asking him about his association with the housebreaker. But I'd also like to know who he works for, and what he knows about the places he took the housebreaker, especially Clemens' house and, of course, ours. And why was he driving past Chatto's just as Clemens was walking down the street?"

Holmes nodded and said, "Yes, those are all good questions."

"In fact, Holmes, I have wondered what we are to do if we *do* see the driver. For one thing, even if he is seated in the van, how can we know he is the same man? Clemens' description isn't much help, and as far as I know, you didn't get a look at him during your brief pursuit of him."

Holmes shook his head. "No, I did not."

"For another thing, considering that he is complicit in housebreaking—twice—should we try to detain him? And if that's our mission, wouldn't we have been wise to involve a constable or two in this outing? We have no official standing. I am unarmed." Until Holmes asked, my unease about our plan had been suppressed by the thrill of the chase; we were at last on the track of something, even if only the van. But now I found myself wallowing in uncertainty.

"Important matters, one and all, Watson," Holmes said. "And what if we are not so fortunate as to meet with the driver? What then?"

"Then, surely the manager or an ostler will be able to provide us with information about the van in question. He may well have its registration, and then we can quickly trace its ownership." But something in Holmes' tone of voice had aroused my curiosity. "Why do you ask, Holmes? Do you have something else in mind? Is there some other element of the case you hope to pursue? Are we to interview the goat?"

Holmes smiled, and with an uncharacteristically abashed expression said, "No, not the goat—though we may wish we could ask him a few questions before we're done. No, Watson, there's no use hiding from you that at this point I am as unsure as you are. Everything that has happened so far is all out of proportion. "No," he reconsidered his words, "the word I want is not proportion. Everything is all out of *line*. It has no sense of some underlying direction, no sensible common thread, other than that in some way which we cannot discern, it all matters. Consider these things about the situation, which at this point I even hesitate to call a 'case' because for all I know it is not a case. Or perhaps it is five cases. Who can say, now that the housebreaker is dead? But let us consider the things we are concerned with."

He began ticking off his list on his fingers. "There is the peculiar involvement of a world-famous man for no reason that even he can fully justify to himself. There is the improbable unleashing by the higher police authorities, if not by the higher authorities above *them*, of both Gregson and Lestrade on the case. There is the utterly inexplicable appearances of the housebreaker at such unexpected locations. There is his equally inexplicable attack on us with firearms—*firearms*, Watson! There is the strange matter of that huge brute who, with no provocation that we know of, tried his best to brain us in the passageway last night." He paused for breath, then, moving to the forefinger of his other hand, he added, "There is the perhaps meaningless and yet disturbing concurrence of these things with the impending Jubilee. And, as if that's not enough of a muddle, there's *Marston*." He added that last as if just stating the name itself made clear why Marston should be included in his list of puzzles.

"You know my devotion to systematic, rigorous thought, Watson. I am ill at ease with hasty or unbridled theorizing, much less with what the Americans refer to as 'hunches.' But it is not rigorous thought that drives me today. It is, how shall I call it, just a *feeling* that we are caught up in something of enormous significance—that all these things not only relate, but relate with great urgency."

"Holmes, you astound me with your candor. I know I often chide you for your closeness during our investigations, but it is only because I am so sure that you know infinitely more than you will tell. Yet here you sit, admitting that you are at a loss; that you are, in fact, falling back on hunches."

"And I, on the other hand," Holmes said with a sigh, "am equally unaccustomed to the bewilderment I confess. To answer your original question about my hopes for what we shall find at the cabyard, all I can tell you is that I hope we shall find *something*."

The first thing we found at the cabyard was a surprisingly full central court, which reminded me that it was Sunday morning. Yards on this side of town primarily served commuters from the inner suburbs. The demand for transport of people and goods would naturally be much lower today. The cabs were generally fine ones, including several with the new solid-India-rubber tires. The yard, even packed with cabs and a few vans, was a model of efficiency. Holmes' explanation about the goat had led me to expect a rather outdated if not seedy establishment, but this location, so near Paddington and neighbouring hotels, was primed for a loftier clientele.

We had time to walk the perimeter of the open part of the yard. A number of handsome horses and, yes, not one but two goats, occupied connecting stalls along the back side of the yard. We had just determined that the gray van was not there when a man emerged from a small, tidily constructed shed that adjoined the street at a corner of the yard. He was, as predicted, elderly, with thinning gray hair oiled down to one side, but his figure was trim, his step was lively, and his posture was erect and dignified. I found myself happily anticipating a conversation with him.

But when he was still a few steps off, and Holmes was just opening his mouth to address him, he held out a hand to Holmes, who reached to take the small proffered envelope. Before Holmes could thank or question him, the man abruptly turned on his heel and marched back to his doorway. Our surprise at this was lost in the sight of what was written on the front of the envelope: "Mr. Sherlock Holmes/Dr. John H. Watson."

"What can this mean, Holmes? You were never out of my sight from the moment you learned the address of this yard from Wiggins. I know you did not notify anybody of our visit."

"What it means, Watson," Holmes said, "Is that my hope for our visit has been fulfilled. We have found something."

"Well, let's see what it is," I added eagerly, pointing at the envelope.

He gave it another long, appraising look. "First, I'd wager it's the finest paper to pass through the hands of that man in his entire life." Holmes was staring at the envelope as if suddenly confronted with a photograph of a long-forgotten but beloved old friend. Noticing that the yard manager had come to his doorway and was standing there watching us discuss the envelope he had handed us moments before, I said, "Perhaps opening the envelope would help, Holmes; we're rather attracting attention here."

He emerged from his bemused state, saw what I meant, and agreed. He called to the watching man, asking him if a cab could be arranged. The man turned to the interior of the shed and spoke. A cabbie appeared immediately, directed us to an especially fine cab, and we were on our way toward Baker Street by the time Holmes again took up the matter of the envelope. He separated the flap and drew out a small slip of paper identical to that of the envelope. The same hand had written on it "Mr. Holmes and Dr. Watson: it is time we spoke." There followed a Kensington address and the signature, "Constance Wakefield." Smiling, Holmes called the address up to our driver, who, either by chance or design, was already heading that way. In a few moments we were hurrying along Bayswater, then turning down Palace Gardens Terrace toward our destination.

Chapter Fourteen
Something Big

It is well known among the students of London geography that mere proximity of a given residence to great wealth is no guarantee of similar financial resources. It is a short stroll from many of the city's most exclusive neighbourhoods to quite different social and financial environments. Thus, knowing that we were headed for an address so close to some of the city's most palatial residences still left me no sure way of knowing just what appearance, much less condition, the Wakefield address might have. Remembering Black's foul nest by the docks, I was braced for the worst.

I needn't have worried. The Wakefields occupied one of the grander homes the whole length of the street. Set back just enough to allow for a screen of the first and second floors by a few well-trained horse-chestnuts and cammelia, the house itself was a double-lot white-stuccoed block, some parts three stories and some four, with perhaps a few more bay windows than any amount of need for sunlight might justify, and with a few not quite sufficiently subdued Moorish touches around the windows. A pair of rooks squabbled along the highest roof line.

Our driver left us off at a gate, which was promptly opened by a thin, heavily bearded young man who emerged from behind the closest cammelia. He nodded to us and announced with a grandly executed wave of his arm toward the house that "The missus is expecting you." There was something vaguely familiar about the voice, but I was too distracted by his informal terminology and sensational livery to think of anything else. His entire outfit, while fine in cut, was theatrical in the extreme. His linen shirt, a vivid fuschia with pale lime stock, glowed from under a waistcoat of what appeared to be leopard skin. His tights were butter yellow and tucked into elaborately tooled American cowboy boots that reached halfway to his knees. Despite all this, his frock, whose tails reached almost to his ankles, was the great showpiece of this startling ensemble. As he conducted us to the front door, I had a moment to study the rear expanse of this striking garment, which gave every appearance of being genuine William Morris art needlework—an exquisite vine-and-blossom motif in subdued blues and grays. Most odd of all, I must admit that the overall effect of this bizarre combination of garments was not as unpleasant as it might sound, perhaps because the man wore it with such assured bearing.

The front door stood open to the mid-morning breeze that, running over the cammelias, was pleasantly scented. I wondered at the seeming carelessness of this casual attendance to residential safety for an instant until it came to me that we were in fact entering what was in all likelihood a sort of command post for the very people who might be tempted to take advantage of such carelessness and that, therefore, the door signaled by its openness that only an imbecile, and indeed an imbecile who had only arrived in London that day, would even think about burgling these premises. It was not a comforting thought.

We were conducted down a wide hallway whose walls were covered with a strange but wondrous assortment of objects. In our brief passages in and out of the house I had time to notice several large heads of exotic species of game, probably African or Asian, that I did not recognize. Two very large oil paintings by one or another of the recent French *plein-air* radicals faced each other midway down the hall; a few antique firearms were hung butt-to-muzzle above an impossibly enormous snakeskin, and a section of the wall beyond the door to the sitting room appeared to be entirely covered in feathers of every imaginable colour. Holmes gave this outlandish cabinet of curiosities barely a glance, again causing me to wonder if he had had previous dealings with the Wakefields.

When we came to the sitting-room door, our colourful guide stepped smartly to the side and with another broad sweep of his arm directed us into the room, then, without announcing us, retired deeper into the house. Holmes led us into a room that was, in striking contrast to the extravagances of the hallway, the very soul of probity in its furnishings. Our hostess, elegantly but much more conservatively dressed than when last we had seen her at the ratting match, rose from a simple Windsor fanback in the centre of the room and said, "Gentlemen, thank you for coming on such short notice."

Upon closer inspection in this calmer setting, I had no reason to revise my earlier assessment of the spectacular Mrs. Wakefield, whose age could have been anywhere between 25 and 35. I will resist a mighty urge to rhapsodise further on this woman's breathtaking good looks, though they were of the sort to make normal conversation all but impossible for the many men who are susceptible to such things. Recognizing myself as among that group, I mentally braced up to concentrate on our case, and found myself wondering if by keeping Sam Clemens' face in my mind I could reduce the distraction of Mrs. Wakefield's presence.

Holmes responded to her greeting with a slight bow, then said, "It is good to see you again Mrs. Wakefield. I trust all is well with the children?"

She unleashed a devastating smile of pleasure at what, to me, had seemed only a polite bit of small talk on Holmes' part. "Yes, thank you, Mr. Holmes. They still speak with great enthusiasm of you and their big adventure."

At this response, I looked questioningly at Holmes, who said, "A few years ago I was able to assist the Wakefields when their boys were in a bit of trouble."

Mrs. Wakefield laughed a small but stirring laugh of objection. "Though I appreciate Mr. Holmes' discretion, Dr. Watson, you should know that it was much more than a 'bit of trouble' when the boys were kidnapped and carried all the way to the Near East before he extricated them from what at the time seemed a dire and hopeless situation. I do hope that some time he will share this story with you, even though," and here her look sharpened ominously, "it is most decidedly not for publication."

"By all means, Holmes," I said, "I will look forward to hearing this tale."

Holmes nodded to me in apparent agreement, but changed the subject. I was suddenly aware that even in this disorienting setting we were now necessarily engaged in saying the "proper nothings" preliminary to settling down to business. But even the nothings were proving of considerable interest, and continued to do so when Holmes said, "I see that Wiggins is thriving. The cowboy boots are a new touch, I think."

My near-recognition of the footman's voice came back to me and I broke in with, "That's the senior Wiggins, Holmes!"

"Yes, Watson. I'm sorry I didn't introduce him. I thought you recognised him."

I shook my head. "There were too many, well, layers of interference."

Mrs. Wakefield again laughed, then said, more to Holmes than to me, "I gather that you have taken my request to say nothing about our dealings to a generous extreme. The doctor knows nothing of us?" I assumed that by "us" she referred not to her and Holmes alone, but to Holmes and her entire circle.

Holmes said, "Except for our disconcerting and ultimately tragic adventure at the ratting match the other night, I don't believe that Watson has had any prior acquaintance with the Wakefields and their various enterprises. And, alas, I fear that some of what little he has been told is erroneous." At this I glanced back and forth from him to her, determined not to verbally showcase my apparent ignorance any further until one or the other of them chose to elaborate on the apparent mysteries between us.

Mrs. Wakefield spoke first, and to me. "Would the two of you please be seated? Tea will be along momentarily." As we made ourselves comfortable on a long and well-sprung settle opposite her, she continued. "Charles—that's my husband, Dr. Watson—my actual husband, in case you've heard otherwise—and I oversee a very large number of what

113

Mr. Holmes has graciously referred to as 'enterprises.' Many of these, like the cabyard you visited earlier today, are respectable even in the eyes of polite society. Many others are not. We make no apologies for either type, and are disinclined to quibble over the minor illegalities that are to a great degree our worst transgressions against convention." She paused for a moment's thought about how best to continue. "In short, during the past twenty years, these enterprises have generated both great wealth and great independence. In fact, 'independence' is a gracious way of saying that we are utterly separated from the mainstream of wealthy society. That being the case, we have chosen to craft our own manner of living, one that combines the best of what seems to us sensible about the way rich people live with our own little preferences and habits. We live precisely the way we like, and find our work all the more satisfying for it. For example, this is only one of several very comfortable residences we maintain in the city. I happen to be here at the moment because of business I have with some nearby embassies, whose occupants are more comfortable transacting our business off premises. These are people for whom appearances and a certain amount of formality are matters of deep personal, even cultural, importance, and I can provide them with those ceremonial niceties here while at the same time making our business convenient for all concerned."

Though this was all quite vague, it was fascinating, all the more because of the heart-melting animation it brought into her until-then rather restrained facial expressions. I redoubled my efforts to rein in my awe.

The tea arrived, delivered by a young maid whom Mrs. Wakefield thanked but sent out immediately and prepared our tea herself. As she did so, she continued, "That is probably more than I needed to say about what we do, but it bears directly on the matter of Frances—we prefer to call Wiggins by his given name, as we do all our people—and his, what did you call them, 'layers of interference'? You knew Frances in his childhood, so you know the enormous promise he displayed. I can tell you that he is now fulfilling that promise. Occasional footman duties are the most mundane of his responsibilities with us. When he first came to us"—she nodded in apparent gratitude to Holmes—"we put him to work at the door. Now I let him continue those duties occasionally because he enjoys them so much. He is especially fond of materializing from unexpected directions to greet guests. And he relishes the chance to play at the ceremonies and rituals that all through the random brutalities of his childhood were as remote to his life as, well, whatever sort of society flourishes in the *piazzas* that border the canals of Mr. Lowell's Mars. But combined with his joy in exercising such little social rituals is a delight in the same sort of unorthodoxy that characterises so many of our *enterprises*"—another glance at Holmes. "In short, he decided to design his own livery. He kept the basic form of the traditional garments, but with our blessing and, I must admit, continued amusement, he has found his way to the present combination of fabrics and styles by experimentation. In winter there is also a very becoming fur cap, 'coonskin,' he calls it, which provides another happy effect similar to that of the boots."

"I had no idea Wiggins could be that original," I continued. "Forgive me for belabouring this when I imagine that we have more important things to discuss, but was that Morris fabric?"

"As to his originality, Mr. Wakefield was, I am sure, his inspiration; he also enjoys playing at the gentleman while parodying gentlemanly conventions. Perhaps you noticed that peacock suit he wore at the ratting match?" I nodded as she went on. "And yes, the fabric came directly from Mr. Morris' shop, though in that case I bear most of the culpability. I used the same pattern for some hangings in one of our other homes and Frances fell in love with it."

"Speaking of the ratting match," Holmes at last interjected, "I am not sure that the events of that evening are what you brought us here to discuss, but I trust you won't mind clarifying a few points for us."

"No, not at all. I have hoped to do so ever since I learned of the tragedy. The evening went horribly awry, and Charles and I are still upset about it. Where would you like to begin?"

"Let's start with your big fellow, the one who attacked us," I insisted. "What prompted that assault?"

"For that we owe you our deepest apologies. I am sure that you," and she looked directly at Holmes as she said this, "do not for a moment imagine that we directed Gilham to detain you, much less to assault you."

"I did not imagine so," said Holmes, "but that made it all the greater surprise when it happened."

"What became of him? I don't think any of us got back to him later that night," I asked, looking at Holmes.

"No, we did not," he said. "I'm not sure that I, or even Marston, could have navigated our way back to him."

"Oh, you wouldn't have found him there anyway; he has been taken care of," she said.

The suspicion on my face must have betrayed my lingering memory of the sinister Wakefields described by Marston, for she immediately bridled and spoke with only thinly restrained indignation. "No, doctor, you misunderstand me. You misunderstand everything about us, in fact."

"I didn't say . . . I didn't intend to mean . . ."

She took a breath, seemed to gather herself. "Perhaps you didn't, and I apologise if my anger is uncalled for. When I say we have taken care of him, I am not speaking in sinister euphemisms. We do not regard human beings as disposable. When I say that we have taken care of Gilham I do not mean that some mudlark will be snagging his corpse from the river come the next tide. I mean that he is in hospital, where, I fear, he will remain for some time. It may be that your defence of yourselves has deprived him of his livelihood—perhaps, God forbid, even his ability to walk. I can hardly blame you, considering that he admits that he was trying to deprive *you* of your heads, but the fact remains that we are at something of a loss as to finding him a useful living once he has recovered

enough to get about with a crutch. His pride will not stand . . . "
Here she paused only a second, then changed direction back toward the original question. "He attacked you because it seemed to him that you were about to harm Alexander."

"A name at last, Holmes!" I said, having grown heartily tired of referring to our peculiar subject as "the housebreaker," or "the walleye," or by any other feeble substitute for the actual thing.

Mrs. Wakefield looked at me sadly. "A name that did less justice to its owner than most, because it was just a name we gave him."

"You *gave* him the name?" I asked.

"We had no choice. He came to us unbidden and unintroduced, so of course we had to organise *something* for him."

I could make little of this, and my bewilderment only increased until Holmes had mercy and said to Mrs. Wakefield, "Dr. Watson has not yet understood that your Alexander was an inarticulate mute and utterly deaf."

"Oh," she said. "Of course I didn't really know how much you knew of Alexander, only that he was of interest to you in your inquiry regarding Mr. Clemens. And I must say, he was not really *my* Alexander."

"Holmes," I objected, even though it seemed that Mrs. Wakefield had paused only for breath and was about to continue, "He was most definitely not mute. You were there. You saw him as well as I did, though the very thought of it makes my skin crawl. He was talking to those rats."

"Not talking, Watson. He made many sounds, yes, but think—did you hear a single real word?"

"Well no, I suppose not. I could hardly hear him at all in that racket. But the meaning and emotion of his intentions were plain, no matter how mad they may also have been. I call that the power of speech."

"Mr. Holmes is correct, Doctor. Alexander made many sounds, but I never heard him utter a single recognizable word. Nor, I am sure, did he ever hear one. His lack of hearing was absolute." When I made no additional attempt to interrupt, she continued. "He came to us about a month ago. It was Gilham who found him making himself at home among some old shipping crates behind one of our warehouses at the docks. Gilham kept an eye on him as a matter of course, but then early one morning he caught him attempting to pry open the front door of the warehouse, so he had to act. He could tell that Alexander was not accustomed to living rough, so he took pity and brought him to Black's, one of many establishments in which we maintain a business interest, where he was fed and given a place to sleep. Gilham, unable to communicate with him and recognizing his physical limitations, named him Alexander, I believe for a deceased brother. I first heard of him from Gilham about two weeks before the ratting match. We have many people in our employ, and many more whom we in some way watch over. Alexander was a little of both types, and I encouraged Gilham to carry on with helping him. Mr. Black found some simple chores for Alexander to justify his tenancy in a small room. He enjoyed tidying up around the place—not that any amount of tidying could ever make Black's actually tidy. But he seems to have roamed at large during the day. That was no problem because we had taken him in without any serious intention of making him earn his keep, at least for the time it might take for us to gain a clearer understanding of his prospects. We do not operate any of our enterprises"—I wondered if Holmes was beginning to tire of this word—"as pure charities, but they do provide us with opportunities for patience when the circumstances seem to justify the effort. Alexander was special, and under normal circumstances, quite sweet-natured." She smiled and added, "Charles accuses me of excessive good will when it comes to these waifs and foundlings. He may be right; it is no doubt the result of my own childhood experiences. But, like Gilham, I sensed something in Alexander that made him seem worth our attention. I am still not sure what it was."

Her face saddened and she said, "You may then imagine how I feel about his death. It has not escaped my

118

notice that it was because of our well-intentioned kindnesses toward Alexander that he soon became acquainted with the ratting matches at Black's. Within a day or two of his arrival he became a fixture at the matches, even an attraction, and there, of course, a darker side of his nature emerged."

"You learned nothing of his background, his home?"

"We could tell from his clothing that he was a recent arrival from South Africa. Gilham's attempts to communicate with him were unsuccessful; there was something in Alexander's unusual combination of impairments that limited not only his ability to learn but even his ability to pay attention. He looked at written and printed words as if they were small pictures he couldn't quite make out. He had some hand gestures to which Gilham tried to respond, but the main features of his story were either hidden in his own troubled memory or perhaps lost even to him."

"Did you know he was armed?" Holmes asked.

"I know he was *not*," she said. Her tone was firm, but almost hurt. "Neither Gilham, Mr. Black, nor I would have tolerated weapons in the possession of a guest of his sort. I would swear that even as he stood by the pit that evening before you chased him, he could not have been armed. Besides, Gilham had already told me that Alexander showed no inclination to try to use any sort of mechanical device, though he was charmed by small, pretty things. He picked up almost anything of the like within reach, usually turning it this way and that before putting it down." She paused, as if suddenly remembering something. "He put things down with great care, almost ceremony. Anyway, Gilham doubts that Alexander had the mental wherewithal to understand how a revolver works; or, if he did know how to make it work, he wouldn't understand what it did."

I said, "That would go a long way toward explaining his remarkably poor marksmanship that night. Under the circumstances of that moment, even a mediocre shot, having the element of surprise entirely on his side, would have disposed of two if not all three of us before we could have fired a shot."

Mrs. Wakefield seemed disinclined to continue on this subject, and I wondered if she found discussion of gunplay too distasteful or even painful, but she disabused me of any idea that she might be squeamish when she said, "Speaking of weapons, Mr. Holmes, your handling of Gilham's attack has raised considerable professional interest among some of our people. Gilham has spoken in the most admiring if regretful terms of your cosh."

Holmes seemed unsurprised at this line of questioning. "It is of my own design, a lighter alternative when carrying a stick is inconvenient. I have found the common steel-handled coshes too heavy and unresponsive, so I have replaced the metal with bamboo."

"Whole cane?"

"No, the handle is a laminant of several small, long slivers shaved—or, perhaps better said, split—longitudinally from the outer portion of the culm of certain species of Chinese bamboo."

"Like the slips of a bamboo book?"

"Roughly that size, but three-sided rather than four. I am told by the city's foremost craftsman in this material that there is no other species in the entire plant kingdom that can match these Asian bamboos for the extreme density of fibres along their outer skin. The resulting shaft, once these small slivers are glued up together, shaped, and polished, has both great flexibility and an unparallelled strength. I understand that similar shafts are just coming into vogue among sportsmen for golf club handles and fishing rods, especially in America. Watson will no doubt be replacing his greenheart trout rods before long."

"And the head?"

"The heart of an oak knot I found a few years ago along a stream in the Cairngorms. The water had shaped it into a slightly elliptical sphere. Wrapped in gutta percha and inserted into a hinged leather harness at the end of the bamboo shaft, it is quite my ideal of such a weapon.

"Wood, even oak, seems a curious choice," she said. "Most professionals prefer lead, or at least brass." Her plainly expressed confidence on this point brought to mind the improbable image of her sitting in this same elegant room surrounded by half a dozen shabbily dressed toughs as they calmly compared notes on alley combat techniques.

"True," said Holmes, "and for their purposes the preference must seem the logical one. But for mine, I find lead and unshielded brass unnecessarily lethal. My studies indicate that they result in death or severe brain injury in many circumstances when simple unconsciousness would serve as well. Cushioned oak is more than heavy enough, especially at the velocities achieved with the long whippy bamboo handle."

"Gilham would agree, I'm sure. I admire your sense of sportsmanship in the matter," she said without the smile that I thought such a remark deserved. "I will pass both your technical advancements and your insights along," she said.

I listened to this matter-of-fact technical disquisition with my mouth half open, again struck by the meandering and improbable nature of our conversation with this woman whom only days before I had been credibly informed was a leading force for great evil in London's most sordid underworld. Passersby seeing us through a window would have assumed that we discussed some grand ball of the past season, rather than the finer points of criminal weaponry.

Holmes nodded at her remark and then asked her if there were a gray van kept at the cabyard, and if so did she know the driver, but she was unable to help us, though she did assure us that her own inquiries, presumably with the cabyard at Paddington, had been unproductive. "The van is not one of ours; it did indeed bring Alexander to the cabyard yesterday, but I have no other information about it or its driver, who seems to have left almost unnoticed. My manager could only tell me that he was a very slender man of average height.

Mrs. Wakefield looked toward a nearby mantle clock, then abruptly abandoned the subject, saying, "I would enjoy further conversation, but I fear I have a luncheon engagement, so I must hurry us along to the reason I invited you here." Her demeanor and tone of voice became grave. "You are correct, Mr. Holmes, in your surmise that I have another concern than the sad death of Alexander. Our common interests compel me to alert you to something, though I hardly even know what to call it. There is, let me say, a great restlessness in London. You may object that of course there is, and the Jubilee is the cause, but this is another thing. You know the magnitude and breadth of the Wakefield business interests. You have some idea of the sensitivity of our needful scrutiny of the city's ways. I am certain that something extraordinary is happening. No," she shook her head as she corrected herself, "it is not happening. Not quite. It is about to happen. Underneath the happy anticipation and logistical frenzy of the Jubilee there is another current, and there are hints of another kind of expectancy. It is sinister in the extreme, Mr. Holmes, and it exasperates me that all I can tell you is that something is up."

"Surely your sources have narrowed it down more than that?" Holmes said, in a tone that left no doubt that he took these vague forebodings as perfectly reliable.

"Not much; not as much as I would normally expect. Of course it seems most likely to have to do with the Royal Jubilee. As you know, at any given time there are many undercurrents, or perhaps I should call them crosscurrents, among the city's criminal communities. Indeed, if we—people like you and me, I mean—had only to think of our resident criminal population, we would be surprised if our native entrepreneurs were *not* making plans to take advantage of the wholesale diversion of the regular police that is already occurring."

"To say nothing of the opportunities provided by millions of strangers, many of whom will be relatively unfamiliar with the city's ways."

"Yes."

"But you anticipate more than that," said Holmes, as half-question, half assertion.

"I am sure of it," she said. "The greatest concern surely must be some sort of violence or other disturbance. I fear the worst. You know the obvious target. Her Majesty has survived five or six publicly acknowledged attempts on her life during her reign, and probably twice as many attempts that were never let out. There is always that risk. But whether she is a target or not, the other risks of the occasion are inestimable. The sheer volume of innocent humanity that will be crushed together along the procession route—millions, they're saying . . . ." She shook her head in wonder at the awful thought. "You've seen the papers." I looked at Holmes who, unlike me and except for fussing over his old clippings, had not been paying much attention to any newspaper in recent weeks, but he gave no response. "So many people, packed so vulnerably together, would provide any lunatic with a few sticks of dynamite countless opportunities to express his insanity in horrors of almost biblical proportions."

I came near to physically reeling at the prospect of such wholesale atrocity. Holmes had not moved a muscle since his last words.

Anticipating our need for details, Mrs. Wakefield continued. "Sad to say, I have few specifics to add. I have tried. I can tell you that I have unquestionably sensed an unusual, or perhaps I should say inappropriate, tension among my acquaintances at three embassies, two from the Indian subcontinent and one from the Far East. But more than that, my people tell me there is a definite air of unrest among the city's international populations; it is no surprise that the Americans are included. Frances himself, who is widely travelled in the city these days, says it is as if these diverse and scattered people, most of whom have no contact with one another, are uniformly uncomfortable about something that they don't consciously even know is wrong. I wish I could give you more than that, but it is all I have."

"It is a great deal, madam, and I will act upon it immediately. I have been so absorbed in this Clemens business that I have had my nose to the grindstone when it should have been to the wind. Indeed, thanks to this alert I now wonder if I might see a little more light directed toward the Clemens problem too. I will make urgent inquiries, and we must, as usual, keep each other posted of any new developments."

"Certainly," she said, and rose to see us off. Frances materialised at the door, but before we turned to go she addressed me. "Doctor, you seem troubled. I sense that we have left questions unanswered for you."

"There is nothing especially new in that, madam," I said, giving a resigned nod toward Holmes. "But except for these tremendous and disturbing revelations that you have just shared with us, there is only one other question that nags at me. It just seems indelicate of me to ask it."

"Delicacy is always appreciated, but by now you may realise that we are not always obliged to honor it here. Perhaps you should set it aside just this once."

I nodded and said, "I have learned much here, and I feel almost as if I owe you an apology merely for the hearsay about you that has come my way." Her eyebrows raised a bit at this, and I saw that I was near to dithering. I started again, to the point: "You are a cultured, refined woman. And yet you came to the ratting match. You sat there through that whole wretched nightmare of gore and cruelty. You and Holmes sit here calmly discussing the finer points of the most brutal violence . . . ." Realising that I was almost sputtering and not really asking my question, I paused for a moment, then simply added. "It makes no sense. Indeed, forgive me for saying it so bluntly, but for all your obvious intelligence and insight, *you* make no sense."

"I see. I will take your words as a compliment, doctor, but again it appears that we have not been sufficiently introduced. The sense it makes—the sense I make—is political. Consider that my husband and I oversee what the newspapers would in more polite contexts call a business empire, one that in good part involves our city's most neglected and shadowy realms and, I freely admit, exploits some of human nature's least savory impulses. We have interests in several other trades more or less like the ratting matches. But our stature in the community is not measured solely by our reach, or our wealth, or even by whatever actual power, legitimate or extra-legal, that we may exercise. It is dependent upon our presence, just as the ancestrally titled royalty of this nation are enslaved to the rituals and ceremonies that march them in front of the great mass of people they rule. I go to the ratting match because it is, in the strange manners of *my* London, the right and necessary thing for me to do. Does that help?"

"Yes. It does. I see your point; but still . . . ." Again I was almost at a loss for how to continue, and just blurted out, "It's the bloody savagery of the thing." My eyes strayed to her glorious features, her perfect coiffure, and her elegant dress. "You shouldn't have to see that."

"You are kind to say so, and well meaning, but again I can see that you have not had a fair opportunity to know me, or my life. By the time I was eight years of age, I had seen things, and known savagery, that would make the ratting match at Black's seem like high tea at St. James."

"I find such a thing impossible to imagine," I said.

"Then, doctor, please believe me when I say that you should regard the failure of your imagination a great blessing. Frances, will you please see that our friends find a good cab?"

Chapter Fifteen
A Chaos of Conspirators

Once in the cab and on our way, I asked Holmes what he made of Mrs. Wakefield's alarming warnings. "I hardly know enough specifics except the most important one: if she, of all people in the city, is alarmed, there is reason for all of us to be alarmed."

"But this is London, Holmes. What could happen?"

"Surely you have not forgotten ten years ago, Watson," he said, "and the so-called 'Jubilee Plot' that had the press in an uproar prior to that celebration?"

"Of course, but it evaporated, didn't it? All that talk of some kind of reign of terror during the celebration, but nothing came of it. From what I remember, the Fenians could barely even get into the country, could they? The government—the police, I suppose—took appropriate notice. I assume they must have acted upon the threats and it all fell apart. No doubt some of the plotters were serious in their intentions, but the conspirators whom the police collared were locked up tight, and the Fenians were broken, or tore themselves apart with their usual in-fighting. Parnell is dead, and that other chap, too. There's hardly been a peep about any of them in the papers for years."

Holmes looked at me patiently. "It was much more involved and unresolved than that, Watson, and still is. But we are not concerned here with something as easily identified as Irish discontent, as distressing as that continues to be for all concerned."

"You're saying there are others? Other nations, or just other plotters?"

"Watson, no individual, political group, or nation has a monopoly on dynamite. Mrs. Wakefield tells us that there is unease scattered throughout the international community in London. 'Something big,' she said. As big as the Empire, perhaps?"

"But what are we to do this late in the game? I gather that Mrs. Wakefield's resources are considerable, and if she hasn't been able to learn what is going on, who can?"

"At least there I know where to start," he said, then leaned out and called up to the driver, "Pardon me, but we must change direction—the Diogenes Club, please, in Pall Mall." Then, settling back into the seat and speaking more to himself than to me, he frowned and added, "We should have heard something from Barber by now."

The afternoon was wearing on by the time we reached Pall Mall and stopped in front of the odd little club to which Holmes' older brother Mycroft belonged. Holmes' movements were brisk, even hasty, as he led me up the steps, through the small door, and into the cramped and starkly inhospitable guest chamber that was as far into the sanctum of the club as non-members were allowed. It was also the only place in the club where spoken communication was permitted, though even there conversations were invariably conducted in whispers. The doorman told us that Mycroft was just then having a late luncheon, and after Holmes introduced himself and emphasised the urgency of the situation, the man reluctantly went to fetch the elder Holmes.

While we stood waiting, I asked Holmes if his brother still occupied his quiet backstage position at Whitehall, where he long had functioned as a great synthesiser of disparate bits of information from all corners of the government, indeed of the Empire. Holmes nodded and said, "If anything, his reach has extended. The last time I called at his office, a few months ago, he was just seeing the American ambassador out." His expression darkened and he added, "Let me caution you that though he still seems up to the task intellectually, I fear that his health is beginning to suffer. He is barely in his fifties, but you may be shocked by his appearance."

And so I was. In the two years since I had last seen Mycroft Holmes, his weight had declined dramatically. His obesity, which I had always regarded as worrisome even in so robust a man, had not all disappeared, but the earlier effect, of a nearly slothful inertia, had been replaced by an alarming gauntness. I immediately made a mental inventory of a variety of lethal diseases that I would consider if a man of his appearance came under my professional care. He still carried a fair amount of extra weight, but it hung on his face and body like old draperies.

The sharp gaze I'd been so struck by during previous meetings had taken on an almost feverish aspect.

But his voice was hearty, and louder than would normally be tolerated in this room. "My dear Sherlock, I can't say what a happy surprise it is to see you, and a most fortuitous coincidence. You know, for the past couple days I have frequently had it in mind to call you in, but, well," he smiled humourlessly and gave a long sigh, "things have been rather more busy than usual. You are lucky to catch me here; I only stepped over from Whitehall for a breath of air and some food." Turning to me, he stretched out a still-massive paw and added,"Dr. Watson, I am pleased to see you too. Until the recent excitement I'd been catching up on some of your tales of Sherlock." He nodded toward the door into the club's inviolate silent spaces. "Not my usual reading, you know."

Then began one of those exchanges that these two men were uniquely capable of making. For them it was simple conversation, no matter how bewildering or disjointed most bystanders might find it.

The younger Holmes began, "You have been alerted for some days now."

"Others too. Many others, the past few days."

"It is grave, then."

"I wish I could say. For all its inevitability, gravity is tricky. As you plainly have come directly from Kensington, perhaps you have points of value to add."

"She has gathered only rumblings."

"And he?"

"Apparently abroad."

"Which is odd timing, but she is more attentive alone than when he is in residence, so it may be better this way."

"Not much, I fear. She has discerned only the outline of the alarm."

"You hadn't? I thought to hear from you a week or two ago."

"I was enjoying a few weeks of *in*attentiveness to London as I caught up on my references."

"Your winter was indeed difficult, but you seem in the pink now. You are not back at it any too soon."

"Not at the right 'it,' perhaps. I have sensed that somehow the Clemens affair obscured something larger but less substantial."

"We have kept an interest."

"As you should. He is, in his way, one of us."

"Oh, he is more than that."

At this point they seemed to have caught up on their most pressing common concerns. The conversation slipped back into a more conventional mode. "You both had best come with me back to the offices. There is a meeting later; you should wait for it." He glanced at me, and I wondered if he were unsure precisely how much I could be told. Then he spoke somewhat distractedly to the space between us. "Forgive me, I must have a few more minutes. I will need the energy for a long night." He hurried out, presumably to finish his meal.

I said, "As important as all this sounds, surely they could have provided him with something to eat right at Whitehall, wherever he is there, and saved him the running back and forth to the club."

Holmes said, "To the best of my knowledge Mycroft has never run anywhere, back or forth, in his life. More important, his dietary philosophy is inflexible. Outside this club, I doubt there is another chef in the city who could satisfy his tastes. I suspect he also uses these little dining outings as opportunities for reflection." My own growing hunger was apparently well below the scope of even slight interest in this strange crisis, so we stood and waited.

Mycroft returned in minutes and led us down to the kerb where a government brougham waited. The Holmes brothers took the seat and I perched on one of the front-corner fold-downs for the short ride. In moments we had skirted Trafalgar Square, turned down Whitehall, and stopped at the great pile of the Admiralty just short of the Horse Guards. We were ushered to the nearest door by Mycroft, who led us up a floor and toward the rear of the building, where he put us in a small cramped office. "A moment," he said, as he hurried out.

The office was apparently his. The walls were lined floor to ceiling with shelves piled with document cases of various sizes and conditions. Every flat space, including much of the floor, was likewise occupied. Though the place overflowed with paper, hardly a bookbinding was to be seen. Mycroft clearly dealt with massive quantities of information, little of it published for general consumption, though I did notice, with just a bit of pride, a small stack of back issues of *The Strand* piled on a corner chair, presumably the issues with my stories.

"I am confident there are reasonably comfortable chairs here, but I would be reluctant to disturb the documentary architecture," I said.

"Documentary sedimentation might be more like it," Holmes said just as Mycroft hurried back in.

"We have a few minutes," he said. Glancing between us again, he said, "You are both welcome at this session, but I feel compelled to insist that no word of what is said be repeated. And the attendees should under no circumstances become known either." Looking at me, he added, "For reasons that you may well understand, doctor, these deliberations must remain unreported. There is little point in developing strategies and tactics if later they are published where the wrong sort could read them and thus anticipate them on some future occasion. As well, there will be others at this meeting whose part must remain unknown."

"Of course, of course," I said. "I understand."

"In his tales of our experiences," Holmes added, "the doctor may not always have emphasised the proper aspects of a given case, but his discretion on a great many sensitive matters relating not only to individuals but to the state has never failed."

I turned to thank Holmes for this, which was about as close to a compliment as he had ever come in discussing my stories, but Mycroft was on the move again. We were led down a corridor whose space was in good part crowded with temporary benches and desks, at which sat a number of men and women, all working furiously at piles of paper whose subject I could not determine. There were city maps everywhere.

Mycroft Holmes' admonition to me about the secrecy of what I was to hear is all the explanation you will require to understand the extreme vagueness of my account of the meeting to which he was taking us, though I make no apology for the times when I do name names. We were conducted into a long, high-ceilinged room. We had obviously arrived at the rear of the building, because the windows along the west wall gave a view toward St. James Park. Slight sparkles of the water glinted through the trees from the lake, but we were not elevated enough to see the palace beyond the park. A long table, capable of comfortably seating at least forty, occupied the centre of the room, though only about a dozen people were scattered in small groups around the half of the table closest to a simple podium. Many more chairs lined the walls on three sides of the room. There were stacks of papers on many of the chairs and on the unoccupied end of the table. Maps and other large documents had been tacked crookedly here and there on the walls. The remains of what appeared to be more than one meal were also discarded about, and a large wheeled cart holding kettles, baked goods, and sandwiches had been left near the door. Now that I was at least semi-officially a guest, if not a participant, at this meeting, I resolved that I was within my rights to investigate these provisions at the earliest opportunity.

Judging from the many people already in the room, the meeting was apparently a more or less continuous affair, with a changing list of participants as required. "I assumed that the work of planning such a gigantic event as the Royal Procession would require a large number of people, but somehow I didn't expect the work to look like this," I said to Sherlock Holmes.

But it was Mycroft Holmes who replied. "Oh, we aren't concerned with the ceremonies and the bunting here. That's being done elsewhere, and," he looked around the room, "by many, many times as many people as you see here. Though I do wish our task were as simple as that."

"This is the security planning, then," said Sherlock Holmes.

"Yes, in all its fractious glory," Mycroft said, again looking sternly at me, but my wandering attention was drawn to some of the people in the room. Seated side-by-side on chairs in the most distant corner of the room, and looking rather like two children isolated for misbehavior, were Lestrade and Gregson. By their postures, I guessed that they may have been feeling as insignificant and out-of-the-picture as their remoteness from the group around the table seemed to suggest. Neither Lestrade nor

131

Gregson showed any of the usual air of self-importance that had become so practiced in their normal work, so I assumed, rightly as it turned out, that they and a few other individuals likewise spaced randomly along the walls were here only to listen.

The greater shock came as I scanned the half-circle of men at the table. I recognised two or three prominent figures in the government (I write this trusting that Mycroft would certainly have tolerated such a low level of specificity). Several independent conversations were underway among these men, so even though it was apparent that some level of work was still underway, there was clearly a *hiatus* in the main deliberations.

But then my scanning vision unexpectedly was caught and held by the broad and unrestrained smile of Constable Marston, seated right in the middle of this august group! He had obviously noticed us enter, and once he caught my eye he promptly gave me a vigorous wave of greeting. The highly distinguished personage to his left looked up at that motion, gave us a quick look, said something to Marston that made Marston laugh and nod his head, and went back to his other conversation. Looking at his pocket watch, Marston rose and walked over to us.

Still grinning broadly, he shook our hands in turn, saying "Cat's out of the bag now, isn't it?"

"It had partly escaped before we got here," Holmes said. "Though I am impressed at your ability to sustain your supposed status as a constable, you must have known that it wasn't completely convincing under the circumstances."

"No, I'm sure it was not," Marston said, "at least not to you. There are some here for whom the discovery seems to be a complete and overwhelming revelation." He nodded in the direction of Lestrade and Gregson, who were now watching us as closely as possible from such a distance.

"It was time that they be briefed in the bigger issue, I suppose," said Holmes.

"Yes. Holmes," Marston shook his head and started over, "Mycroft, I mean; must be precise now that there is more than one Holmes in the room." Mycroft had moved to the table and was standing speaking with another of the seated figures-whom-I-dare-not-name. "Mycroft thought it was time they were brought on. The top echelons of the police force, from Bradford on down, have been engaged from the beginning of course, but Mycroft and the Colonel thought that at this stage these two might have something to contribute, and at least could do no harm. They only just arrived a few minutes before you, and I fear that they are still trying to figure which is the bigger shock: that this is all going on, or that one of their apparent inferiors—me—has been involved in it all along."

As he finished speaking I noticed that the room was rapidly filling with an amazing variety of people who were entering from the door behind us and from a second door at the other end of the room. Many went directly to the table and took seats that they were apparently accustomed to occupying. Others found seats in the chairs along the walls. Others crossed the room and stood by the windows. Quite a few others came in as if for the first time, looked uncertainly around, and were quietly greeted by a few people apparently delegated for that task and directed to an appropriate location.

Marston also noticed the growing crowd. I reached over and grabbed a random sandwich and a bottle of something just as he said, "Time to start. Come on," and led us to chairs next to his at the table. I looked for Mycroft but he was not in sight. I later noticed that he had taken a chair along the far wall, one or two seats down from Lestrade and Gregson, whose earlier stunned expressions were if anything intensified as they recognised many of the new faces. I now understood why Mycroft's admonition of secrecy had been so stern. What a gathering this was. While I can hardly even characterise the stature of the government people without names and offices coming immediately to the reader's mind, I can say that they were matched by the most distinguished array of other citizens of the empire, many if not all of them household names for their achievements and adventures in the most distant, exotic, and violent corners of the world. I leaned toward Holmes, who was also looking about the room at this dazzling parade of notables, and whispered, "Who is running the empire today?"

He gave a slight shrug and said, "The people who always run it, I suppose."

There was one last rise in the volume of conversation and general stir, then the room, with upwards of 100 men crowded into it, subsided into near silence. As if awaiting that quiet, one last figure entered the door we had passed through moments before, a man whose attendance at such an event seems to require no violation of my pledge of discretion: Prime Minister Robert Gascoyne-Cecil, 3rd Marquess of Salisbury. He moved quickly to the head of the table, glanced about the room, and began to speak.

"Gentlemen, I thank you for your attendance here, and for your vital work. I know that some of you have been long involved, while others have more recently arrived from great and I am sure dreadfully inconvenient distances, but all of you are essential. As many of you no doubt already know, and as the rest of you can just as easily imagine, the arrangements for the public side of this event have been long and demanding. As for that work, I am gratified to be able to report to you that despite our best efforts to the contrary, it is becoming apparent that the upcoming festivities stand an excellent chance of giving the lie to the legendary British inability to organise anything." Never having heard of this man exercising such pointed sarcasm or even humour publicly, I gave Holmes a quick look, but his expression was unchanged. "And now that the countless logistical arrangements for the great day have been largely completed . . . " Salisbury gave an audible sigh and continued in a patient tone, "that is to say, now that the learned men who so earnestly lead your government have exhausted the subtleties of such portentous issues as whether or not the term 'jubilee' can accurately and thus officially be applied to a sixtieth-anniversary event;" a few knowing chuckles met this, "and whether even Her Majesty's horses are highly enough esteemed to be permitted within the nave of St. Paul's"; more chuckles, "and whether the Empire, indeed western civilisation generally, can survive should the Metropolitan Police Courts be given a holiday on Tuesday," some open laughter, over which the Prime Minister continued to speak, "we can concentrate on the more serious, indeed extremely urgent, matters upon which you have been working and will continue to work in these last hours before the Jubilee is underway."

"This week we celebrate sixty glorious years. But of those sixty years, not one day has been free from the violent application of our military authority somewhere on the globe. Many, I dare say almost all of us in this room," he said, his eyes scanning the faces, "have participated in one if not several such exercises. There are none of us here but have lost dear compatriots, or still suffer other unhealing wounds from those experiences. And though we all hope and pray that the mass of our citizens may continue to enjoy an idealised national recollection of this grand pageant of conquest and benevolent administration, in which happy endings abound, all of us in this room are painfully aware that in every part of the mighty Empire that we have created there are men much like us in their vigor, their intellectual power, their determination, and the sharpness of their memories—men who harbour overwhelming bitterness and a long-nurtured craving for retribution—for justice, as they see such a thing. Her Majesty's Diamond Jubilee presents such men with an unparalleled opportunity. Our sacred responsibility is to keep that opportunity unfulfilled.

"In the present effort you are honor-bound first and foremost to protect Her Majesty. Her person is inviolate. There is no possibility in our most dire imaginings that anything may be allowed to happen to her—nor even that anything may be seen *almost* to happen to her.

"But we are likewise determined, and with no less uncompromising a commitment, to protect this *occasion*. Nothing must mar it, nothing distract the attention of the world from the message and the lesson Her Majesty will represent as she makes her way around the city. We celebrate and honor the Empire, gentlemen. There is no room for any disturbance of that celebration.

"You, in your respective experiences throughout the empire, represent our collective awareness of the supposed grievances that someone, whether a single raving madman or a brilliant strategist at the head of a professionally accomplished movement, might hope to redress during the commemoration. You are too aware of history to underestimate the range of sources of

135

peril, and too experienced to underestimate any of the possible threats.

"Apparently, I was asked to speak to you at this late hour in your work in the hope that some exhortation from me would somehow inspire you, or heighten your skills. I have no illusions on these points, however. You need no further inspiration, much less instruction, from me. Your skills are unparalleled. But I come here anyway, just to exploit this one occasion when you are all gathered in one place. I am here selfishly, to savor the honor of thanking you, on behalf of our Queen and our empire, for your service. On Wednesday, as the laurels are dispensed to the countless functionaries and horse masters and banner bearers and other worthies who will have seen to it that the public pageantry went as planned and advertised, the only sign of your success will be the absence of any public awareness of it. That, and my thanks here today, will also be your only reward. Many of you are accustomed to this level of gratitude, and fully appreciate its greater values."

As the Prime Minister delivered his remarks, the room had gradually achieved that level of silence so often described by melodramatists as deafening. Not a soul moved as he looked about, somehow giving the impression that he caught and held the eye of each of us. Then he added, "At that, I will leave you to it. God bless you." He turned and hurried from the room, trailing two or three men who had silently entered shortly before he did.

Even as we relaxed into our chairs, there was no resurgence in conversation among the group. It was as if an earlier meeting, which had been adjourned for only a few minutes, suddenly resumed.

The next four hours were a bewildering and exhausting series of reports and discussions on the apparently infinite list of potential sources of unrest, disorder, and outright catastrophe facing the Jubilee. It was no wonder that Mycroft Holmes appeared to be in the final stages of nervous collapse. The "something" that Constance Wakefield had sensed was up was a sprawling mishmash of facts, confidences, conjectures, rumors, and shadowy reports of a global array of known plots, half-confirmed conspiracies, long-festering concentrations of hard feelings, and newly ripe fields for unrest.

One by one, attendees rose to offer succinct status reports. Local officials described, first, the taking into custody of various chronically suspicious individuals and groups. Such a wholesale roundup involved some fairly flimsy evidence but was seen as worth the legal and perhaps even moral compromises involved just to "clear the field," as one investigator put it.

From there the discussions moved along to analyses of the currently perceived risks of several perennial if relatively innocent activities like the possibility for unseemly outbreaks of suffragist placards or humane society congregations along the procession route. From a quick summary of these the meeting turned to the most dreadful possibilities imaginable.

I saw that Myrcoft's concerns about taking me into his confidence were irrelevant. I pride myself on my ability to absorb and retain the details of many conversations, but I could no more retain the details of this endless barrage of horrifying possibilities than I could come to terms with the casual observation offered by one of the first speakers, that on Jubilee Day there would be upwards of 40,000 armed military personnel in London. Ten thousand of our own troops would camp in Hyde Park on Monday night, but many of the others were freshly arrived native units from some of the Empire's most distant and troubled outposts. The speaker did not have to ask us what the odds were that none of these thousands of well-armed individuals suffered from divided loyalties or concealed hostilities, much less that none of them was part of some brilliantly organised conspiracy that awaited only the right moment—presumably the close approach of Her Majesty's retinue—to act with ruinous consequences. Once the statistical probabilities presented by the sheer number of such anonymous military professionals had been presented to me, I heard the rest of the proceedings through a fog of dread.

The worst was in how little could be known. Several problematic political elements of the Indian subcontinent, still reeling from the previous year's historic famine, had suddenly become unreachable in the aftermath of the unprecedented Assam Earthquake of June 12. I had paid little attention to the sketchy

137

early reports in the previous week's papers, and indeed little was yet known of the 150,000 square miles of countryside, villages, and cities from Burma to New Delhi that had been reduced to dusty rubble in a matter of moments by that awful chain of seismic shocks. What was known, and was especially on the minds of many at our meeting, was the way in which such disasters feed whatever discontent happens to be simmering right then among the victims and their distant compatriots.

But there seemed to be similarly ominous reports, minus only the natural cataclysm, from throughout the empire. Salisbury's allusion to the lingering hard feelings of 60 years of imperial wars and policing actions was illuminated in reports from China, Afghanistan, Africa—all over Africa, not just the south—Ireland, Scotland, eastern Canada, and so on. The potential for trouble was everywhere, and it was not confined to strange races of people whom many of my fellow Londoners knew only as almost fantastic fairy-tale characters.

There was for me a personal revelation in this. As the recitation continued, it occurred to me, again recalling a remark of Lord Salisbury's, how comfortable we Englishmen had become in the forty-plus years since any of our citizens had fought and died in a war against our own kind, which is to say other Europeans—and that war had taken place in the Crimea, which most of us did not regard as properly Europe anyway. Before the Crimea, one had to think all the way back to Waterloo to find Englishmen fighting and dying in a war near to home. Since then, to our great and largely unconsidered convenience, Her Majesty's military forces had concentrated on expanding and consolidating the Empire among people we all rather mindlessly thought of as "natives," and about whom we knew essentially nothing and did not care to know more. When it came my generation's turn, I was among the immense ranks of Englishmen called upon to participate in these far-flung imperial ventures, but as we sailed off to the lands of said natives, the idea that some day there might be consequences visited upon our own lands never occurred to us. However wretched or heroic we may have perceived our adventures in the far corners of the empire, we ceased to fear retribution the moment we stepped aboard the ships that would take us home. I was taken by an overwhelming sense of naked vulnerability.

Some of the speakers were able to report not only the discovery of a plot of some substance but also the apprehension of the ringleaders. Others reported on the circulation of vague but convincing rumors, and the pursuit and scattering of apparent conspirators. Others could provide no certainty of the seriousness of the potential threat they were investigating, but identified groups or individuals whose movements would be closely watched in the coming days. The final report of the evening, presented by Marston himself just after midnight, was one of the most hopeful; the Fenians, while still "long on talk" about dynamite (which Marston described as "the most brutish and stupid of weapons"), seemed not to have been able to organise a plan of any substance.

I welcomed having the meeting adjourn on this modestly positive note. It gave me the bit of extra energy still needed when it was finally time to file out of the room with Holmes and the rest.

Mycroft had vanished about an hour earlier. He was among the many who over the course of the evening left the room now and then for whatever personal reasons, but this last time he had not returned. I thus thought that we should look for a cab immediately, but as we made our way down the hallway, Mycroft appeared coming the other way, breasting the exiting crowd and bringing us to a halt in the middle of the hallway.

As the rest of the attendees flowed around us, Mycroft said, "Doctor, I would like to borrow Sherlock, for only a moment." Needing no real permission from me, he took his brother by the elbow and led him back into the room. I could not miss the obvious unspoken command that I was to wait where I was. As the Holmes brothers re-entered the now almost empty meeting room, my narrow field of vision through the open door allowed me to see them join three or four other men then engaged in an intense and guarded conversation. It had just dawned on me that one of these men looked remarkably like Lord Salisbury himself when the door closed and I was distracted by the passing of Gregson and Lestrade, trailing after the busier attendees at the meeting with shell-shocked looks on their faces. As they passed me, both nodded a subdued greeting and hurried on.

Holmes, my Holmes that is, was now clearly an initiate, part of whatever constituted the inner circle of this effort, and I wondered if I would be left standing there the rest of the night. But in only a few moments the door opened and he reappeared alone, and joined me. His mood seemed unchanged by whatever had just passed between him, his brother, and the others, and as we entered our cab he said, "I hope that Mrs. Hudson has left us something. That sandwich cart you had the foresight to raid before we sat down was stripped to the boards by the time I got to it just now."

Chapter Sixteen
A Case of Chimney Pots

Mrs. Hudson had indeed left something, quite a lot of it, on a tray in our rooms, and we pitched into it with considerable enthusiasm despite our fatigue. Holmes, however, took only two or three bites of his sandwich before starting as if suddenly remembering something, jumping up and hurrying out the door and up the stairs. With a groan I levered myself from my chair and followed to the door in time to see him stop at the landing between the second and third floor, where I had interrupted him lingering a day or two earlier.

"Watson, would you please close the door behind you? We must keep the hallway here dark."

I did so, and he immediately turned to look out the window, though he stayed in shadow, well back from the pane. As I started up the steps toward him, I said, "What's going on, Holmes?"

There was only the softest light coming in the window, most of it diffused from the lights of the streets and the few windows that were still lit in nearby buildings, but Holmes stayed to one side of the window and motioned me to join him there in the shadows. "Stay back, Watson, but look over at the roof, right there." He indicated the roof of a house almost directly behind ours.

"Yes?" I said. I was of course curious what he was about, but now that I was half a flight of stairs nearer to my bed my strongest inclination was to continue up rather than participate in whatever new puzzle had engaged his attention. Besides, I could see nothing but the same roofline we'd seen out this window for years. "It's dark, Holmes. I'm sure you've noticed." What little light there was made the roofline of the row of houses that backed upon ours little more than a silhouette of right angles decorated with the usual ranks of chimney pots.

"See that cross-chimney there, the long, narrow one that runs perpendicular to the roof line?" I could see it, of course. It was one of the few interesting features to be seen from this window, and I had been attracted to it for years. Once in a fanciful mood I'd noticed its resemblance to a great ocean liner, the long narrow brick chimney angling toward us like the rising prow of some mighty ship with the row of pots resembling the liner's smokestacks. They were tall, straight-sided crown pots, more reminiscent of one of Sam Clemens' Mississippi sternwheelers than of our modern ocean-going liners, but no matter. It looked even more ship-like in midnight silhouette.

"I do. I've seen it before."

"A few days ago I noticed a change. The second pot toward us is out of line; see its tilt?"

"You're right, Holmes. I haven't looked for a while. Is this somehow significant?"

"I believe so. It has happened in the past week. But keep watching."

We had stood there unmoving for a good ten minutes when suddenly the outline of my ocean liner changed; a low bulk appeared on the deck amidships. "Holmes, something, . . . some man is on that roof!"

"He has been there at least four times in the past week. I suppose that the first time, as he was still learning his way, he must have unknowingly bumped the one pot, tilting it but not dislodging it completely from its terra cotta flange."

"But why? What's the use of being there this time of night? Or in daylight, for that matter."

"To keep an eye on us, of course."

"But again—why? Why us? Why now?"

"Ordinarily, but especially these past few days, it is very likely that we are the only residents of the block whose comings and goings might matter enough to set someone there to watch us."

"You mean this has to do with Clemens? Or with the Jubilee?"

"Perhaps both. Have you your field glasses handy?" I ducked under the window and hurried up to my room, returning in seconds with my prism binoculars. Putting them to my eyes I focused on the shape by the chimney pots. "It's hard to make out."

"Can you see a face?"

"I can see a front end of the form, and if I am not just mentally manufacturing details out of the darkness I can see a head with a soft hat of some sort pulled low over the forehead. There's so much shadow under the hat that I can see nothing of the face. My overall impression is of a short, somewhat bulky fellow in heavy clothes. What shall we do? I'd love to find out what he's up to."

"As would I, but we have no chance of catching him when he comes down. He could descend any number of ways that we could not detect if we tried to wait for him in the street."

"So? What now? Do we just watch him watch us?"

"We must act quickly," Holmes announced, scurrying back to our common room and into his laboratory corner. I heard him rummage through his cabinet and trunk, give a little "Ah!" of success, then hurry back my way. As he passed me on the landing with an unidentifiable armload of bottles and other things he said, "Keep looking Watson. I am going to attempt to shed some light, as they say. If our intruder will only maintain his post for two or three more minutes, we will know him better. Keep your glass on where you think his face is. Don't lose sight of it!" he urged as he hurried past the door to my room and continued up to the attic trapdoor.

He disappeared through the trapdoor and almost instantly I heard the creaking of the window in the front attic dormer. I could only assume that he was on the roof on the front side of the house, shielded from view of the mysterious spy. As he later explained, he worked his way along the front of the roof above two or three residences, then silently crept toward the back.

I could see or hear none of this but I did all I could to keep steady and not let the glass slip from its view. Just as my nose began to itch and I wondered if Holmes had fallen from the roof, there came a sudden and almost painful blast of white light, flooding the entire scene with a nearly colourless brilliance. I jumped, but somehow kept my focus on our man as his features came into sharp and unmistakable view. It was none other than young Wiggins, captain of the Irregulars!

The light was gone from the rooftop instantly, but not from my vision nor, I am sure, from the vision of our chimney pot spy. It took all of a minute for the sparkling outlines of chimney pots to fade from my sight before I could make use of the binoculars again. Through them I saw the dark form of Wiggins slip from view—I reflexively scaled down my estimation of the size of the chimney pots to match his boy-size frame—and by the time I had recovered sufficiently, rubbing my eyes for several seconds, the roof top was deserted. Holmes reappeared then, climbing quickly through the trap door.

"It wasn't a man, Holmes, it was a boy—Wiggins! It was Wiggins! What do you think of that?"

Holmes stopped short at this announcement, plainly shocked by the news, and without another word we returned to our tray of sandwiches and cold tea to discuss this remarkable and dismaying turn of events.

He didn't immediately respond to my news. As if to give himself more time to absorb the information, he talked about his idea to use a flash of light to identify him. "I could see right off that we had little chance of getting him in hand," he said," So I decided that we must at least get a look at him. Naturally, I sought the necessary ingredients for a makeshift magnesium flash pan. Once I was up there I carried the ingredients two houses down before mixing them and setting them off. I thought it best to move down the roof from our window, on the chance that our friend wouldn't necessarily associate the location of the flash with us and know that we're onto him. But, it being Wiggins, I doubt I fooled him."

Holmes' expression was troubled. I had never seen him look so openly hurt as he did right then. "You're sure, Watson? It *was* Wiggins?"

"There was no mistaking him, Holmes. I hardly know what to think. There is nothing about that boy that would ever have made me think him capable of this betrayal. There's no possible other explanation for why he would be up there, is there? He must have been spying on us?"

"I fear that is so," said Holmes. He thought for a moment and then added, "We were warned, you know."

"You mean Clemens' remark about the lying?"

"Yes. But now that I think of it, it is in the good Mr. Clemens' reading of the boy's behavior that we may also find a little hope."

"How's that?"

"You may remember Clemens' parting remark, that what worried him was not that the boy was lying, but that he did not seem to be enjoying himself. At the time I took that to be a bit of whimsy on Clemens' part, but now I wonder. I share your conviction about Wiggins; he is at heart an honorable fellow, besides being a thoroughgoing professional. We should take Clemens at his word. He is the expert on such matters after all. I suggest that we withhold judgment on the boy until we learn just what his circumstance is. Perhaps he is under some duress. His world is not simple just because he inhabits it as a child."

"But we must learn what he is up to."

"And we shall, as soon as possible. However, Mycroft and his associates have guaranteed me a very full day tomorrow. They seem to think I can assist them in various projects they have underway. I must start out early, so I suggest we retire at once."

"I would rather not sit here and await developments," I said. My extreme fatigue may have made me a bit pouty at the thought of Holmes going off and leaving me with no apparent role now that it seemed all the irons were in the fire. But if my words came out a little fussier than I intended it was because my injured shoulder had renewed its aches during our hours of sitting earlier this night. Holding my arm up while using the binoculars had put me past my threshold of patient forbearance of pain.

"By no means must you do that, Watson!" Holmes objected with considerable feeling. "You are essential to this whole business now, and most immediately to the prosecution of our investigations of the Clemens mystery. First, you must get a good night's sleep, no matter how long that takes. I need you in fighting trim here in the home stretch. Take something for your shoulder, which was obviously plaguing you most of the evening, and get to bed. At whatever time tomorrow morning that you feel rested enough to begin your day, please go to Tedworth Square. I will let Clemens know to expect you."

"To the Clemenses? Now? But what of the conspiracies and plots we've just been told about?"

"Watson, everything that has happened today has only strengthened my conviction that the Clemens' household is somehow crucial to the resolution of this mess of a case we find ourselves in. I have little idea of their role, but we must be prepared. Keep close to them, and communicate frequently with the constables who are guarding them. I am assured that the constables will not be pulled away by the demands of the Jubilee. Expect Marston's support there some of the time, though I gather that his attention will be divided, which is no surprise. Should I learn of developments tomorrow I will arrange to get word to you at Tedworth Square. We can reconvene here tomorrow evening, perhaps in time for a late dinner. Please explain our plans to Mrs. Hudson, and make sure to thank her profusely on behalf of both of us for this," he said, indicating the meal she had left us.

"Fine," I said. It was about all I could muster now that everything that could be said and done had been said and done, and especially now that sleep was both my most urgent need and my assignment. Holmes was still puttering about his desk as I slouched up the stairs to my room.

What with the draft I administered myself and my utter exhaustion, I expected to fall instantly to sleep, but for the second time in a week the day's singular events kept me awake. First, my mind, which must have been working on this worrisome little detail subconsciously all the while I attended to other things, presented me with questions about that moment during our conversation with Mrs. Wakefield when Holmes asked her about the gray van. Did I remember right? Hadn't she revealed that she knew that Alexander had arrived at the cabyard in the gray van even though neither Holmes nor I had mentioned that particular specific? I was pretty sure that Holmes had asked only about the van, and had not connected it to Alexander. I resolved to ask Holmes about the point; how could she have known about the connection between Alexander and the van? This question led me to wonder: Was the younger Wiggins working for her? Had he been recruited by the older Wiggins?

Then, in a completely unanticipated moment of lucidity, I finally wondered why Wiggins would choose such an awkward and even unhelpful location as a neighbouring rooftop from which to conduct his surveillance of our house. Couldn't he have done the same job, and more effectively, from somewhere down Baker Street in either direction of our front door?

And, last, under the inspired spell of Sam Clemens, whose slow tutelage of us in the ways of boys had apparently started to take hold in my mind, I at least had the answer to that question. Crouching in a nearby doorway to watch 221B from street level would be nowhere near as adventurous as sneaking past the residents of the neighbouring street to find a suitably precarious spot on the rooftop amidst the pigeons, the ash, and the chimney pots, from which to accomplish the same thing under considerably more daring circumstances. Smiling at that realisation, and at how fulfilling such an approach sounded even to an aging, aching boy like me, I thought momentarily of Tom and Huck's unnecessary and elaborately contrived "rescue" plan for the all-enduring slave Jim, and fell asleep.

Chapter Seventeen
Talking Shop

I involuntarily obeyed Holmes' order that I sleep as long as I needed to. It was nearly noon when I awoke. My shoulder was stiff but the pain had greatly subsided, and I was ravenously hungry.

Of course Holmes was long away. When she heard me thumping around, Mrs. Hudson brought me a late and generously grand breakfast and coffee, informing me that "Mr. Holmes left very early. I had only just risen myself and was unaware that anyone else in the house was stirring when I heard the front door close."

I had no more than set to my late breakfast when Mrs. Hudson returned with an envelope. "Doctor, this just arrived by royal messenger."

"How do you know he was royal?"

"If ever that grand a coach has stopped at this house before, I did not notice it," she said. "Besides, I know my own Queen's crest, I'm sure," she said, carefully handing me the envelope. As I took it, she added, "Oh, and the coach is still there and the messenger says you are to use it—'at your earliest convenience,' was how he put it."

I went to the window for a look and was both pleased and a little mortified to see a huge town coach, looking for all the world like some grand and misplaced frigate moored along the kerb of Baker Street. I returned my attention to the message in my hand. The square envelope, of the finest, was unmarked, not our address nor even my name. I tore it open and extracted a twice-folded piece of equally fine but dissimilar paper with writing on both sides but in different hands. Recognizing Holmes' script, I read his side first:

Watson:

A great entangled hurry here. I will try to see you later today but now I cannot guarantee when. There is more to tell than we heard last night. And our own news is bad—see reverse. You must act swiftly. I was right in my surmise. We dare not abandon the Clemens family. They are not out of this. <u>Arm yourself</u> and get to Tedworth Square as quickly as you can. Support the constables. I will communicate further as events develop.

SH

I turned the sheet over and read a second letter, dated earlier this morning.

My Dear Mr. Holmes:

My people report that our sometime associate Harold Barber has been found in the river a few hundred yards below Tower Bridge, dead about two days, shot precisely. I have not engaged him for several months but I know that you also occasionally do. What with the general unease among the authorities that you describe in your early note (for which I thank you) I thought it best to inform you.

Yours,
Constance Wakefield

P.S. Had Barber any family who should be notified?

It took only a moment to gather some toast, my revolver and some spare rounds, coat, and hat and hurry down the stairs and out to the street. The "messenger" held the door as I entered the coach. I said, "Apparently you know our destination as well as I do."

"Yes sir," he responded, and turned to climb up beside the driver. As I settled in the plush of the coach's immaculate interior, I wondered when last I had sat down to a meal and finished it uninterrupted. I wished I'd brought more toast.

Had I brought it, I would have had plenty of time to enjoy it on the way to Tedworth Square. Though it was easy enough for us to bypass the Jubilee procession route—which was by all accounts a clogged frenzy of workmen, official functionaries exercising or rehearsing or whatever it is that official functionaries do at such a time, and other last-minute preparations—it was impossible to avoid the general disorder and disruption of the impending celebration. Indeed, judging from the crowds spilling from many public houses, it appeared that an unofficial celebration was already well underway on many of the city's streets. Crowds, particularly at busy intersections, seemed to have been distracted into a nearly bovine inertia by the occasion.

As well, my coach attracted a great deal of attention. I could not have travelled the streets of London in any greater comfort, but I could have travelled a great deal faster in the first anonymous cab I might have flagged down. Pedestrians were so keyed up for a sight of any royal personage or official that once the carriage came into view they ceased normal movement and were glacially slow to stand aside. On more than one occasion, when groups of these idlers finally caught a clear sight of me through the coach's windows, their disappointment was palpable, and their resentment—that I did not fulfill their hopes for a more privileged glimpse—was plain on their faces.

At Tedworth Square, Katy Leary greeted me as I climbed the front steps. She conducted me past the constable stationed just inside the front door to the comfortable room where Holmes and I had first interviewed the family, but as soon as I was seated she immediately abandoned me, explaining that the Clemens' women were all upstairs, preparing for the Jubilee. I sat there a few moments, assuming that Sam himself would be in presently, but it was Mrs. Clemens who arrived first. In one of the very few conversational exchanges we had during the entire case, she very cordially apologized for the lack of hospitality. "Jean especially wanted to come down and visit with you, but I told her you would have business to attend to, and so does she, what with the celebration to prepare for." She came as close to smiling as I was to see during our brief acquaintance. "You would think that we had not been preparing and sewing and planning for this very day for weeks now; but I suppose a little panic now and then is good for the circulation."

I was about to leave the room and make the rounds of the constables when Clemens, walking by in the hallway, glanced in and noticed me. "Why, Doctor, how good to see you. Holmes sent word that you would be over. I'm sorry no one thought to tell me you were here. We are in royal disarray here, you understand."

"Yes, Mrs. Clemens has already explained. I am sorry to intrude and add another complication, but Holmes thought it best that I stay close today."

He came into the room and sat down opposite me. "And is there progress to report?"

I was utterly unprepared to answer this perfectly reasonable question. I was so preoccupied with the great crisis I'd suddenly become immersed in yesterday that I'd given no thought to sorting out the Clemens case. Last evening I'd been bombarded with secrets by the dozen. They had all run together in my mind and gotten mixed up with the baffling happenings and occasional revelations of the Clemens case. What could I tell him and what should I not?

A passing remark of Holmes' came to mind and rescued me for the moment. "Let me start by setting your mind at ease on one point at least. Holmes thought you would be especially glad to hear of it, though it is a small matter compared to all that is going on."

"Do tell," he said, all interest and good cheer. I do not mind admitting that even after our hectic and eventful past few days, looking into the attentive face of Mr. Samuel Clemens—of actually speaking with Mark Twain—right then brought back to my mind and heart the adulatory excitement I'd felt at our first encounter. It was only with a good deal of restraint that I was able to contain my excitement that here, for a little while at least, I was free to sit and converse with this giant of our age—even to have his undivided and enthusiastic attention. Heaven knows what demented expressions may have crossed my face in the pause of a few seconds as these thoughts came home to me, or what Clemens may have made of them.

"When first you told us your story of the man you called the walleye," I started, but then could not help interrupting myself by adding, "whose name, by the way, we now know," Clemens' face lit up at this, until I added, "well, sort of . . . ," at which point he tilted his head, then shrugged slightly as if to say to himself, "if I listen to this idiot long enough everything he knows will finally come out."

I started again. "I will come to that presently. First I want to reassure you on a point that, as I say, may seem minor right now. But I think you'll be pleased with the news anyway." This unhelpful repetition of my previous statement had no visible effect on Clemens. I said, "Your first experience with the walleyed man; you found it humiliating that he was so unaffected by your lecture, and seemed immune to your humour."

"So he did. And, yes, it seems a trivial matter even now, as much as it troubled me at the time. You have something to explain it?"

"I do. The man did not respond to you because he did not hear you. Not a word. He was stone deaf."

"You interest me greatly, doctor. I can understand how that would make him invulnerable to my remarks, but I can't understand why, under those circumstances, he sat there giving me what appeared to me his intense and undivided attention for an hour and a half."

"To understand that, you will need to know more about him. We don't yet know as much as we should like, but maybe it is enough for this purpose." I went on to explain to Clemens what little we had learned about the man we called Alexander, especially his mental limitations and the peculiar habits that Holmes had identified as such an important part of his personality. "Whatever his reason for being there at the theatre that evening, it is certain that he was obeying some instruction or other that totally guided his behavior. We know that there was a stern kind of discipline to his habits under some circumstances, and it seems safe to assume that his attendance at your lecture must have been such an occasion." To that I added, "By the way, you might also like to know that your own Miss Leary was as quick as Holmes to see the signs of this strange fellow's peculiarities. She brought them to our attention very early in the investigation."

"Did she?" Clemens said with a smile. "Well, that doesn't surprise me. Katy seldom misses anything that might have some bearing on the family."

From this beginning I made my careful way through the labyrinth of other information I had accumulated since last we saw Clemens. With a mental image of Mycroft Holmes glaring over my shoulder, I gave Clemens only the lightest summary of the apparent threats to the Jubilee and the Queen, saying only enough to convey to him why Holmes' attention was divided today. It seemed the better part of discretion not to dwell upon all the plots, real or imagined, but just to say that Holmes had been recruited to assist with certain important police matters relating to the Jubilee Procession the next day. I alluded only vaguely to Holmes' suspicion that the Clemens case might have some connection to these matters.

Clemens took all this in with more than polite interest, but sat forward most attentively when I recounted our midnight adventure with Wiggins. I told him that Holmes remembered his remark about Wiggins not enjoying lying to us, to which Clemens responded, "Good. Nice to learn that my guesswork has proven out. But I'm alarmed by this news. My impression of the youngster was based only on moments of observation, of course, but I never would have taken him for a rat."

Assuming I properly interpreted this American slang, I said, "Nor would we. He has no doubt had numerous occasions in the past when he could have betrayed us, but all indications are that he never before has. Holmes and I agree that some extraordinary circumstance must apply here. Our best guess is that Wiggins is under some kind of pressure or threat. Holmes is confident that we will find out, though I don't know when he will find time to pursue the matter considering how busy the Jubilee people seem to be keeping him."

Sam Clemens had a way of absorbing all the attention in a room. He entirely occupied mine. The deaths of Alexander and poor Barber (which I did not mention to Clemens), the feverish secret activities of so many heroes of the Empire right then underway, even the weight of the revolver in my pocket, receded from my mind.

I think that Clemens welcomed the distraction too. After a little more discussion of Alexander, in which I gave Clemens the highlights of Mrs. Wakefield's account of her acquaintance with him, our conversation drifted here and there in what was, for me at least, the most delightful way. How I wish I had a transcript of all Sam Clemens said to me on that afternoon. As Holmes and his associates were engaged in the most desperate matters to preserve the order of the Empire, and as the nation's leadership underwent a great breath-holding until the Jubilee celebration was successfully concluded, there we sat happily chatting of this and that. It all raced by too fast and in too great a volume for me to retain in memory all of Clemens' fascinating and varied observations, but a few things still ring in my memory as if they happened yesterday.

"Your mention of Wiggins reminds me of something I've been meaning to ask you," he said at one point. "Your portrait of Reverend Beecher; I can't help wondering what brought that to your wall."

"I remember you noticing it. You knew him and his family."

"They were neighbours in Hartford for years. I benefited from my acquaintance with Reverend Beecher especially. He advised me on the negotiations for the publication of one of my first books. His advice was priceless."

"I came to admire him," I said, "because of his anti-slavery work during your Civil War."

"It was not mine, personally, you know. I had very little effect on the outcome. Except for a brief dabbling in it there at the beginning I managed to avoid the whole thing."

I smiled and said, "Just a manner of speaking, of course. I didn't mean to blame you for it. But it's true about Beecher. I probably wouldn't have formed such an admiration for him if it weren't for the mistreatment he received when he came over here to solicit support for the anti-slavery cause during the war."

"Yes, that mistreatment was quite the scandal in American cities," he said. "In the North, anyway."

"You know, I was just a child at the time, but thanks to my father's interest in such things, I actually heard Beecher's London speech. I recall nothing of the specifics, of course, but the power of his feelings stuck with me."

"Your memory serves you well," said Clemens, nodding. "He was a spectacular orator, one blast of stunning language after another. He was also a smart man, so his sermons were meaty. But even if he'd been a complete dullard without a thought in his head he could have gotten by just on the rhetorical athletics of his delivery."

"I'm sure it was the memory of that speech that predisposed me to sympathy and admiration for the man later, when I was old enough to understand what his visit had been for. Slavery has always seemed to me the vilest perversion of human society. Anyway, not long after I first moved in at Baker Street I happened to notice the engraving of him in a book. It brought to mind his heroism, and we had not yet decorated the walls here, so I took it out and set it in a frame I had handy."

"I hope you don't mind me asking," Clemens said, "but I wonder what you thought of the scandal. You must have heard about it."

"You mean that adultery trial," I said, recalling the enormous controversy that raged on and off in the mid-1870s when one of Beecher's parishioners and closest friends accused the famous preacher of having inappropriate relations with his wife. "I was still at medical school then, and there was endless hooting about it in the papers here. Downfall of the mighty, dark underside of sainthood, and so on. There was a good deal of irreverent student humour, too. I don't remember paying much attention to it all at the time. I suppose it happened before I'd read enough to put his visit during the Civil War in perspective. But later, giving it all more thought, it seemed to me that whatever happened between Beecher and that woman was the least important part of what, even from here on the other side of the Atlantic, I could see was mostly a tussle over greater political and social campaigns—women's suffrage, personal privacy, the press's obsession with celebrity and giant-killing, and all that."

"Perhaps the Atlantic Ocean helped give you the necessary distance on the whole affair," he said. "The clarity of your view was not so evident in New York."

"No, I gathered that." Then I recalled that I was neglecting my rounds. I admitted feeling guilty that I wasn't attending to my little duties around the house.

Clemens stirred himself and stood. "I have some things I must tend to as well. I am finishing my book again today and I should get back to it. Please make yourself at home, and don't hesitate to bother whoever you can find if you need anything."

"I may trouble the kitchen for something. I was swept off from Baker Street in some haste."

"By all means, do so. The constables have not been shy about that; no reason you should be." With that he excused himself. I made the rounds of the constables, pausing in the kitchen long enough to put in a request for a sandwich that was forthcoming in moments. In keeping with the past few days' pattern of interrupted meals, a note from Holmes arrived as I was enjoying my sandwich, but it was only an exhortation to continue my vigilance and a tentative suggestion that he might see me late in the evening, or, more likely, early tomorrow, presumably back in Baker Street.

The short remainder of the afternoon and early evening passed in such peaceful routine that I began to wonder if Holmes hadn't assigned me this duty just to keep me

157

occupied and avoid hurting my feelings. At about 5 a new shift of constables replaced the three that had spent the day at the house, and I took my time discussing things with them, though in fact there was precious little to be said. We were all waiting and watching for something unknown, or for nothing.

As the light through the windows weakened, Clemens joined me in the sitting room, where I'd retreated for want of any other place to go. My shoulder, though not as painful as the night before, was slowly wearing me down. At the sight of my face, he recalled my injury and encouraged me to take a rest on the couch. I thanked him, but declined. "Well," he said, "I've finished finishing my book for today, and I don't imagine I'll have time to finish it again tomorrow, what with the Jubilee. I'd be content just to sit here for a while, if you don't mind the company." I was about to assure him that I didn't mind at all when he continued, saying, "Oh, and speaking of company, I should explain that the family is in the habit of dining alone these days. I have managed to go out now and then these past few months, quietly, just to keep up with some old friends, but I most often go alone. And except on those rare occasions when Livy or the girls join me, I find myself almost immediately eager to get home. I suppose that my socializing has increased since I started finishing the book, and because of that it is only natural that more and more people have become aware that I am here. You may have seen that silly report about my death in the spring."

"I did, and I enjoyed your response, that 'the report of my death is greatly exaggerated.'"

"That isn't what I said, you know, but never mind; how did we get onto this? Oh, yes, what I was starting to tell you is that of course you must stay for dinner, and that you must forgive the family for not joining us."

"I understand."

"Besides, I am confident that you and I can make a go of dinner by ourselves. I've asked for something to be served in my study in a few minutes," he added, and we moved down the hall to that room.

We ate hastily and with little conversation, but afterwards we returned to the sitting room and he poured us each a brandy and lit a Manila (I gratefully accepted his offer of one, having forgotten my pipe in my hasty departure that morning). I was as content as I'd been in days. In an hour or so I could make one more round of the house and immediate neighbourhood, to fulfill my responsibilities, and then return to Baker Street. Holmes' very brief instructions, while insisting I be vigilant in my attendance at Tedworth Square, also seemed to intend that I would return to our rooms for the night. In the meantime, I felt free to indulge myself. After all, I had just eaten a complete meal without interruption, and imagined (most foolishly, as it turned out) that this late in the day no further interruption could be forthcoming.

After a moment of companionable silence with our brandies, he revived from the lethargy of our sizeable meal. He sat up with enthusiasm and asked, "So, doctor, here we are, you and I, smack in the middle of one of Sherlock Holmes' famous adventures. I assume that some day you may want to write it up. Tell me; what is your method?"

"How do you mean?" I asked.

"I'm talking shop, Doctor," he said, "you know—one tradesman to another. Carpenters comparing rasps. How will you tell our story? I mean, how do you work? During our times together the past few days, I have yet to see you make a note," he said, "not even to transcribe any of my famously pithy observations. Far be it from me to try to pry loose your trade secrets, much less accuse you of playing fast and loose with the details of your experiences by just making up everything you need later. I know how *I* do it, and how some of my other friends do it, but how do *you* finally get it all down for the printer?"

Remembering his apparently lukewarm attitude toward my stories in earlier conversations, I was flattered by the question. "I am told I have a good memory for certain kinds of details. Not the sorts of things that Holmes notices; nothing as esoteric or penetrating as that. But I do seem to be able to

159

recall a lot of *routine* things very accurately. And you're right; during a case I hardly ever make notes, certainly not extended paragraphs of what might be called narrative. When possible I scribble a thought, or set aside a clipping or a letter or whatever other little memory-jogger comes my way. I took the sheet of paper containing the Holmes/Wakefield notes from my pocket and waved them once. "This note from Holmes is what brought me here today, and it will no doubt make its way into my files and probably into the story if I do write it up. I even made sure to save that little slip of paper, the one you wrote your address on during your first visit to Baker Street, though I suppose that was more along the line of a memento than a helpful piece of the story. By the end of a case, a number of these little things have usually piled up in my pockets and on my desk. I work from those for the outline and the rough chronology of events. But when it comes to the spoken words, pithy or not, memory must serve for the conversations I quote, and I feel pretty sure of them. Holmes, for all his other skepticisms about my stories, at least has never challenged my recollection of conversations."

"That must be gratifying for you," he said. "I wouldn't want to have an observer of his powers double-checking my memories when I write out experiences he and I shared."

"Quite. When I finally sit down to write up a case, any verbal exchanges I may have had with Holmes, and any of his interviews and conversations with other people that I witnessed, just seem to be waiting there in my head." I had never given this process much thought before, and as I explained it to Clemens something occurred to me, so I said it aloud. "It is as if they perform themselves again in my head."

"This is an enviable gift," he said.

"And I have been grateful for it, though I sometimes wonder if all that talk just stays in my head because there is so little competition for the space." He smiled at this as I continued. "Of course what I finally write is nothing much compared to *real* literature, but the public response has been gratifying beyond all my hopes."

"Ah," he said, "I appreciate the implied compliment in your humility but I fear now that during our first meetings I may have given you the impression that I believed that your work was somehow beneath my dignity."

"But it is!" I objected. I was about to elaborate when there was a sudden clatter of hooves and wheels in front of the house. Seconds later there were deep and agitated male voices, and one female voice I immediately recognised as Katy Leary's, discussing something somewhere near the front door. Then came a pause, and I distinctly heard the constable who was posted there say, "Yes sir!"

A second later, Marston appeared at the door to our sitting room, with Katy peering around his shoulder. "Dr. Watson! Mr. Clemens," he almost shouted. We rose instantly. He was breathless, his entire demeanor a wild contrast to that of the man whose coolness under deadly fire I had personally witnessed only a few nights ago. Before we could speak, he continued, "Mr. Holmes, both of them in fact—and higher authorities galore, I must say—have sent me to bring you. There is no time to be lost. We must leave instantly. I can explain on the way."

Chapter Eighteen
Sam Clemens Follows Orders

Leaving instantly occupied several minutes. Clemens was adamant that he not go anywhere without explaining this strange turn of events to his wife. Marston said, "Yes, yes, of course; I didn't mean . . . tell her you'll be back soon. A few hours at most. Nothing to alarm her, but very urgent, very urgent!"

As Clemens hurried up the stairs, and before I could question Marston, he looked directly into my face and burst out "Constable Stuart!" as if that would make all the sense in the world. Turning from me, he rushed toward the back of the house, Katy Leary marching along unbidden behind him, presumably to confer with said officer, who had been posted toward the rear of the house. A moment later Marston returned. Katy was right behind him but this time she whisked past without a glance our way and hurried to the stairs, where she met Clemens donning a dark overcoat as he came down. She gave him a quick look, then ran up the stairs as Marston greeted Clemens with, "No need to worry, sir; Inspectors Gregson and Lestrade are right behind me with additional men who will stay here."

Clemens gave me a pained look that plainly asked why the imminent and apparently essential arrival of additional police should in any way reassure him that there was nothing to worry about. Marston caught the look and added, "Just an additional precaution, you understand. Mr. Holmes insisted, said that taking you away from your family was inconsiderate and some additional constables might make you feel easier about it." He paused for a deep breath and shrugged apologetically, then added, "Looks like Mr. Holmes missed that call, eh?"

Marston's humour helped. Clemens—who though he had heard a good bit about Marston from Holmes and me, had for all I knew never had a conversation with the man before—seemed to relax just a bit and we hurried out the door and down the steps. Before us stood a plain but smart black two-horse coach, unmarked but emanating "official business" from every line. Two smartly uniformed soldiers sat stiffly above the coach, one holding the reins, the other glancing around as if on watch. I couldn't quite place the uniform, but every imaginable military uniform of the Empire was represented somewhere in the city right then, and I assumed that any of their occupants might be recruited for special duties as needed. Clemens, too, seemed curious about the officers, stopping in mid-stride to give them a closer look before proceeding to the coach.

Marston had just opened the coach door for us when a police van rounded the corner down the street in some haste and soon came to a noisy stop behind ours. We watched Lestrade, Gregson, and four more constables emerge from the front and rear of the van. As it pulled away they hurried toward the house, nodding importantly to us (and particularly to Marston) as they passed. They directed the constables to positions in the park opposite the house and around the corner to Tite Street. By this time, a number of people, men and boys, had drifted out of the park and were goggling casually from the sidewalk. Two or three boys darted in and out of the shadows cast by the street light as they played catch-the-ball over the heads of the gawkers.

Clemens and I had barely entered the coach when I heard a familiar female voice shout, "Mr. Clemens! Sir! Hold on!" Marston, still holding the door, saw Katy hurrying down the steps and stood unmoving until she reached us. "From Mrs. Clemens," she said, and handed an envelope past Marston's face through the window to Clemens. I could make out the words "Youth (personal)" written on it in a firm but fine hand. As if her words would make perfect sense to Clemens, presumably as part of some earlier conversation, Katy said, "She remembered just now and thought you would want to know." She gave Marston and me each a quick sharp look, then hurried back to the door, where she turned to watch us go.

Marston entered the coach behind us and took the seat next to me, opposite Clemens. He rapped on the roof and we were off. "A fine woman, that," Marston said wistfully. Then, resuming his businesslike demeanor, he added, "Doctor, would you please close and fasten those shades," indicating the windows on my side of the coach. I did so as he did the same for the ones on his side, adding, "Perhaps a needless precaution, but Mr. Holmes was quite specific about these things." The interior of the coach darkened even further, though small oval windows set high, front and back, above the seats did admit a little light. Settling back in his seat, he looked at me and added, "I trust you are armed?"

"Yes, the same as at Black's the other night."

"Good choice," he said, then turned to Clemens, who had already opened the envelope and unfolded a single sheet of paper, and said, "And you, Mr. Clemens, should I assume you are unarmed?" Clemens looked up from the note, frowned at no one in particular, glanced down again, then back up as he said, "Yes, assume that. Never had much use for them." He looked at the note again, then added "Guns, I mean."

Marston, seeing Clemens' distraction, nodded at the note and said, "Not bad news, I hope?"

"News?" Clemens asked. "Oh, this," he said, waving the note a bit. "No, not at all. Things are fine. Well, more or less. As I age, I just find it hard to move with my former agility between the world's weighty affairs and equally weighty domestic crises. Are you married—Mr. Marston, isn't it?"

"Yes sir, I am. Marston, I mean; I'm Marston. But no, I'm not married, though it is a dream of mine," Marston said. I thought he might say something about Katy Leary then, but he let it go at that.

"And so it should be," Clemens said. "I am the luckiest of men in that regard, and yet I also provide a vivid example of how complicated inhabiting such a wondrous dream can become on a day-to-day basis." Here he gave the note another little wave, folded it back into the envelope and slipped it into an inside pocket. "That's not a complaint, mind you. I sometimes think that the distraction provided by the choice of new draperies, or precisely the right hat for a Jubilee"—he patted the pocket into which he had just placed the note—"or some other equally earth-shattering matter has been all that stood between me and madness." Marston smiled, obviously pleased with this privileged glimpse into the life of the real Mark Twain.

All this time we had been rumbling through the streets at a good but not breakneck clip. I wanted to peek out, but there was little point. There were many routes to Whitehall, and I could only assume that our driver knew the most efficient course better than I. Marston checked our course every few minutes, slipping his finger tips under the edge of the shade and pulling it back an inch or so to look out, but I could only assume that he knew what he was looking for. Clemens sat quietly. I could see his face, but not well enough to read his expression.

It must have been approaching 10 p.m., and I thought we must be getting close to Whitehall, when it finally occurred to me to wonder if that were even our destination; perhaps Holmes was waiting for us somewhere else. Remembering that Marston had promised to "explain on the way," I was just about to ask him to do so when Clemens stirred and said, "Doctor, I confess to a novelist's curiosity. You say you are armed and yet during all our time together today I never noticed any evidence of a weapon anywhere on your person. I don't have to know much about guns, even small ones, to know that they are heavy. How do you conceal it so well?"

"It's this tweed that does it," I said. "Stiff weave, thick fabric; it holds its shape. Perfect for a pocket gun." I reached into the right inside pocket of my coat and brought out the compact revolver I favored for these occasions.

"Not a Colt, is it?" Clemens asked, almost airily. I could just barely see him squinting at it. "That's what I used to see the most of in Nevada and California, though there weren't nearly as many of them as legend now makes out."

"No, it's a Webley. A Bull Dog, they call it," I said, turning it over in my hand. Its dull metal managed only a faint glint in the coach's low light. It's what you have, isn't it?" I asked Marston.

"Not exactly, but along the same lines," he said, eyeing the Webley with great apparent interest. "In my work I am willing to sacrifice a fashionable profile for the additional bulk of a longer barrel and one more chamber." He patted his chest just below his left shoulder to indicate a holstered revolver there.

"Venomous looking thing," Clemens said, still looking at the Webley. He reached over for it and I gave it to him handle first.

As Clemens examined it and idly spun the full cylinder, Marston said, "You would have no reason to know this, Mr. Clemens, but a gun very like that one, in fact it was a Webley now I think of it, was used by that lunatic who killed your president in, let's see, 1881. Terrible thing."

"No, in fact I do remember that," Clemens said. "I read in the papers that he claimed to have bought the pearl-handled model because he thought it would make a better impression than the standard wooden-handled one when they put it in a museum after the assassination."

"I never heard that," Marston said with professional appreciation. "Remarkable."

I happened to be watching Clemens as Marston spoke, and was startled to see, even in the poor light, that the writer's entire bearing suddenly underwent the most extraordinary change. His casual posture became firm and to my utter astonishment he lifted the revolver, thumbed the hammer back, aimed the deadly weapon directly at Marston's face, and said, "Sit back, sir, and please don't move. You will know I am serious."

Marston slid back in his seat and said in a calm and businesslike voice, "I do."

"For Heaven's sake, Clemens!" I cried. "What are you doing?"

"Following orders, Watson," he said, not taking his eyes from Marston, "and you *must* trust me. I have delayed too long. We have to get out of this coach as quickly as possible. Call the driver to stop."

I reached up and gave the roof a few hard raps, yelling "Driver stop!" in as authoritative a voice as I could manage. The coach immediately gave a lurch, which threw us all forward enough that Clemens' aim swung away from Marston, who quick as a striking snake grabbed the older man's wrist with one hand while reaching into his own coat with the other.

But he grabbed too hard. With the unexpected jolt on Clemens' wrist a shot roared up and forward. Right then I had no time to think the consequences through but could only imagine that the heavy bullet must have ripped through the coach's flimsy ceiling and struck the driver, for I heard a yell and the coach swerved and teetered dangerously. As this happened I took the only action I could think of: I grabbed Marston's other hand before he could bring his own revolver free of his coat and into play. He was by far the younger and stronger man, but Clemens now had both hands on my revolver and desperation gave him the strength to keep his grip, though Marston's twisting hold on his wrist must have been very painful. I was shocked at Marston's strength, as I could barely keep my grip on his other arm with both my hands, and I think that Clemens and I would have fared the worse had not the coach, having veered hard to one side, put a front wheel around something, probably a stone hitching post, which stopped us hard. The horses, panicked by the shot and misdirected by the slumping driver, rushed on and thus immediately pulled the coach's frame apart with a screech of rending wood and twisted metal. Over we went, the three of us tumbling around in our wordless struggle. We all hit hard when the coach crashed down on its side. My injured shoulder bore most of my weight and I gasped even as I felt Marston's arm go limp. Somewhere near my feet, Clemens cried, "Watson, are you still with me?"

"Yes! And you?" I answered incoherently.

167

My guess was that Marston's head had hit the pavement with only the thin layer of the window shade for cushion as we all slammed against the street on that side of the falling coach. As Clemens struggled free of Marston's inert bulk and climbed toward the door on the upper side of the wrecked coach, he said, "Yes, I'm still with me too. Let's get out. You'd better bring his gun if you can find it. I've lost yours somewhere." But Marston's pistol must have rattled loose in the fall too. A quick groping around was fruitless so I followed Clemens up and out.

With each passing year I have looked back on this whole episode with growing wonder. As we undertook this life-and-death struggle, I was in my early forties, but Sam Clemens was twenty years my senior and not in the best of health. As I approach that age and condition, I realise that the demands he had just successfully placed on himself were beyond heroic. It was probably that overwhelming strength of conviction in his actions that convinced me to follow his lead without hesitation.

It took us some moments to clamber out the upper door and then slide down the underside of the upended coach onto the deserted street. I recognised nothing of our surroundings. As far as we could see in either direction, the street was lined with tall, shabby, and uniformly unlit buildings, probably warehouses somewhere near the docks, by the look and smell of them. There were only a couple of functioning lights, and those were too far off to be much help, but we could see one of the uniformed men piled in a heap on the street where he had been thrown when the coach swerved or tipped over. I assumed he was shot. The other man was nowhere to be seen. I thought I could see the horses standing a hundred feet down the street near a light post.

While I was taking all this in, Clemens hurried over to the fallen man—injured or dead, we didn't know—and had just bent over for a closer look at him when we were both startled out of our skins by a bright, young, and very confident voice coming from just behind the wreckage of the coach. "You gents'll want to do a scoot right quick," said Wiggins.

As surprised as he must have been, Clemens' first words were not addressed to the boy. Still looking at the dark heap of the uniformed man, he said "It's not him." Then he stood up and joined me in staring at Wiggins. "As desperately as I may need to have a long talk with each of you right now," I said, "I am inclined to agree with the boy." Turning to him, I said, "I assume you have something in mind?"

He turned without a word, waving us to follow, and the three of us set out back the way the coach had just come. In a moment it became clear that neither Clemens nor I were in any condition to keep up with him. My shoulder was burning with pain, and Clemens was almost immediately fagged. Wiggins was already twenty yards ahead of us when I called to him, "Here, Wiggins, we can't follow you if you leave us behind." He slowed at that, and I added, "And what's the great rush?"

At this he stopped and turned toward us. Clemens and I kept on, struggling to catch up as Wiggins said, "Let me ask you. Did you kill that Jack you was ridin' with?"

"No," said Clemens, "he was hit in the arm, but I think he was knocked out when the coach went over."

"But now you pegged him, he'll be wantin' his back."

"Yes, that's why we're leaving," I said.

"The other, though, the blue bottle up top, the one hain't down flat. I jumped off afore the growler went over, see? So I sees him jump clear too, see? He come off runnin' and it wasn't for fear. It was for 'elp." He nodded at the dark buildings around us to indicate the roughness of the neighbourhood. "Wherever we was headin'. . . ," he said and paused meaningfully.

"We were almost there," I answered, finishing the thought.

"So?" He asked, like a nanny who has finally talked a dull child through a puzzle to the obvious answer.

"They'll be back after us soon. Right. Lead on," I said, with a wave of my hand. We headed off again, this time at a brisk but manageable pace, Wiggins a few steps ahead of us. He seemed to have a destination, purposefully turning this way and that, dodging down alleys and then apparently backtracking onto other ways. Some of these were neither alleys nor streets, just narrow rubbish-cluttered passages between black walls. Except for the lack of a ceiling and the stone street rather than a wooden floor it was much like being back in the dingy labyrinth at Black's on the trail of the doomed Alexander. We saw a few people, but, also as at Black's, they were interested only in being of no interest to others, and hurried off on their own errands.

"That was you in the park at Tedworth? One of the ball players?" I asked Wiggins.

"Right. Hitched a lift on t'back as you's pulled away," he said. "Can't pull that off in the day, but nobody's to see this time of night."

"You seem to be paying an awful lot of attention to us these days," I said, breathing heavily, "but I must assume for the moment that you mean us no harm. The thing is, Wiggins, we need to get help of our own. It isn't enough for us to hole up somewhere. We have to get word to . . . " I took a breath as I tried to figure out who all we needed to alert, and finished with "a lot of people, including Holmes. Right away. Get us to a busy street with lots of cabs and constables."

"Considering our last experience," Clemens added, "I'm not sure we want to rush into the arms of just any policeman right now."

Wiggins spoke over his shoulder to the two of us, plainly exasperated. "I gets you your help, just a bit here!" But before I could ask what he intended, we were all brought up short. About fifty feet ahead of us, turning into the narrow street and walking toward us, came two men whose silhouettes clearly identified them as bobbies, one fairly bulky and the other lean. When one blurted to the other, "There they are!" Clemens' doubts were confirmed. Random constables on duty here would have had no awareness of us; these had to be more of Marston's men.

For just an instant we froze. I longed for my Webley. As we did not move, the men continued to approach us at a brisk walk, the big one calling, "Oi, stay where you are!"

I turned to Wiggins and said, "Get him away. That fat one can't run and I'll delay the other."

Before Clemens, who I fear was already quite fatigued, could cast a vote in the matter, Wiggins said, "C'mon guv," grabbed his sleeve and all but dragged him back a few yards, then into a side passageway I hadn't even noticed when we passed it.

At that, the big constable yelled, "Get'im!" and the thin one came galloping our way. Resigning my shoulder to yet another wicked jolt, I stood still, feigning surrender until he was almost beside me and concentrating entirely on pursuit of Wiggins and Clemens. As he passed, I threw myself at him, wrapping my arms around his waist and easily bringing him down on the rough stones. He struggled against me, trying to loosen my arms, but I outweighed him by a third. Making no effort to strike or otherwise fight him, I simply kept my hold on him and let my greater weight encumber his movements and prevent him from rising to continue his pursuit. This worked admirably until the other constable came huffing up. He was behind me and I couldn't turn to see him without losing my hold on his companion, but I could hear him shuffling around. There was an impatient grumbling, a rustle of cloth and leather, the snap of some sort of fastener coming loose, then a terrific "whack" on the back of my skull excused me from further awareness of the situation.

Chapter Nineteen
A Triple Life

I awoke slowly, brought around partly by an unfamiliar restriction of my movements and partly by a dull throbbing in the back of my head. I felt myself seated with my arms held unaccountably behind me, and was roused to full consciousness by the pain in my wrists. Memory of Wiggins and Clemens fleeing and my little scuffle with the bobbies came to mind all at once in a sense of sudden panic.

Opening my eyes to a dim light, I found myself alone in a small room, unfurnished except for a heavy wooden chair in one corner. I sat in the middle of the room in another apparently similar chair, my arms tightly bound around its back. My legs were likewise bound, each to one of the chair's front legs. What little light there was came from behind me, and by twisting painfully I could just see a long and heavily streaked window of many panes high on the wall there.

It was obviously still night, though I had no idea if a few minutes or even a few hours had passed. There was little else in sight to recommend itself to my attention. The walls and ceiling were some dull, long-faded, and generally stained colour, and the floor was roughly milled wide boards. There was a closed door to my right. The low light allowed no further inspection, but it seemed most likely that I was in one of those anonymous buildings somewhere near where our coach had toppled over. I hoped that the fact that I was alone indicated that Wiggins and Clemens had not been apprehended.

The pain in my shoulder was now approaching the familiarity of an old friend, though through some odd quirk of posture the manner in which I had been trussed up seemed to relieve the ache a bit. The same couldn't be said for the pain in my head and wrists.

I immediately began to consider the possibility of escape. The first thing to do was somehow loosen my bonds, but a few minutes of furious twisting and pulling revealed that I was tied too professionally for that. Nor was I able to tip the chair over; it was either too heavy or was actually attached to the floor. I saw no point in calling for help, my captors having been so careful with these other arrangements it seemed unlikely they would have put me within earshot of anyone with enough sense of civic responsibility to react favorably to such cries. I began to suspect as well that I was probably several floors up from street level.

I waited for perhaps another two hours. The building was silent until, faintly at first, I heard movement somewhere, then the gradually louder footsteps of two or three people who were speaking as they approached. I couldn't understand a word, just a rumble of voices mixed with the rumble of footsteps.

Then the door opened, flooding the room with light from a wide corridor in which I caught glimpses of at least four people before the entry was blocked in silhouette by the bulky figure of a man I assumed must be Marston. He entered, but right behind him came an identical form, like a second Marston, who also entered, closing the door quietly behind himself. The first man slid the other chair from the corner to a few feet away and sat down. When his face came into the light I could see it was Marston. The other man stayed standing by the door.

Marston drew a long-barreled revolver from a coat pocket and kept it casually in his hand, the barrel resting on his thigh in front of him but aimed off to the side. "Doctor, I cannot express, nor, I am sure, would you believe, how deeply I regret having to treat you this way. But you must believe me when I tell you that there is no chance of your escape." Turning to the other man, he said, "There is no need to keep him tied. Would you please remove the ropes?" The man promptly came and bent behind the chair. In a few seconds I felt the ropes go slack and brought my arms around and bent forward to rub my ankles, whose ropes had also dropped.

I felt a great need for an epic outburst of indignation but was at a loss for where to start in such an extraordinary situation. Before I could begin, Marston again addressed the other man. "I'm sure we'll be fine here. Perhaps you and Denison should go see if the others need help with the van." I assumed that Denison was guarding the door from the outside, and I wondered if he had been there all along. The man nodded and left, but after he closed the door Marston got up and went to it, re-opened it, looked up and down the hallway, and then closed it again.

"You must have questions," he said, returning to his chair, "and probably a good deal of justifiable outrage."

"I hardly know where to start, man," I finally said. "You are obviously deep into some horrible conspiracy, and I must assume that you are somehow responsible for much if not all of the trouble that we have been wrapped up in these past few days." Then, in what now seems to have been an almost irrelevant note, I added, "Whatever awful plans you are hatching, I must say that in our brief acquaintance I never once took you for a murderer."

"Robert was a necessary sacrifice," he said. "Again, you will with good reason not believe me, but I must say that my sense of loss at his death nearly broke my resolve."

"Who the devil is Robert?" I demanded. "I'm talking about Barber!"

Marston's expression was blank. "Who the devil is Barber?"

We sat facing each other in exasperated bewilderment for several seconds, then he shook his head and said, "Let us begin again. There is much for you to hear, and much I am eager to say. We have time and I want you, of all people, to know what you have become embroiled in. If you will allow me, I shall attempt to explain."

"I could hardly stop you if I wanted to," I said angrily, "but I admit that I could very much use an explanation. In fact, you are not the first on my list of people who owes me one just since leaving Tedworth Square. What in blazes is going on, Marston? What have you done? Why did Clemens . . . " I faltered momentarily, then blurted out, "And where *are* we?" My head had now taken a commanding lead among my aches, and I winced as I touched the swollen bruise on the back of my skull.

"In good time, Doctor, in good time. This is a tale that takes some telling." I said nothing, and he continued.

"I might as well start with Robert. You have known Robert as the walleye. As Holmes' 'tidy burglar.' He is, or was, my brother."

Shocked by this, I said, "But you and I killed him. We shot him. Your *brother?*"

"Please, Doctor, if you interrupt me every time I surprise you, we will be here a week. Let me get on with this.

"Robert was a year my senior. Adelaide, of whom I have spoken before, was two years older than he. We were raised in considerable comfort on an estate north of Durham. Robert was as you knew him, mentally and physically damaged from birth, poor soul, except for his eye. That came on when he was only a year or two old. Of all the injustices in the world, that such a sorrowful and star-crossed little fellow should be inflicted with that additional curse seems all the indictment a cruel providence requires.

"My family was quite wealthy but otherwise a damnable mess. When we three were still nursery inmates, my father vanished at sea during a business venture in the West Indies. My mother, fragile at the best of times, slipped permanently over the deep end at the news of his death and was committed to some awful asylum. My father's younger brother, who was also his business partner, assumed proprietorship not only of the estate but of Adelaide, Robert, and me." Marston was warming to his story, and added in a most conversational tone, "and by the way, Uncle Alasdair was also afflicted with the leucoma. Apparently it runs in families, but I suppose you know that. I feel fortunate it missed me." I could think of nothing to say, and he continued.

"My uncle ran a bizarre household. He was a remarkably free-thinking man, and probably more than a little mad. The staff loved him, some quite literally. He openly fathered children among the servants like other men might breed their hunting dogs, and happily incorporated those offspring into the household. Of course as a child all this meant to me was a perpetual abundance of playmates, but among the large staff of the estate it must have been strange almost beyond comprehension.

"Anyway, among his other unique perspectives, my uncle entertained a democratic conviction that children of privilege must receive a thorough grounding in the life of the common people, as he called them. Even before we were of school age, Robert and I were trained and indoctrinated as servants along with various of our half-brothers and -sisters who were also learning these same skills as the logical course of their eventual lives as domestics."

"Holmes predicted that something like this must have been the case," I said, "that your brother was the product of an unorthodox but well-off household."

"Did he? What an extraordinary person. I have so enjoyed seeing him work," he said, smiling happily as if we were just friends discussing a cricket champion, then returned to his story. "Well, as you know, Robert's capacities were naturally quite limited, so throughout his childhood he mostly followed other household staff around until he learned to mimic their activities. Then he was turned loose around the house with endless busy-work duties of his own. We all shared the role of his overseer, outdoing each other in finding things he could straighten up. It absorbed him totally.

"I underwent an identical but rather more advanced apprenticeship. Though our training, and I might better say conditioning, was never unkind, it was relentless. Even yet I have trouble resisting impulses that were verbally pounded into my brain before I was twelve, especially when I am agitated." He stopped here, as if about to digress from the narrative, then continued. "Robert always exercised those impulses without restraint."

"You refer to his reflexive tidying," I said.

He nodded in agreement. "He lacked the capacity to absorb much education, so he continued, quite happily I like to think, doing his many little chores and assignments. He stayed on the estate, where he was treated no better or worse than the rest of the staff. All things considered, it was perhaps the kindest future anyone could have hoped for him.

"I, in the meantime, had been sent to good if not distinguished schools. It was assumed that I would return to the estate to be groomed to take it over when my uncle died or at least chose to step back from his duties.

"But the very week of my final examinations I received word that disaster had struck. By some means that I never did manage to learn, my uncle suddenly lost everything and found himself in appalling debt. The shock of knowing that he could no longer support the estate, his brother's children, and all his tenants and servants, including his own sizeable brood of beloved bastards, was too much. Without so much as a word of written instruction or fare-thee-well, Uncle Alasdair shot himself and left us all to land however best we might.

"Luckily, the good will that my uncle so indiscriminately displayed to everyone on the estate was not forgotten, and Robert was taken in by a kind tenant family. Adelaide had already married the young man I have told you about and moved here to London. And I found my way into the military, where for some years I had the very career that I described to you when we first met. But you will not be surprised to learn that I left some things out of that account. I have lived what I suppose could be called a triple life.

"The first was the life that everyone saw, that of the cheerful, forthright fellow you met at Tedworth Square—the diligent and ambitious constable of humble means to whom dolts like Gregson and Lestrade condescended at every chance.

"The second was the life that Holmes, at least, had begun to suspect I led—as an agent of Her Majesty's Secret Service, a life into which I was recruited, by the way, even before I left Afghanistan, thanks to Roberts' personal interest in my career. I suppose that you and Holmes first discovered me in that guise at the meeting in Whitehall, when Salisbury came and bestowed upon us his approval." He uttered the name "Salisbury" with obvious distaste. "My apparent career in the police, at least when I have not been abroad on some assignment, has proven a consistently effective masquerade for my real work."

"But it is the third life that brings you and me here on this pivotal night in the history of the empire. It is a life that until this moment only I have known about. You, doctor, are the first to share the secret of that life." At this he drew himself up and proudly stated, "All else about me has been fraud and ruse. For the past fifteen years, my good doctor, I have had only one true profession underneath all the posturing and dissimulation. I am the assassin of Her Royal Highness Victoria, Queen of the United Kingdom and Empress of India."

Chapter Twenty
Only One Man

I sat speechless as Marston continued his tale. "I embarked upon this career—for as such I see it, and a noble career at that—in Afghanistan. There I witnessed horrors so unimaginable, and cruelty so unforgivable, that I came to despise the very idea of national pride. I am sure that you, as a medical man, probably saw worse than I did. I don't know how you came to terms with it, but I couldn't, at least not in any accepting way. Rather than succumb to the helplessness of it all, or become dulled to it the way most men must if only to preserve their sanity and some bit of their souls, I was instantly resolved upon an action that would finally give our smug and bloody English world pause.

"I can already see in your expression that you think me merely mad. But I say to you, of course I am mad. How could any caring man who saw what we saw not be? For that matter, why aren't you? You were there, you experienced the worst and barely made it home. The madness of it was not lost on you. You have not escaped it. I could see it in your eyes when we first met, and I see it now." At this confrontation with my own long-suppressed anguish, I almost broke his glance and looked away, but I steeled myself not to give in to his ranting and looked steadily back at him.

His speech had gradually become more vigorous and indignant. "It wasn't merely the immediate effects of such violence, the hellish suffering and waste of life, though that was in itself unspeakable. It was a sudden terrible realisation, one day on the battlefield, that all this was the result of the cold whims of the privileged few who administered our wholesale slaughter and infamy in diffident luxury from the other side of the planet." He paused, looking off into some painfully imagined distance. "That day on the battlefield, there was a ferocious barrage. By strange chance, one of my many half-siblings from my uncle's estate had wound up in my unit. He was a perfect young man, full of life and joy, and somehow still innocent of evil despite his participation in the vile doings of the campaign. We were only yards apart, separated by the crumbled ruin of a low stone wall, and were right then sharing some small terrified joke. He was still smiling at me when a shell hit just beyond him. I flattened myself helplessly under the wall as the shattered fragments of my dear half-brother, this cherished childhood playmate, rained down upon me. Kneeling there dripping with gore and horror, I knew past any possible doubt that no political creed, no sense of imperial destiny, no absurd delusion of glory, could possibly have justified the loss of this happy young man's life."

He stopped and shook his head as if frustrated at his inability to better convey his argument to me. "I know that I am saying nothing that has not been said by thousands of soldiers in a thousand wars. But unlike the rest, I resolved not to stand for it, and once I had so resolved, everything changed. I had a higher, finer purpose, one that seemed to mock the most lofty and preposterous sentiments of public and national good expressed by countless generations of bloody leaders of every supposedly civilised nation since time began. That purpose was to remind the world that the spreading of such terror, no matter how noble the supposed goal, had greater consequences than the miseries of remote battlefields and the injustices endured by faceless populations of the conquered. England, indeed all such arrogant governments, could in fact be held accountable in a way that, though only symbolic, I know, would bring home the truth of the violent death they so casually administered. There, I saw, was the real madness. Not mine. Theirs. I was only one man, but I could deliver that message.

"With that purpose held privately in my heart, I embraced the opportunity provided me by working in the secret service with every fibre of my being. And I was superb at the work. In the next few years I was sent off to the far corners of beyond on desperate missions where I distinguished myself for my ingenuity and resourcefulness, and especially for my ability to play any role required of an undercover agent. Under the expert tutelage of the very government whose heart I intended to break, I developed precisely those brutal skills of battlefield and back alley that I so loathed.

"But I knew better than to risk hasty action. My plan stayed largely unformed as I accumulated the array of knowledge needed to formulate the most perfect strategy possible. Indeed, the most important lesson I learned was the value of flexibility, of not surrendering to a rigid plan that could not instantly adapt to changing circumstances.

"Through it all, while my ultimate purpose never wavered, I played the unassuming and passionate patriot hero to the hilt and was rewarded with ever more important and dangerous roles. At the time of the Golden Jubilee, I was so deeply ensconced in the inner circles of the Fenians that Caron himself, now heralded as our greatest undercover agent for all his years among that rightly vengeful society, did not even know of me. In fact I kept watch on him almost as much as I watched the Fenians squander opportunities and effectiveness with their incessant internecine bickering.

"And I was learning all the time. By the last jubilee, having at various times smiled and finagled and lied my way into several of these fanatically passionate organisations around the globe, I had come to the inescapable conclusion that they did not provide the route to my goal. Right or wrong as any of them may be in their cause, the revolutionary organisation is too volatile, too apt to accumulate over-wrought and combative personalities. The larger the group, the worse its operational efficiency and the greater its chances of self-destruction.

Marston had now slipped into a formal manner of address, almost as if he were lecturing new recruits to the secret service. "I don't doubt that to win a revolution and displace a government, the organised and determined group, or network of groups and cells, is the best course. But for a single devastating stroke you want your smart, clear-thinking individual with passions firmly in check and plans totally unknown to the world. No shared secrets, no complications of scheduling. You mark my words, doctor; the future of assassination is in the workings of such individuals—not some clumsy fraternity of silly secret codes and surreptitious lurkings. These gangs of plotters will be caught out ten times where the careful individual will not. The proof of my words will become evident tomorrow. As you know, right now our most capable counter-spies are busily sweeping up half a dozen gangs of just such idealistic fools. Even your Mr. Holmes is hot on the trail of a genuinely weird combination of American and Persian maniacs—which, by the way, is why you should not hold out any hope that he will be bursting through that door any time soon."

This was not the first time in the past week that I found myself in an inconceivably unlikely conversation. It was odd to the point of fantastic, to be sitting there discussing assassination strategy with this passionately deranged man while so much hung in the balance. But it occurred to me that if I couldn't escape, just such a conversation was what Holmes would have encouraged me to continue as long as I could. For all I knew, help of some sort was on the way, whatever Marston said, and even if it were not I very much needed to know more, so I asked, "But you are *not* alone, are you? You've co-conspirators, apparently a fair number of them, right here." I nodded toward the hallway beyond the closed door. "And what about those thugs of yours in the uniforms who collared me?"

"Oh," he grinned, "Yes, it would look that way, wouldn't it? But no, those men only make my point. I needed some help, it's true, and I've recruited them into a conspiracy, it's true"—I had hoped he might let on precisely how many men there were, but he was, as he said, an expert, and far too smart for that—"but it's not the real one. No, you see," he said, smiling even more broadly, "they're just crooks; best in the business, I admit, but nothing more than crooks." He chuckled. "They think we're getting ready to rob the Bank of England—you know, during the confusion and distraction of the Jubilee celebration. I've let on that I'm from the Secret Service, and I dazzled them with a lot of insider's babble about security displacement and redirected traffic and vacated corridors. You should see the maps and blueprints they're studying. But no, they are not my co-conspirators. They have almost completed the tasks I needed of them without the faintest idea that I'm planning something quite different.

"In fact, I suspect that one or two of these men are principled enough that they would try to stop me if they knew what I really have in mind. Right now they're loading dynamite and stone-cutting equipment into our van. At the appointed time, they'll scatter enthusiastically on various assignments, and then reconvene later this morning at a rendezvous at which I simply won't appear. I will have gone on to a very different rendezvous."

After a pause he remembered the rest of my question. "As for the bobbies, you forget who I am in the second of my lives. I have today exercised law-enforcement authorities long entrusted to me in ensuring that this neighbourhood is practically crawling with bobbies, all of whom answer to me. Those two men who apprehended you may have been thugs but they were official ones, the best kind for my purposes—real bobbies doing their duty. I turned them and a number of others loose to find you as soon as I regained consciousness after our little crash. They think that the two of you are members of an international conspiracy of communists. There's an irony, don't you think—you and Mark Twain as notorious communists? Naturally I warned them to ignore whatever wild tales you might tell them." I took some comfort in the hope that the bobbies had not told Marston that there were in fact three of us when they encountered us. Somehow I found it hopeful that Wiggins was not only at large but unknown to this man.

I did not have to pretend to being amazed by Marston's narrative, even impressed, but there was still much unexplained. "But your brother," I objected. "The break-ins at Tedworth Square and Baker Street. The whole Clemens affair, in fact. And that awful shootout, man, what sense did all that make? Your brother killed. For what?"

"That was my biggest gamble, I think, that you or Holmes would be suspicious about Robert's little escapades. But as far as I know neither of you stopped to wonder."

"About what?"

"The coincidences, of course. Think, man. What were the chances, in all the city of London, or in all of the world for that matter, that Clemens would come out of his publisher's office just as Robert rode by for him to recognise; and then that Robert would come rushing out of Clemens' house just as Clemens came in sight of the house on his walk back from the smoke shop; and *then* that Robert would come rushing out of your Baker Street apartments just as you and Holmes came within sight of your front door? Didn't it ever occur to you that such exquisitely precise timing was suspiciously convenient?"

"Perhaps it did to Holmes, but not to me. After all, we were caught up in a baffling mystery at the time," I said. "You must mean to say that those encounters were not coincidences, but I can't see how that could have happened."

"Of course it could not have happened!" he said cheerfully, "but it could be arranged, and arranged it was. By me. Or, I should say, by me and my fellow bank-robbing conspirators," he smiled again at the thought of his misled men. "They believed me when I said that by arranging these little encounters for Robert we were setting up distractions to confuse and distract Holmes and the police. It was easy enough for a few of my men to station themselves out of sight along the right streets and signal ahead so that the van driver could appear just at the right moment to be seen but not caught. And of course it was all just a lark for Robert, who was a sweet child and had no idea of the role he was playing."

I was unconvinced. "I think you're just trying to flummox me again. Surely you didn't need to construct such an involved ruse just to keep your men preoccupied. Besides, why would these little pranks necessitate the murder of your brother? And what about Clemens? He saw Alexander, I mean

Robert, where was it, Johannesburg? You arranged that, too? That was last winter, thousands of miles away on another continent. None of this hangs together, Marston."

"Yes, it does," he said, "and Clemens' appearance in Johannesburg was the spark that ignited my whole plan. The only authentic coincidence in this whole affair was finding Robert and myself in that city when that wonderful man came to town."

"You were there too?"

"Of course I was. How else could Robert have been there in the first place? I was there on duty, nosing around the nasty little disaster of the Jameson Raid. You know, the ugly shambles that came of Rhodes and his cronies trying to stir up an insurrection among the British in the Transvaal—to overthrow the Boers?"

"Yes, of course, I read about it," I said. "Jameson was lionised here, but I thought he behaved little better than a gangster."

"Now you're getting in the spirit. He was a gangster, but who wasn't? Rhodes was the worst, but of course Chamberlain and *his* cronies were in on it too, though they whitewashed themselves out of the whole thing." He looked at me severely, as if about to shake his finger at me, and said "Every assignment I have had as an agent has been like that one. It merely confirmed my conviction that power and privilege can make the finest human being a demon in a matter of hours. And it can turn a bad man to start with into a monster.

"Anyway, because it seemed a harmless enough assignment with no serious risks, I arranged to bring Robert with me. I dearly loved him, boy and man, and hardly ever had time with him, you know. For years I'd looked for an opportunity to spend more time with him. So I went to Durham, retrieved him from his adoptive family, and brought him out to the Cape with me, arranging care and entertainment for him whenever I couldn't have him along on my work which, frankly, wasn't very often.

185

"Shortly after I arrived I saw the advertisements about the approaching visit of the great Mark Twain. I'd always admired his writing enormously, as I believe you do, Doctor. Anyone with the sense God gave a goose could see past the entertainment to the profound power of his deeper messages. He seemed to me to speak against precisely the human tragedies I was so concerned with. And that was when I finally hatched my plan.

"Most important, while thinking about Mark Twain I sensed what I had been lacking; not a co-conspirator but a kindred spirit—a literary counterpart. I decided that I would recruit him, the world's most popular and widely read author, to tell my story."

Seeing my look of shocked dismissal, Marston said, "Oh, I knew he would never voluntarily endorse the assassination. I didn't even want him to. This wasn't to be a business arrangement. I just wanted him to put the whole story in print, in his own way. To explain how I, and the world, came to such a tormented moment, you know? That is why I knew that I must do what I did this very night. At just the right moment, no sooner or later, I must kidnap him and compel him to hear my tale. I was sure that he could not help telling that tale once he had heard it all."

"But you lost him in the street," I said, triumphantly.

"Which is why I brought you along too, doctor," he said. "I am nothing if not adaptable, and though you are neither as skilled nor as beloved as Mark Twain, your stories are enormously popular. They have, if you'll pardon me, an innocent, almost naive credibility among the public. Readers all over the world trust you. In my mind, the great good chance that you were also at the Clemens home last evening"—he thus inadvertently confirmed my assumption that it must at least be past midnight—"seemed fortuitous beyond my hopes. When I arrived at Tedworth Square I had not one but two world-famous storytellers at hand, so I immediately determined to bring you both. Clemens' escape is regrettable and, I must admit, a little puzzling. But, and you'll have to pardon me again for putting it this way, you will do splendidly in a pinch."

"Again I must tell you," I said, "You're mad. And you're all the more mad if you could imagine that the great Samuel Clemens—or even the mere John Watson—will be the tools of your insanity. We simply wouldn't do it. I won't. You shan't recruit me."

"Won't you? I can't?" he said. "I disagree. I know you both better than you know yourselves. Think about it. Clemens would have written my story if only for his immense and brilliant sense of history. How could he not? The age's greatest storyteller could not resist the age's greatest story, especially as he was such an intimate part of the story himself. I imagine that he may write it anyway, even though he missed out on this part of it.

"And you won't be able to resist it either, Doctor. I'm sure of it. It's not as if I am hoping that either of you would portray me as a hero. This isn't about Richard Marston," he said, the indignation in his voice rising. "It isn't even about Her Majesty, though she's the one who must die so visibly on her very doorstep in full view of her adoring subjects and the people whose oppression she has so graciously symbolised all these years. No. It's about injustice and evil. It's about the tragedy of a world that can only sustain itself by turning good men into monsters." He looked away for a moment, then said, "But let's not quarrel. There is more of the story you must hear."

"Now I'm not sure I should listen so willingly," I said.

"You might as well," he said, and I knew he was right.

"Robert and I attended the first Clemens speech we could. We sat toward the back, the only seats we could get. Robert couldn't hear a thing, of course, but he has the most astonishing capacity for proper behavior. I could take him anywhere and he would stand, or sit, or be attentive, or otherwise give every outward appearance of fitting in. It was during that speech that my plan began to firm up, and Robert became central to it. I decided that while Clemens must not see

187

me, he *must* see Robert. I wasn't even sure why, but I knew. Once seen, Clemens would not forget Robert, and somehow I could make use of that memory. You know," he added, interrupting his own story, "it has been through such little intuitions that I made my way so successfully through many a complicated and perilous mission in many a foreign outpost.

"That is how it came about that Robert was so visible on the stage the next time we attended, which was Clemens' speech at the Standard. I made sure that Clemens couldn't miss him, and having done that I knew that he wouldn't forget him. Even from my seat in the balcony I could see that Clemens kept glancing over at Robert.

"What had finally congealed in my mind there in Johannesburg was to make the Diamond Jubilee into an event that the world truly would never forget. It was the chance that I had unknowingly been looking for.

"This had never been about simply doing in some royal personage. In my career with the secret service I'd had Her Majesty within reach several times when a quick moment of suicidal action could have accomplished that. But as I say, that had never been my entire purpose. The statement that I intended had to be made as publicly and symbolically as possible. The approaching Jubilee promised to be the best, and possibly the last considering her age, such chance I would get. This thought had been nagging at me for some time when Clemens clarified it all for me.

"It was easy enough for me to determine with a good degree of certainty that the Clemens family intended to come to London at the conclusion of their trip, and live here for several months at least, while he wrote his book. There were some tense moments for me right after they arrived in England and learned that their daughter, in Connecticut I think, was dreadfully ill. Clemens' wife and daughter rushed off to see her, and for a moment I feared that the whole family would all go home and stay there. Sad to say, the poor thing died before her mother could reach her, and at that point the women seemed to decide that there was no real reason for them to stay there so they hurried back to Clemens and took up their secluded mourning in Chelsea. I knew then that, what with Clemens working on his book, he would be in residence right through the Jubilee. I could proceed.

"By the time they moved into the house in Chelsea, I had formulated my strategy. All I needed to do was manufacture a panic for Clemens that would ensure my comfortable involvement in his household and enable me to choose just the right moment to haul him off for this very conversation. The rest you know."

"Hardly," I said, "There is much more. I mean, did you even see to it that Clemens came to Holmes and me?"

"Oh, well, no, but that was lucky for me, wasn't it? I know the workings of my trade, doctor, and I don't mind telling you that I was more concerned about Sherlock Holmes somehow finding me out than I was about the entire police force and Secret Service. I had the official forces well in hand and completely gulled. In the highest ranks of my profession your Holmes is justifiably revered for his unique facility at uncovering the most unsuspected problems. I was delighted to have him drawn into the mysterious and unsolvable Clemens situation. Talk about a red herring! What a delicious irony. I couldn't have planned that better. Of course I knew how to take advantage of it, and to gently encourage you and Holmes in your misdirected inquiries, absorbing all your energies while my own plan moved ahead."

"So the murder of your brother," I pressed on; "that also was necessary to keep us distracted?"

Marston abruptly sobered. "Perhaps not, but at the time it seemed for the best. You see, once back here I had to separate myself from Robert completely. I couldn't risk anyone, especially you or Holmes, seeing Robert and me together. So I arranged for him to ingratiate himself with the Wakefield people at Black's. "

"This is not becoming in the least clearer to me," I complained. "For one thing, the man was both deaf and mentally limited. He would not seem in the least useful as a co-conspirator," I said.

"No, no, it wasn't as if we ever sat and conspired. He and I had developed a kind of sign language of our own as children, and I was able to convey to him the idea that he should stay there around the docks, you know—camp out in the crates at that warehouse; try to enter the building. Robert is utterly guileless and trusting, which I think must have been recognised by the Wakefields. They're not so evil as I led you to believe. I simply encouraged him to accept their kindnesses. It was a safe enough place for him while I worked. I had no idea he'd become obsessed with the ratting matches, but I was also able to make use of that unexpected development, as you know."

"But why involve him in that sordid scene at all?" I asked.

"To give you and Holmes someplace to pursue him, of course. I thought you were following my thinking here," he said with some disappointment.

"Apparently not," I said. I began to wonder if this man's entire effort wasn't some wild combination of incredibly convoluted planning and simple random happenstance that in retrospect he had shaped, in his own addled mind at least, into a brilliant "strategy."

While we were speaking the light had begun to increase. It was when I plainly saw the expression of disappointment in Marston's face that I realised that early morning light was coming through the smeared windows. Marston must have noticed too, for he broke off the conversation and stood up, returning the pistol to its holster inside his coat. I could see that the long barrel was the reason he had been unable to extract the revolver more readily during our struggle in the coach. Reaching into an inner coat pocket, he extracted a thick sheaf of folded papers and handed them to me.

"It's time for me to go," he said. "I admire you, doctor, and I am sorry if I haven't adequately explained all the finer

190

points, but I have given you the necessary outline of my story. For your additional information I have prepared this statement," he nodded at the papers, which I had not yet unfolded, "so you will have a more rigorously articulated account of my position and how I arrived at it." I looked down at the paper as he added, "Make no mistake; it's not some desperate defence of my actions. They require no such justification. All it does is lay out in more formal and considered terms why it is right, in some higher sense, to do what I am about to do."

Before he could turn to go, I despaired of rational discourse and shouted, "Right? Higher sense? For God's sake man! For the sake of all that is decent and good come to your senses! Don't do this! You can still walk away from it. You're gifted, a resourceful man. You could leave London this very night with nothing in your pockets and still make yourself a productive life anywhere in the world."

"I'm sorry, doctor," he said, crossing the room and reaching for the door. "It is too late for any of that." Then he paused and said, "If you'd like, Denison can fill you in on the shooting of Robert. He'll be with you on the boat, he and Brown."

"Boat? What boat?" I asked.

"No need to worry. I'm just removing you as far as possible from further involvement. Well, no," he added, correcting himself, "That's not quite all I'm doing. Brown, the fellow who came in with me; you probably noticed his resemblance to me. It's quite uncanny, actually. He is dressed as I am now, and should there be any chance of someone wanting to know where I am, he will give them the wrong impression. Just a precaution. But as for you," he said, "they'll drop you off well downstream at some isolated and inconvenient spot far from any hope of communication with any help. You'll miss all the pomp and pageantry, and of course the unplanned conclusion of the procession." Then, as one more proof of the man's absurdly twisted reasoning, he added,

"You ought to get that bruise looked at as soon as you can. I can tell it's bothering you."

"But Marston," I said, intending to give it one more try, but he cut me off sharply.

"No more, doctor," he said, his voice firm. "They will be in to get you soon. Good luck to you, and do give my best to Holmes."

The door closed and the lock clicked loudly, then there was silence again, not even the sound of his footsteps going down the hall. As desperate as I was to get away, I admit I was just as desperate for those men to come. It had been many hours since Sam Clemens and I had enjoyed our drinks, and my bladder felt about to burst.

Chapter Twenty-One
A Plan of Their Own

Denison and Brown arrived mercifully soon thereafter. I now saw the remarkable resemblance that Marston had told me about. As Brown opened the door, I could see that he was nearly a twin, not only in build but in facial features, and he was dressed identically to Marston.

But it was Denison who held most of my attention. My first thought was that here, finally, was the mysterious van driver. Slender, almost skeletal, he fit the hasty observations Clemens had made of him. Without even thinking and before Denison was through the door behind Brown, I burst out with, "You're the van driver!"

Denison smiled and said, "At your service, Doctor, but this morning I shall pilot another conveyance, if you will please come with us." I rose to follow him out the door, with Brown maintaining pace about three steps behind me. As we walked, I said to Denison, "You're an American."

"I know," he said.

"Sorry, I just didn't expect. . . " but I didn't know what else to say, so I changed the subject. "Marston said you could explain a few things to me."

"And what might those be?" he asked, without breaking stride.

"Well, now I'm also curious how an American got involved in this, of course, but he said you could tell me about the death of Robert. You know, his brother?"

"The walleye. Yes, that I can." We were walking down a long corridor toward stairs. "I expect you'd like to make a stop first. You've been cooped up all night. Right in here," he waved toward a door and added something I did not quite catch that sounded like, "It will mean less of a mess later," which I supposed was a lame attempt at humour.

"Yes, thank you," I said with relief. They waited outside the door of the windowless privy, then we continued down three flights of stairs. As we walked, Denison commenced to tell me his story.

"Marston and I first met some years ago in New Orleans, where I was able to do some work for him. I have a number of specialised skills, unlike Brown there, who pretty much concentrates on one kind of work." Brown said nothing. "We ran into each other once or twice after that, but we'd lost touch for a few years until last year. I'd come over to Africa for, well, certain opportunities I'd heard about, but foolishly got myself involved in that stupid military uproar in the Transvaal. Not out of any political convictions, mind you; some friends had told me there might be some opportunities coming up if the government changed, you know. Well, it was all a mistake, what with Jameson's little escapade. I suppose you know about that."

"Yes, a little," I said as we turned the corner to the lowest level of stairs.

"Then you know what a disaster it was all around. But I weaseled out of it, thanks to Marston. He was nosing around down there on some government business or other, not long after the raid this would have been, and somehow found out that I was jailed along with the rest. Arranged for my release and offered me this job."

We came off the stairs directly into a large gloomy space with high windows, obviously the main floor of the warehouse. There was little light but I could see that much of the floor was occupied with stacks of various sizes of crates, great piles of sacks, and raw lumber. There was a strong scent of coffee, which I suppose must have occupied the sacks nearest us and made me wish for a large serving. I could see no door.

I could imagine some of Denison's unnamed "specialised skills" that might have been of interest to Marston, but rather than pursue that question I again asked him about Robert. "Oh, that," he said, "The oddest job I've ever had, that. And the best paying, it has to be said. That fellow gave me the blithering willies just to see him; to have him stare at you the

194

way he did." He gave a bit of a shiver. "Oh, I know he meant no harm. Didn't know any better, had no idea what he was. But I always tried to clear out when he was around."

We were now just standing, Brown maintaining his position a few steps behind me while I talked with Denison. Wide aisles of boxes and other goods radiated out to the dark corners of the room. Denison didn't seem to be in any particular hurry, and continued his story. "Marston mostly kept him out of our way; the rest of his crew, I mean. We didn't see him much, thank Heavens. But then that day you're talking about, Marston came around and told me he had a special chore for me, let on that I'd be getting a special bonus for some work, you know. He kept using the word, 'special,' so I knew something was up. He took me to Black's first thing that morning and showed me the lay of things, then told me what I was to do. Said that Robert would come running to me. I think he'd worked that out with Robert, too. The poor fellow could follow complicated directions, simple as he was, I'll give him that.

"So that night I waited right where I was supposed to and sure enough, Robert came loping in all winded and even more crazy looking, like that big eye was finally going to pop clear out of his head. This was in that bar-room, you know. Well, Marston had told me what to do, and that I would only have a minute or two to do it. I took Robert over to that pillar and stood him with his back to it, facing towards where you all were supposed to come in. He was still pretty wound up from whatever he'd been doing, maybe just from being chased by all of you, but he knew me, so he was still as biddable as ever. I gave him a pat on the shoulder and put those pretty little revolvers in his hands and made him understand that he should hold his arms out to the sides. Once he knew he was to obey you, you could move him around like a mannequin."

I interrupted him. "But didn't the other people over by the bar take notice of any of this?"

"Couldn't tell you. Not the sort of establishment where it pays to look around much, you know? If a couple fellows want to be alone, who's to care? Besides, it was mighty dark back in our corner," he said. That was true enough. We hadn't even noticed Robert until he started firing at us.

"Once I had him situated, I went around behind the pillar. It was a hefty one, but I could reach around easy enough. I just put my hands out on each side and took Robert's hands in mine, from the back you know." He wriggled his very thin fingers in front of himself, then demonstrated the motion of reaching them out and grabbing Robert's hands. "I put my trigger fingers on top of his, plenty of room for us both in the trigger guards. Robert must have figured this was a game; he moaned his little loonie noise he always made when he was having fun."

The horror of what was being described to me sank in, but before I could say anything Denison continued. "We only stood there a minute or so when you all came running in. I gave you a few seconds, then began scattering rounds in all directions. Marston was very specific about that. No shots anywhere close to the three of you." He chuckled. "At first Robert decided to help or something. I had no idea what he thought he was doing but he kind of pulled my hand around toward you before I could yank it back. That's why that one shot almost got you. Sorry about that, though I guess it would have all worked out the same anyway.

"Well, you were there," he said, "You remember the rest. I wasn't more than half done shooting when you all opened up. I felt safe enough behind the pillar, but I did worry that one of you might shoot through Robert's arms and, you know, hit my arm or my hand. But you were both real Dead-eye Dicks—Marston's famous for it with that long cannon he carries. But you didn't do bad either, Doctor. Anyway, I could feel Robert sort of grunting as he took all that lead and started to fall, so as soon as I finished shooting I just slide my fingers off the triggers and let go of his hands. He just flopped over right there. Easy as that.

"Then all I had to do was sneak back through the door. I knew what was coming, so I'd closed my eyes when I started shooting so's not to be blinded, you know. I guess that after all those muzzle flashes you probably couldn't have seen me if I'd do-si-doed around the pillar a couple times. But I kept it between me and you as best I could and tippy-toed on out of there. That answer your questions?"

"Yes," I said, shaking my head. "What a sad waste of life. If ever there was an innocent man, we shot him that night."

"Can't argue with that, doctor," Denison said, then turned to Brown and said, "Time to go, don't you think? He said to wait until there was just enough light so people could get a bit of a look at you." Again Brown had nothing to say, but he did nod, then turned toward a chasm among the crates, letting Denison lead me and taking his usual position behind me as we proceeded to a door leading outside.

We emerged from the building directly onto a platform above the river. The motion of the occasional glint of current told me we were on the north bank. I could see only dark looming silhouettes of buildings on the far shore. A hasty glance upstream and down revealed no bridges, and no immediate hint of just where we were. The river was quiet, with little moving traffic. A good many lighters, barges and other unidentifiable craft were anchored here and there out in the current, sometimes singly and sometimes in straggling bunches. A longer shape at midstream suggested what was probably an excursion steamer. On our shore, upstream a hundred yards or so, probably in front of the next warehouse, there were a few lights and a tugboat seemed to be getting up steam. Otherwise there was no visible activity on the nearby docks. I could hear the metallic thrum of a small engine down below us. Now that I was moving around, I felt very tired and was eager to get off my feet and have a seat in the boat.

"Time to go," Denison said again and started down the stairs to the water. Brown gave me what I thought was an unnecessary nudge on the back of my sore shoulder, and I followed Denison slowly, watching my footing on the dark and uneven wooden stairs. At the bottom there were two or three wherries rubbing alongside one another, and one small steam launch from which the engine noise emanated.

It was a trim little police launch with no cab and a thin stack raking back at that affected angle meant to indicate speed. I knew from previous experience pursuing criminals with Holmes that these little boats were among the swiftest on the river. Brown stepped in first and uncovered the green police lamp on its pole. Its light reflected on the bright brass among the engine works. He then activated a powerful flood light in the bow and aimed it down to illuminate the water a few yards in front of the boat. I could almost admire Marston's genius for planning. Any constables nearby would make the most trustworthy possible witnesses to observe "Marston" departing on this official police launch. I wondered just why he was so eager to falsely place himself here in official eyes, and for the first time wondered if this passionately deliberate man even had a plan for his escape following the assassination. What life might he have in mind for himself following such a devastating act?

As I stepped into the launch, Brown put a light hand on my shoulder and held me in place while Denison followed me into the boat and moved immediately to the stern, where he took a seat by the rudder. With a light push, Brown then directed me toward the stern as well, where he seated me on a low hard bench facing Denison. I was barely seated when Brown pulled my arms behind me and tied them savagely tight. I started to object but he brought a heavy cloth gag over the top of my head and pulled it just as tight over my mouth. My inability to move my arms indicated that Brown had somehow secured my hands to the bench.

Denison watched these proceedings patiently, then said, "We're in the open, now, doctor, and you are tied because I would prefer that you not communicate with any of our neighbours." I could hear Brown move a step or two toward the middle of the boat, presumably to tend the engine, which soon began to chuff more energetically.

"And now that we're underway I feel obliged to inform you that Mr. Brown and I have changed the plan. As Marston probably told you, he asked us to take you downstream well out of things and maroon you somewhere. But Marston operates in a different business world than we do. For reasons I just can't imagine, he is unconcerned about all the people who will know him or recognise his face when we are done with our work this afternoon. We do not share his disregard for that risk. Our careers depend upon us maintaining a fair degree of anonymity. I am sure you understand, and I am sorry to tell you that your trip will be considerably shorter than he intended. Once we're well out in the current and clear of some of these boats," he waved toward the big clots of vessels dotting our side of the river, "Mr. Brown will practice his limited but highly expert skills and then we will sink you to the bottom."

I greeted this information with a determined effort not to panic. For a moment I pointlessly wondered if these two men had killed Barber, but remembered that he had been shot, so I turned to thoughts of escape. My legs were still free, but I could see no point in attempting to bolt, either back onto shore or into the river, even if I could drag my bench with me. Denison was out of reach even if I had been able to extend my feet in a vigorous kick, and I was sure that Brown would have me instantly in hand if I showed any such sign of fight. I looked desperately around but the only signs of life I could see in any direction were on the dock by the tugboat some distance upstream, where it appeared the crew were casting off the lines. If the noise of our launch did not drown out any muffled shout I might be able to make through the gag, the greater noise of their engine surely would have. Worse, I knew that any constable or other officials nearby would simply disregard any noise I made as the unremarkable ranting of Marston's prisoner.

Then we were underway, Denison expertly taking us away from the dock. He kept us near our shore for a while, perhaps to make as sure as possible that "Marston" was seen in the boat by any observers, but after a hundred yards of slowly promenading in close this way, he signaled to Brown for more speed and turned out toward midstream. As we passed among the first little flock of anchored skiffs, Denison's face lost its soft green light. Brown must have covered the police lamp and the flood, presumably so these villains could not be identified by any chance observer when it came time to dispose of me.

Even without the floodlight showing his way, Denison slipped around and among several groups of barges and a pair of sizeable steamers with a sure hand. He kept in close to whatever vessel we passed, putting us in the darkest shadows for much of the way. I could hear movement and voices on some of the barges, and once even the sound of someone warning us off, but Denison ignored them. In my mounting desperation I sensed the latent power of the launch as the little engine seemed almost straining to be let loose in open water where it could sprint as it was made to. My case seemed more hopeless by the second. The engine ran steadily on under Brown's management.

After a few moments, Denison made his way between two more strings of lighters and came in under the deeply shadowed stern of a large steamer. Judging from the distance and time we'd travelled in our winding course among all these boats, I guessed that when we came around from behind this steamer we would probably find ourselves in the open lane of water in the middle of the river. Denison was concentrating on his course, which may be why I alone thought I heard another noise over the sound of our own energetic little engine—a deeper and more formidable rumble that seemed to come from somewhere over our heads but could only be another boat of some sort, and almost certainly a much larger one.

As we cleared the stern of the steamer I proved to be correct. Denison, angling the launch out into the open channel and downstream, still seemed not to hear it, but there it was. A large tugboat—I guessed it to be the one I'd seen casting off moments ago—was coming fast on a course that would converge with ours in a matter of seconds. My frantic shout of warning through the gag was muffled and lost in the noise of engines, but Brown must have looked up from his work right then, for there was a frightened bellow from behind me. Denison gave a start and turned quickly. Seeing the oncoming tug, he leaned hard on the rudder, hoping to swing us back among the anchored vessels. As he did so, I heard Brown scrambling. In an instant the green light again illuminated Denison's terrified features, and then, I suppose in his desperation to get the attention of the tug's pilot, Brown also uncovered the floodlight and swung it around 180 degrees. Denison swore and raised his arm to shield his eyes as the brilliant column of light washed over him, but I ignored his antics in favor of what that blast of illumination revealed looming over us—a sight that will stay with me in glorious memory to the grave and beyond.

In the pilot house of the tug stood Sam Clemens, but it was a Sam Clemens we had not yet met—Mark Twain himself, old-time Mississippi River pilot, straight and tall, eyes afire, jaw set, hands firm on the wheel—at last back in his own element and carrying on the battle from ground he knew so well.

Chapter Twenty-Two
Mark Twain

My instant of admiration and wonder at this legendary sight was in the next heartbeat replaced with abject terror as the foaming bow wave of the tugboat rolled over the stern of our little launch, drenching me in place. Denison and Brown had already leapt into the river. It was only later that I learned that in his panic Brown had jumped directly into the path of the oncoming tug, but I could see Denison make the wiser leap, back toward shore. I could hardly rise from my bench, and in that instant I had the exhilarating and dismaying thought that I had been rescued only to drown as the little launch was crushed under the steel hull of the bigger craft.

But I had underestimated the seaworthiness of the launch, the skill of the tug's pilot, and—most certainly of all—my luck. Instead of simply steaming right over the top of the launch, the tug nudged it a bit and began to slide by with the launch scraping along the tug's port side. The launch's screw was no doubt still spinning wildly, and upon first contact with the hull of the tug the launch "came alongside" with a loud slam, its gunwale then grating noisily against the tug's passing hull. The friction of that passage tilted the little boat dangerously downward toward the tug, and it shipped even more water. Having survived what I had assumed was the certain death of the initial collision, I waited helplessly for the launch to roll the rest of the way over and trap me underneath.

Instead, suddenly the contact eased and the launch, though still banging along the larger hull, rocked back to a level position. As the launch neared the stern of the tug, a man appeared in silhouette on the tug's deck above me. Even in my complicated state of mind I noticed that he seemed to be attired in a large tricorne and a cape that billowed widely as he hopped overboard and down into the launch, landing in a sturdy crouch precisely where Denison had stood only seconds before. Grabbing the rudder, he swung us out from the tug, waited until it was well ahead of us, then turned us toward the far bank. The launch, though none the worse for its noisy passage against the tug, was sluggish from its new cargo of water. The engine sputtered as if about to drown, but we made steady headway toward a low mud bank beneath what I took to be a small shipyard. Unable to speak and indeed unable to think of much to say even if I could have spoken, I simply sat and savored the relief of this unexpected reprieve.

I had by now recognised my rescuer as none other than the elder Wiggins, attired in another of his fantastic costumes, a wild theatrical parody of some forgotten fashion. In my silent jubilation I resolved to buy him an entire wardrobe of such finery at the first opportunity.

In a few moments Wiggins unceremoniously ran the launch directly up onto the soft soil of the bank as far as its momentum would carry it. Once it came to rest at an easy tilt he let go of the rudder, stepped past me to silence the wheezing engine, then returned and kneeled behind me to loosen the gag.

"By God, Wiggins, thank you! That was a close thing," I shouted the instant I was able.

He was working on the bonds around my hands as he replied, in far more cultured language than he had employed during his urchinhood with the Irregulars, "Closer than you may know, Doctor. This perch of yours," he rapped his knuckles on the side of my bench, which gave a dull stone-like sound, "was an anchor. Seen these before. Local specialty. Concrete, you know. There's a man in Wapping makes them for the trade, with a nice little loophole for the rope. Says that when he retires he plans to bill the Lord Mayor for paving the entire river bottom from the Tower to Greenwich."

As the rope came loose, he gently took my arm and said, "No broken bones? Good. We weren't at all sure what those rascals might have gotten up to with you. Here, let's get you up to the street. Should be a coach along soon."

I was grateful for his assistance in stepping me out of the launch. My accumulation of injuries, the sleepless night, and the shock of the near-catastrophe of the last few minutes had now fully caught up with me and I could barely wobble along. My head was pounding again, and even with his arm around my waist to support me, we crossed the mud flat, climbed a substantial stone stairway, and were well along a narrow passageway between two buildings before I could navigate on my own.

"Not far now, doctor, and we'll get you situated with a little refreshment," Wiggins said.

"I would give a good deal for a brandy," I said.

"No sooner said than done," he responded cheerily as we came out into a narrow lane. He waved toward some moving lights that soon resolved themselves into a large two-horse carriage approaching beneath a dully glowing horizon west of whatever part of the city we were in.

The carriage door swung open even before it had come to a complete stop and the utterly unanticipated voice of Constance Wakefield said, "Please, Doctor, take a seat. You must be exhausted. Frances, you had best return the launch, don't you think?"

"Yes ma'am," Wiggins said as he helped me into the carriage. "It needs a bit of bailing, probably some paint on that one side, but otherwise there should be no complaint. I'll just run it across and catch a ride back with the boys." With a light pirouette that I am sure was intended to bring his cape to its most flamboyant life, he spun and hurried off at a brisk walk.

I was seated opposite Mrs. Wakefield in what seemed right then the most luxurious and comforting seat I'd enjoyed in many a year. I closed my eyes for an instant in the simple joy of being not only out of danger but in such competent hands. Mrs. Wakefield released the latch on a large compartment next to her and extracted a handsome crystal decanter. Despite the jerky rolling of the carriage she poured a hefty quantity of brandy into an oversized glass. She handed it to me, saying "As they say in your profession, Doctor: for medicinal purposes. And well earned."

I smiled, nodded my thanks, and drained the glass in one pitch. Her eyes widened in amusement, and I said, "I apologise, but that was nearly involuntary. It has been a long night." She poured me another, which I silently vowed to drink more slowly.

"I must hear about it, but we had best wait until we have one other passenger aboard, so that we all hear everything the first time," she said.

We rode for some minutes, the driver occasionally slowing and once or twice getting down to jog along some boardwalk or other passage between buildings toward the water, then hurry back. Finally he returned from one of these little jaunts and stood at the window as he said, "He brought her in at the next dock down," then climbed up and drove on about a hundred yards before slowing. As the coach came to a stop a familiar face passed into view in the window. Sam Clemens, with no preamble or greeting, announced in a voice redolent with indignation, "Doctor, I've half a mind to hire Holmes and you to track down the halfwit who built that benighted little tugboat and knock him in the head. Nothing less could ensure a wholesome future for the shipbuilding industry of this nation!"

As he climbed in, and before I could properly greet him much less thank him, he added, "The boy was with me just a minute ago, but I suppose he's off on some new mission. Your men seem to have things in hand with the tugboat people." This last was addressed to Mrs. Wakefield, who nodded as if it were just what she expected.

"Sam," I began, "Mrs. Wakefield . . . I am indebted to you both, and you must be assured of my eternal gratitude, but perhaps if I could have some questions answered I'd know better just what all I should be thanking you for."

"Mr. Clemens will be of the most help there, I am sure," said Mrs. Wakefield.

"All right, all right," said Clemens, obviously settling himself in for a good talk.

"But before that," I said, coming to myself, "we are still in a desperate situation here. There is a horrible danger. I must get . . . ." I paused as I realised that I still wasn't quite sure where, or to whom, I must get, then continued, "to Holmes, or to Whitehall. Yes, Whitehall would be best for a start, and it's closer than Baker Street by far. Whitehall?" I concluded, looking hopefully at Mrs. Wakefield.

"By all means, Doctor," she said. "That is more or less where we are headed right now. But in the meanwhile, there is time for you to catch up. In fact, I insist. And since you seem to have the most pressing news to report, perhaps we should hear from you first?" She looked at Clemens expectantly, and he nodded agreement. So I quickly told them of my conversation with Marston, not just his terrible plans but the outline of his use of his own brother to manipulate and distract us. Several times Clemens' mouth came open in surprise or to respond, but he kept quiet. But when I finally came to Denison's account of the killing of Robert, it was Mrs. Wakefield who softly gasped and let a barely audible, "Oh, no," escape her lips.

All this time we rolled on. As I finished my story we turned onto Borough High Street, part of the royal procession route just south of the river. Before we completed the turn, I noticed a bit of the silhouette of London Bridge off to our right, and I thought I could see the incongruous silhouette of a large balloon swaying near the bridge, probably a part of the festivities. There was more light now, but it was diffuse under a cloudy sky. For the first time in many hours I thought of the nation's hope (and my personal obsession only a few days ago) that the storied "Queen's Weather" would hold true for today and it would be sunny. It did not look promising. I said, "This is the royal procession route. It may be difficult to get through to Whitehall what with all the barricades and work going on. There will be huge crowds."

Mrs. Wakefield said, "Yes, but it's early." So far she seemed correct. We moved slowly but without interference. At times we could see that people were already beginning to gather on the kerbs and a few were even silhouetted on the rooftops. Construction crews hurried along with lumber and equipment. Though the buildings south of the river were not predicted to rival the more historic and exclusive parts of the city to the north, some store and factory fronts were in fact quite handsomely decked out with bunting and a variety of signs and banners. "They are keeping the route open for the carriages of late arrivals," by which she meant the socially and politically privileged who were not expected to walk any troublesome distance to their reserved seating. "I think we'll manage. Now, Mr. Clemens, I am sure that Doctor Watson would appreciate your tale as well."

"Yes, but my head is spinning with your news, Doctor. What a storm we have been in! What a wild substitute for a mind that man has! As for my 'tale,' as you put it," he said to Mrs. Wakefield, then turned to me, "I should start with that note, I think," he said to me, "You know, the one that Katy handed me as we left Tedworth."

"The one from Mrs. Clemens?" I asked.

"About half, yes. Livy had addressed it," he said, reaching into his coat and handing me the envelope. The only words on the envelope, in a fine woman's hand, were "Youth (personal)". He said, "It's a name she has for me," and waved for me to open it. I did, extracting the folded note. I read, written in what must be Mrs. Clemens' hand, the underlined words, "You must believe her." Below that, in a somewhat harder and less cultivated hand, I read the following message:

> Sir:
>
> Marston is a complete fraud and a conspirator against us. Do not trust him! Get away from him however you can!
>
> Yrs., Katy

"For me," Clemens said, indicating the note, "that was final. I would no more disobey those two women than I would, well, I don't know what."

"But why did they write this?" I said, returning the note to the envelope and reaching out to return it to him.

"No," he said, "you keep it. It may come in handy." I smiled as I remembered our conversation about my method of saving scraps that I might use in my writing, and he continued. "I haven't the faintest idea what brought it on, but I guess that Katy must've somehow seen through him just then—in some absolutely compelling way, to judge from the certainty of the note." I fumbled a bit slipping the envelope into a pocket. My shoulder chose this moment to reassert primacy over any other discomforts, and I shifted to try to find a more comfortable posture.

"The problem," Clemens said, "was figuring out what to do about it. There we were, for all practical purposes Marston's captives in a moving coach. He was armed, and so were those men up top." As he said this, he checked his conversation and added, "Oh, and that's another thing. I was already worried about what was up with Marston even before I read the note, you see, because of those men, or one of them at least."

"The soldiers?" I asked.

"Well, the men in soldier uniforms, anyway," he said. "I think that you will recall that during our first meeting, Holmes asked me if I could describe the driver of the van that carried that man, Alexander or Robert, or whoever he was."

"I do, yes," I said. "You described the driver as very thin, and also said that his face seemed familiar."

"He was. It was. When we came out of the house to get in Marston's coach, the uniforms of the driver and his companion caught my eye, so I gave the men a look and was shocked to recognise one of them as that same skinny fellow. Denison, you say."

"Right," I agreed.

"But I also remembered where I had seen him before. It was last May, in Pretoria. You see, one day, in a sudden mood that I now wish I had ignored, I went to the jail there to visit the conspirators who were behind the whole Jameson fiasco. I tried to cheer them up with some jailhouse humour, but it fell flat. Mortifying for me, felt like a moron. But I would swear in court that as I was burying myself in embarrassment in front of those people, I saw that same man there in the cells with the others. Even if he wasn't such a bean pole, his face is quite distinctive."

I had a sudden memory of Denison's face in the greenish tinge of the police launch running-light as he gave me the grim news that he was about to murder me. "Yes, I didn't mention that," I said. "He told me he was there, and that was where Marston recruited him for this whole business. I suppose he was one of the soldiers that came down with Jameson, to supposedly liberate Johannesburg."

"No, I don't think so," said Clemens, shaking his head. "The soldiers had all been shipped back to England by the time I got there. No, this was a different crowd. These were people who were rounded up as co-conspirators, British men who lived in Johannesburg and were apparently supposed to raise up support for the rebellion when Jameson's troops got close to town.

"Yes, that sounds more sensible to me," I said, "though as it turns out Denison was American."

"Really?" Clemens said.

"Yes, and I don't think he was the soldiering type. More a professional criminal type."

"Yes," Clemens said. "But seeing him and finally figuring out why his face was familiar put me to thinking about everything that had happened. As unlikely as it was that Alexan . . , uh, Robert would show up at my door, and your door for that matter, the chances that a second person I saw in South Africa would also be involved in this whole mess was past all reason.

"After that, well, you saw the next part. After we got in Marston's coach and Katy's note confirmed my worst suspicions, I sat for the longest time trying to come up with some dodge that would get us out of there, but it took me forever to think of starting a conversation about your revolver. Once that was underway it was easy enough to ask to hold it, and then I had the drop on our man, at least for a moment.

After that I think we were just lucky that it was his head and not ours that hit the hardest when the coach went over."

I agreed and he continued. "Next thing, let's see, oh, when those counterfeit bobbies showed up and you told Wiggins and me to run for it, he hauled me off up that little alley and around a couple corners. I haven't run that much since the Civil War. I was about to fall over when he pulled up at a door in some alley. He took out a key, opened the door, and hurried me inside, locking the door behind us. He led me down a bare hallway and through another door into an even darker room. Letting go of my sleeve and leaving me standing there, he took a few steps and quickly brought up the gas lights, astonishing me with the sight of a cozy and spotless little sitting room. Indicating a big chair to me, he moved to a little wooden table along the wall, took a seat on the stool beside it, and to my even greater amazement proceeded to operate the telephone that sat in the centre of the table.

"That reminds me," he said to Mrs. Wakefield. "There must be telephones somewhere here," he indicated the streets of the passing city. "Shouldn't we call ahead to Whitehall to get them started on whatever it is they'll do about all this?"

Mrs. Wakefield said, "Yes, we have called ahead," but didn't explain who made those calls, to whom they were made, or what was said. Clemens shrugged and resumed his story.

"That boy operated the telephone like an expert. He told whoever it was on the other end that he was 'at the sittin' room,' those were his words. He said that he had me with him—called me 'Clements'—but that you, Doctor, had been 'run off with' and he didn't know where. Then he rang off and explained that we'd have help pretty quick, then pointed at a cabinet and invited me to help myself. Opening it I found some good Scotch and several tins of biscuits and meat. I had the Scotch."

"Over the course of the next hour or so there were comings and goings of a number of people, including Wiggins' big brother, who showed up looking like d'Artagnan masquerading as Napoleon. He stayed around. The others, three or four men in regular working clothes, asked the younger Wiggins a few questions about our captors and the bobbies, then hurried off. Then Mrs. Wakefield arrived," he nodded in her direction, "and she wanted to send me home, but now that I had been in the thick of things I wasn't of a mind to walk out on you. I pointed out that as I knew the faces not only of Marston but of Denison I might prove useful in the search for you. I don't think she was really convinced of the importance of this, and may have let me come along rather than hurt my feelings." Mrs. Wakefield listened to this account of her actions with a smile, but added nothing.

"She was kind enough to agree to get a message to my family not to worry, and to expect me in time for the festivities today. Looks like she was right about that. By then, as near as I can gather, her people had narrowed the search for you to a few big warehouses right on the river, so the Wigginses and I boarded her coach and hurried over to that neighbourhood, where I was surprised to have the coach stop so that the driver could confer with some bobbies. I would not have dreamed of trusting any of them right then."

At this, Mrs. Wakefield did speak. "Marston isn't the only person with influence among the constabulary. There are a number of bobbies throughout the city with whom we maintain what I might call collaborative arrangements, and they, without violating their specific orders from Marston, could still be called upon for information. Of course they had little or no idea of what Marston might be up to; he was just their duly appointed superior. Asking them a few innocuous questions about his whereabouts, or the whereabouts of his associates, was in no way an unusual matter, and they had no reason to hesitate to tell us what they knew."

"Yes, and they knew enough," Clemens said. "Before long the search had been narrowed down to that particular warehouse where they were keeping you. We had no idea if you were merely a prisoner or had already suffered some awful fate."

"It seemed best just to watch for a while," Mrs. Wakefield added, "and it turned out to be so. But when two of the bobbies arrived in the police launch it seemed most likely that they intended to take you off to some other location, or merely do what they in fact were intending to do with you."

I almost objected that what they were "intending to do" with me did not seem "mere" from my viewpoint, but stayed quiet.

Clemens resumed the story. "But once we saw that boat come in, Mrs. Wakefield and Frances were convinced that we had run out of time. Even with the additional men that had arrived on the scene and were posted in all directions from the building on the chance that Marston might try to make off with you, we were not in a good position to storm such a large building without a better idea of your situation and location. If we tried to break in, they could easily kill you without us even being within sight. But the appearance of the launch changed everything. It was going to get light soon, and if we were right in our surmise that your life was in imminent danger, Frances explained to me that it seemed most likely they would want you out of the way before daylight, especially if they were going to sink you in the river."

"Which they were," I said, grimly.

"The Wapping Wellingtons, was the younger Wiggins' guess," Clemens said with a smile.

"A good guess," I said, finishing my second glass of brandy and wondering if under the circumstances I had been wise to have two such large portions. I felt exhaustion creeping down my limbs like an ague, and was slightly unsettled when the coach came to a halt to let workmen pull a huge lumber-laden trolley across the road in front of us. As they got out of our way, two of the men turned, gave us big smiles, and waved. The people of London, rich or poor, were in a spirited, exuberant mood, whatever may have been occupying the minds of the occupants of our coach.

"The four of us were watching from upstream," Clemens continued, "just peeking out from between your building and the next, on the river side of the building, which was why we saw the launch come in. And when we saw Marston, or as you say the man dressed like Marston, and the other, that Denison fellow, come out with you, we knew this was probably our last chance to get you back. I saw that there was a big tug being warmed up, so I suggested to Mrs. Wakefield it might be of use. She signaled to a couple of her men down the lane on the other end of the building and they came over. She told them to see about our using the tug and they went off and in a minute one of them waved us to come on. This seemed to me to have been a very easy negotiation for borrowing such a big thing," he concluded, looking at Mrs. Wakefield.

"Under the circumstances," she said, "I wouldn't have hesitated to simply commandeer the tugboat by force, but money seemed more likely also to enlist the cheerful help of the crew, which it did."

"Except for that one thing," Clemens said, now smiling broadly. "They had the engineer and a couple other men on hand, but the pilot hadn't shown up yet."

"So you volunteered?" I asked.

"I was ready to, but actually it was Mrs. Wakefield who made the suggestion."

"I have read Mr. Clemens' books, and it seemed an irresistible idea," she said.

"I don't mean to doubt your obvious expertise, Sam," I said, "but hasn't it been a long time? Having never been in a pilot house, I have no idea what it must be like, but surely the things must change, the levers and such?"

"Thirty-some years," he said. "Closer to forty, I would reckon it now. But no, it wasn't all that different once we got underway. The real problem was that we, at least I, didn't have much of a plan. All I could think of doing was somehow getting out in front of that launch and blocking its escape so that Mrs. Wakefield and her people could, well, I guess I still don't know what I thought they were going to do."

"I'm afraid we were indeed that disorganised, Doctor," she said to me. "Our only clear goal was to keep you in sight. I hoped that Mr. Clemens could get close enough with the tugboat so that we could put a man or two in the launch. I had two armed men in the tugboat, and they were prepared to fire upon those men who had you, but of course they wouldn't risk that unless they could be sure of not hitting you."

"And in the event, none of that quite mattered," Clemens added. "The problem there was that I didn't expect Denison to come out from behind all those boats so soon. I knew he was faster, so I was just trying to get down the open channel as far as I could, you know, to try to be ahead of him when he did come out. There were a good many more boats anchored downstream and I thought he would come out from among some of them. When the launch appeared right there under me, it was all I could do to get that thing to turn. I swear, it was like piloting a glacier." He shook his head in indignation. "But that worked out too, didn't it? If I'd managed to separate the tug from you, Wiggins would have had a much harder time getting into the launch and you'd probably still be out there making curlicues back and forth across the river."

All this time we had been moving past busy construction crews and gathering crowds. Daylight was now come, but not brightness. The cloud cover remained dense and solid gray. It couldn't have been much past six in the morning, but many of the windows in the passing homes, businesses, and institutions had at least two or three faces peering out of them. In the papers Southwark was commonly celebrated, and perhaps a little condescended to, as the home turf of "'Arry and 'Arriet," the working-class people whose love for their Queen was no less heartfelt than any other citizens'. And though the flags, flowers, and other abundant decorations were indeed a trifle gaudy here, they were as generous as they could be, if largely lacking the extraordinary illuminations that were to be installed in the old city.

Our conversation continued somewhat restlessly the rest of the way to the river. Clemens and I tried to imagine what could have alerted Katy to Marston's true character during his very brief time in the house last night before he hauled us away. Two or three times Mrs. Wakefield bestowed elegant little waves, and once even a smile, on individuals we could not single out among the pedestrians we passed.

It still being quite early, I had not seen more than a few of the immense ranks of police and troops who were to line much of the procession route in only a few hours. But as we crossed Westminster Bridge, where I was invariably charmed by the sight of Parliament to the upstream side, my eyes were instead drawn to the downstream embankment, which was simply solid with the most colourful array of uniforms, flags, and banners imaginable. "Those must be the Colonials," I burst out with an almost boyish excitement. "I didn't know they were to form up here. The palace is so far! The logistics of this must have been the Devil's own nightmare!"

Clemens was just then giving me a frowning look, as if he didn't understand something I said, but before I could elaborate for him, Mrs. Wakefield spoke. "Yes, they're here to receive the colonial premiers before marching over to the palace. They will lead the procession, at least until St. Paul's. There they step aside in the shuffle that will precede the Thanksgiving Service, and when the procession resumes they will bring up the rear, following immediately behind the Queen's carriage." I was momentarily surprised to hear Mrs. Wakefield speaking so knowledgeably about the day's events, then remembered her remarks a few days earlier about her own place in London society. As we proceeded up Parliament Street, I wondered from what vantage point among the very privileged she planned to view the procession. Then it somehow seemed urgently important to my increasingly foggy thought processes to wonder if perhaps we might just join the procession in this lovely carriage of ours. With more of that lovely brandy.

Mrs. Wakefield said something else, and Clemens might have spoken again as well, but I didn't quite catch any of it. There was a buzzing and then an absolute roaring in my ears and for a woozy moment it seemed that the magnificently decorated buildings and luxuriously appointed grandstands flowed past as if they moved and we stood still.

Clemens had just leaned toward me with that same look of concern on his face when the coach stopped and the door was abruptly opened from outside. Sherlock Holmes peered in at all of us, then gave me a sterner look and said, "My dear Watson, you are all used up!" I invited my face to make what I hoped was a smile toward the approaching floor of the carriage, and as I felt the hands of Mrs. Wakefield, Sam Clemens, and Sherlock Holmes all take hold of me, for the second time in twelve hours I was excused from further awareness of the situation.

Chapter Twenty-Three
Diamond Jubilee

While I was absent from the conscious world, events developed as they tend to whether we pay attention or not, and indeed as they were planned. By mid-morning, under the ferociously organised eye of officials beyond counting, tens of thousands of troops, police, and many other vividly adorned units of adults and children arrived and stood in their designated locations, lining and thus preserving from the pressing multitudes most of the six-mile course of the Queen's coming triumphal procession. Beginning before dawn and continuing up until the last minute and beyond, the vast and brilliantly colourful public, foreign and native, rich and poor, male and female, young and old, poured into the heart of London to occupy every available line of sight, from ground level to the highest rooftops, and to pack the now-finished and gorgeously arrayed banks of grandstands that occupied every vacant space along the procession route.

The mighty lumbering bureaucratic machine behind all this excitement and grandeur, perhaps learning from unfortunate shortcomings in the Golden Jubilee ten years earlier, provided a host of mundane necessaries, including not only law enforcement and organisational direction but strategically placed mobile privies as far beyond counting as the officials themselves, and watchful nurse-ambulance teams whose primary duties would include tending to the many officials and spectators who collapsed after standing for too many hours in the June heat. It was no wonder that scores if not hundreds of the uniformed men, trussed up in beautiful but insufferably unseasonable dress costume—with perhaps a shining brass helmet to ensure that their brains were boiled apace—succumbed to a few hours of what was for them an unforgiving and hostile climate. It was one of the small and unheralded heroisms of the day that so many did not. It was, in fact, one of these happily placed medical teams to which I was turned over in Whitehall when I collapsed just as Holmes joined us in Constance Wakefield's carriage; but more on that presently.

I need not detail all the participants or the order of the grand procession, as many others, including our good Mr. Clemens, have so thoroughly done, but some general outline of the route of the procession is essential for my tale. The Queen's frailty in good part dictated the character of the procession, as she was not mobile enough for extended peregrinations on foot and would stay in her open landau throughout the trip. The procession, which began at Buckingham Palace at about 10:45 AM, was to bring the Queen from the palace into the public eye for about three hours. It first travelled west up Constitution Hill, then back east across the heart of the city via Picadilly, St. James Street, Pall Mall, the Strand, Fleet Street, and Ludgate Hill to St. Paul's Cathedral, where the Queen would remain in her carriage while the Archbishop of Canterbury officiated at the Service of Thanksgiving. Many regarded seating anywhere within view of this service as the *ne plus ultra* of the day's social trophies. From St. Paul's it was on through Cheapside to the Mansion House and a brief ceremony—The Queen again remaining in her carriage—presided over by the Lord Mayor and Lady Mayoress; then on across London Bridge to Southwark and the route that we had followed a bit of at dawn that morning in Mrs. Wakefield's carriage along Borough High Street, then on to Borough Road, and Westminster Bridge Road to Parliament Street and Whitehall. Once at Whitehall the procession would leave the streets of the city, making a left turn onto the foregrounds of the building universally known as the Horse Guards, through the tall archway that divided the Horse Guards at its narrow middle and out onto the great expanse of the Horse Guards Parade. The procession would then curve across the Horse Guards Parade to the Mall, which was literally the home stretch of the procession to the palace. The Queen was to reach the palace at about 1:45 PM.

Throughout this historic journey, the full procession occupied more than an hour passing any given point, providing ample time for the gradual crescendo of public emotion that swelled during the dazzling passage, first, of dozens of brigades and militias and guards and artilleries and aides-de-camp and equerries and other distinguished personages beyond the bounds of imagination, and reached its tumultuous peak at the first sight of the Queen in the seventeenth carriage—the previous sixteen having been laden with a glittering cavalcade of European royalty and envoys.

As I say, all of this was progressing through its long-planned course while I lay inert in a hard cot in the Admiralty building. About 9:00 AM, the Colonials came marching in all their vivid martial and cultural glory up from the embankment through the arch of the Horse Guards and on across St. James Park toward Buckingham Palace and their rightful place near the head of the then-forming procession. During the following hour the looming cloud cover, after making the most dire possible threats of rain, began to break up. About the time the Queen left the palace, the sun, as if saving itself for this particular and most royal of fanfares, broke through and shone on her and on all the adoring hordes who awaited her appearance.

I was finally roused by a raging thirst, but even on my way to a full awareness of my surroundings my thoughts had been in a wild spin. Unwonted fragments of conversation from the previous few days repeated themselves in changing order to no apparent purpose, until my now at least partly rested mind insisted they form themselves into the patterns they seemed so urgently to seek. My subconscious had been at work and was near finding a desperate sense in the madness of the past few days.

The lead soloist in this chaotic chorus in my head was Marston's voice. A few remarks from our last conversation rang in my mind as if I was hearing them for the first time:

"You'll miss all the pomp and pageantry, and of course the unplanned finale."

"She's the one who must die so visibly on her very doorstep in full view of her adoring subjects and the peoples whose oppression she has so graciously symbolised all these years."

I listened to it all again, but this time I heard more. Without meaning to, or even caring, he was telling me his plan. The "pomp and pageantry" of the procession would occur, else how could I miss it? So Marston must intend for the Queen to complete all or most of the procession before his "unplanned finale." And didn't "finale" suggest the conclusion of the procession as well? I suppose that to the extent I had given it any thought I assumed that the Queen dying "on her very doorstep" was simply a rhetorical flourish on his part, meant only to suggest that she would die in the illusory security of her great city rather than elsewhere in her Empire. But now the statement demanded a literal interpretation. She would die at the conclusion of her most triumphant public appearance. The greatest parade the world had ever seen would serve as prologue for the most shocking murder.

These intuitions inspired others. Mrs. Wakefield's explanation of the troops that we saw forming up on the embankment sorted itself from the chaff in my mind:

They will lead the procession, at least until St. Paul's. There they step aside in the shuffle that will precede the Thanksgiving Service, and when the procession resumes they will bring up the rear, following immediately behind the Queen's carriage.

My ideas about Marston's timing were reinforced by this. That the Queen was to die, as Marston put it, "in full view of her adoring subjects" could of course fit any part of the procession route. But to be in the fullest view of "the peoples whose oppression she has so graciously symbolised all these years"—to whom could that possibly refer but the Colonials, the very troops and envoys of the many nations conquered during her reign? And she would not be within the sight of those people until after the service at St. Paul's, at which time they would take up a position immediately behind her in the procession, where they would, finally, at the conclusion of the procession indeed be marching immediately behind her the length of the Mall to Buckingham Palace.

I sat up. I was alone in the room, which appeared to be a spacious office in which the furniture had been pushed to one side to make room for three or four cots like mine; the organisers of the day were well prepared. As I reached for the water carafe on the bedstand, my hand was shaking, whether from agitation or some after-effect of my night I couldn't say, but as I slopped some of the carafe's contents down my shirt while consuming the rest, other remarks and recollections fell into terrifying order in my head.

During his report on the Fenians, night before last, Marston had described dynamite as "the most brutish and stupid of weapons." Unless that was yet another of this man's mad tangle of red-herring exercises, he had inadvertently revealed his opposition to assassination by explosives. Then Denison's hatchet-face came to mind, smiling as he said "But you were both real Dead-eye Dicks—Marston's famous for it with that long cannon he always carries." That led to other memories: during our coach ride, Marston's immediate interest, which I saw now for what it almost certainly was—a morbid fascination—at Clemens' story of the pistol that had killed an American president; and Marston sitting in front of me in the warehouse resting that "long cannon" on his knee; and Mrs. Wakefield's note about the discovery of Barber's body, "dead about two days, shot precisely."

The logic, even the certainty, of my deductions were, I knew, a bit tenuous (during our most recent conversation Marston seemed not even to know who Barbert was), but as I say they were also chilling in their revelation of a kind of mad sense. Sitting there, water dribbling down my stubbled chin, with all these remembered phrases scrambling into place among themselves, I had as close to a Holmesian intuition as I ever would: Marston intended to kill the Queen at Buckingham Palace. And he intended to do it by his own hand, with the professional and un-brutish precision of an expert pistol shot.

Of course. It fit his whole character, his very reason for being. This had to be done personally to fulfill the agonies of heart and soul that he felt so deeply.

I was out of bed in an instant. I found my shoes under the bedstand. My coat was hung neatly across the back of a chair, and I grabbed it as I headed for the door, trying to remember at what point during the night I had lost my hat; probably in the coach wreck. Near the door I reached across one of the desks and turned a small clock my way. It was a little after 1; I had slept for five or six hours. My mind churned through fragments of all my recent reading about the Jubilee, trying to recall the day's schedule. Where was the Queen? When would she reach the Mall?

A plump, red-faced woman in nurse's gray-and-stripes, who had obviously just been hurrying along the hall, met me at the door. She looked me up and down, her gaze lingering on my wet shirt front, and said, "Oh my, sir, are you sure you should be up? They said you have been concussed, you know."

"Where is everybody?" I almost shouted, meaning, really, everybody named Sherlock Holmes.

She naturally mistook my meaning and answered, "Oh, I'm sorry, sir, we all so wanted to see the Queen, you know." I became aware of a low distant roar, as of a great many people singing or cheering, but decided it must be real rather than just another sign of my knock on the head. "I know we shouldn't have left you unattended, which is why I came back, just to check on you, you know, it didn't seem right leaving you, but please don't be angry, it's such a big day, and you were resting so peacefully, there seemed no harm . . ."

"No, no," I broke into her ramble, "I don't mean you. I mean the people who brought me here. I must speak to someone in authority. It is a terrible emergency."

"I'm sure I don't know, sir," she said, less apologetic as she realised that I wasn't upset with her professional lapse. I suspect she feared that I was raving. "I only came up after you were already here; in bed, I mean. They said you were very important and must have our attention, but otherwise no, I don't know. Didn't the note tell you?" She nodded back toward my bed. On the stand by the carafe I finally saw a large unmarked envelope. I rushed over and tore it open, to read, in Holmes' hand:

Watson:
    You gave us quite a fright, but the medical people here assure me you only need a big rest. Well-earned!
    Mrs. Wakefield and Mr. Clemens have given me an account of your night's many adventures, and especially of the discoveries you have made. I have already informed Mycroft, who is setting the proper wheels in motion.
    They gave you something to help you rest, so I will be surprised if you don't miss the procession. I am sorry for that, after all your fretful anticipation, but you should have the happy consolation of knowing that your worrying about the weather has paid off and the day has turned beautiful. If I am not here when you waken, I will look for you later in Baker Street.
    Mrs. Wakefield has taken Clemens to meet his hosts for the Jubilee. I am off in pursuit of one last unresolved and very vexing conspiracy, one worthy of your pen. I can already see your headline in the *Strand*: "The Case of the Persian Yankees!"
    You have done well and bravely, my friend.
                    yrs.
                    SH

"I must get to St. James, "I declared to the nurse. "The park, I mean. Right away. Please show me out of this place."

The nurse at once hurried me down hallways and stairways to the rear of the building, which I now reckoned to be part of the Foreign Office. This put me just a couple buildings south of the Horse Guards, through whose arch the Queen's carriage would pass—if it already hadn't.

My brief acquaintance over the next hour or so with the Jubilee festivities in no way prepared me to add the least detail to the many excellent chronicles of that fabulous event, to which I have already alluded. In the urgency of my mission I was only peripherally aware of what all observers agree were unexcelled glories of decoration and pageantry, except to the extent that they aided or impeded my own desperate progress toward the palace.

I stepped from the door into the gale force of the celebration. I could bear the noise, but the sudden bright light was momentarily intolerable. Stalled there, shielding my eyes, I recalled that the procession was to cross from Whitehall through the Horse Guards arch, across the Parade, and on to the straightaway of the Mall. But from my vantage I could make out little. Grandstands had been erected here as they had at so many other open spaces along the route, and I could only see the rear of those temporary structures, which, from the great noise emanating from them, I judged to be full of people who were just then witnessing the procession. There was no time for me to try to make my way over and through the superstructure of the grandstands. All I could do was assume that the Queen had not yet come through the arch, or the grandstands would already be emptying. Wherever the Queen was, my sole concern was to outrun her the length of St. James Park, to the other end of the Mall.

St. James Park is a narrow triangle of woodland perhaps two-thirds of a mile in length, with an even narrower lake running through much of that length. The forested triangle is at its widest at its east end, where it abuts the parade ground of the Horse Guards, but it narrows almost to a point at its west end, directly across the boulevard from the Buckingham Palace forecourt. I could only assume that

Marston was somewhere down there at that narrow end of the park now, close to the palace and awaiting the Queen.

My chances of finding Marston were further diminished, precisely by half in fact, because whether he was on the St. James Park side of the Mall or the other, I could only search for him on this side. Fate had put me on this side, and even had I wished to cross the Mall to the other side I was certain that at this stage of events the ranks of earnest young militiamen and yeoman and cadets who now lined both sides of the route several deep would not have tolerated any entreaty to be permitted to cross the Mall, even had it come from the most elegantly attired gentleman rather than from a disheveled lunatic, which is what I was sure they would imagine me to be. I could only go on, and trust to luck this one last time.

I later learned that an official effort had been made since dawn of that day to keep St. James Park clear of spectators. This was at least partly because of concerns that as the procession passed certain sections of the route the people along that section would attempt to stampede in all their thousands to a later section so they could witness the whole spectacle again. As the Mall constituted the final portion of the procession route, it would be the foremost target for such an insistent flood of onlookers as could easily result in many injuries among the crush of people.

Whatever the reasons for this precaution, it was true that for much of the length of St. James Park the public was only thinly represented, and those people were concentrated immediately behind the various military units that lined the Mall itself. As I hurried along, however, the numbers of spectators was steadily increasing. Despite the best official efforts there would probably be a sizeable mob close to the palace.

I managed a fairly quick jog for about a quarter mile before my lungs objected and I halted in the footpath, bent over and wheezing, and cursing myself for my poor condition. As I straightened up, there was a hand on my arm and I turned to see the Wiggins brothers giving me serious looks of concern. "Nearly lost you, we did," said Anthony, still puffing from their own run.

"Lost me? How did you ever *find* me?"

"We were waiting for you," said Frances. He was now wearing a kind of velvet beret, deep blue, but was otherwise turned out for a fox club hunt, "Never figured you'd bolt, though." This apparently didn't seem to him sufficient answer, so he added, "Mrs. Wakefield told us to stay close here, just to make sure if you needed something. But we wanted to see everything, the Queen and all, you know, and you were dead to the world in there, so we weren't paying the attention we should and had got up to the top of those grandstands. Lucky thing that Ant here," he indicated his little brother, "was checking back this way and just caught a look at you as you came out of the building. But never mind that; what's up? What's the rush?"

I saw them for the Godsend they were and said, "Do either of you know the man Marston, the one who kidnapped Mr. Clemens and me last night?" Anthony nodded, Frances shook his head. "Well, listen, we must find him. I'm just sure he's up there," I said, pointing toward the far end of the park. "He's going to try to shoot the Queen"—the brothers emitted identical little gasps at this news—"during that last bit of the procession, right before she reaches the palace. We have to stop him." Speaking to Frances, I added, "Marston looks precisely like the big bulky fellow who was in the police launch with me." It was necessary to speak loudly just to be heard over the crowd, whose increasing volume was amazing considering how few people were making it along this stretch.

"The big dumb one who jumped under the tug?" he asked.

"Right. That's the one to look for; same face, same build, same clothes, unless he's changed to throw us off." Frances nodded and we set off, walking as fast as I could manage while we talked.

"What's his plan?" said Frances.

"That's the problem. All I know is he's going to try to shoot her."

"So. No dynamite then," he said.

"Oh, yes, that's right. I'm almost positive he's planning to use a pistol. Evidently he's quite the marksman."

"Well, that limits his choices, doesn't it?"

"How do you mean?"

"Well, I mean look at them," he said, waving toward the dense crowd we could now see ahead of us. Obviously officialdom had despaired at some point and just given in to this last-minute swarming-in of people, probably from both Pall Mall and Whitehall. "Just look. There's thousands of them. What; do you suppose they'll all just stand there while this fellow waltzes up and draws a bead on the Queen?" In my haste I hadn't given this a thought. I was just trying to get there. I suppose I pictured Marston breaking through the crowd and running out into the Mall for a shot, perhaps bellowing some revolutionary nonsense to be quoted in the history books.

"Besides that," Frances said, "there's three or four rows of big cadets standing shoulder to shoulder up there, both sides the whole way. Poke a pistol past a soldier's ear to take aim, he's going to notice, isn't he? All around it seems like a pretty poor place to try to use a short barker, don't you think? I'd have thought a telescope rifle from back farther." He looked around appraisingly but didn't seem to find a high point that suited him, and corrected himself: "The trees are in the way for that, I suppose." This was true. The trees were in fact in the way for almost everything. Trees along both sides of the Mall have long spread their limbs out to meet above the middle of the Mall, so that this entire final stretch of the procession moved through a high-ceilinged leafy tunnel.

Frances' little brother was scanning the landscape at the same time. "Got to be in one of them," he said to Frances, pointing at the nearest of the many grandly spreading trees.

"Thought of that," said his sibling, "but the leaves, they're so thick. Could be a tricky shot."

"No," I said, "I think he's right. This man Marston has been preparing to do this for years. He would have taken care of the details, found just the right tree. He probably even cleared away the necessary lane in the foliage so he'd have the shot."

"But there's more people than him up in there," said the younger Wiggins. "Hain't a private box you know, just him and the squirrels? Bound to be others."

I had no immediate answer to this, and as uneasy as I was with investing our few precious remaining minutes in such a narrow search, I saw it as another matter of necessity, like accepting that I could only look for Marston on this side of the Mall. All we could do was get on with it.

"Right," I said, giving Anthony an approving pat on the shoulder. "And this may help. I believe he will want to be as close to the palace as he can get. So let's stay clear of the worst of the crowd and get to that end, and then work our way back, checking each tree."

As the brothers hared off in front of me, it seemed hopeless. Just the process of moving through the press of people and then peering up into the branches of each tree would consume too much time. But it turned out to be easy now that we had decided what we were looking for. Even before I reached the heaviest crowds where the mall ended in front of the palace, I could see Frances waving his beret at me and hurried through the mob to him.

"He's got to be in that one," he said, nodding but not pointing toward one of the last trees along the Mall. "See? There's bobbies around the trunk. That solves Ant's problem," he said, referring to his brother's question of how Marston expected to have a tree to himself. He had no doubt stationed the bobbies—for a moment I could see well enough through a gap between the onlookers to determine that there were just two of them—presumably on the pretext of having them keep the tree clear while he conducted reconnaissance from the tree's branches. The man was actually enlisting unknowing members of the London constabulary in the murder of their beloved Queen.

"We have to get past them, Frances. I must get up into that tree. Right now!" I said, though I couldn't imagine what I might say to those bobbies that would elicit anything but my immediate arrest.

"A moment," Frances said with a smile, his eye on the nearest bobbie. "Ant's on it." A few seconds later that bobbie's head suddenly disappeared behind the people between us. At the same instant, the other one turned and saw or heard something that made him hurry off into the heaviest crowd, right along the Mall. "Ant's got a mean kick. The other one will be after him now. I think we're clear."

We pushed through to the base of the tree, on the way noticing some men crouched around the fallen bobbie, who was curled up and moaning, his hands clutching his vitals. Without taking the time to look into the higher branches, I stepped onto Frances' interlaced hands and with a combination of my own reaching and his vigorous hoist found myself clinging and crouched in the main fork of the trunk. Through the broken canopy above and out over the Mall, I could see a lone silhouette, a man stretched lengthwise along a hefty branch. Marston had chosen well; his upper body was nearly above the cadets and he faced almost straight across the Mall.

What with the noise of the crowd, he hadn't yet noticed me. My leather soles slid awkwardly on the bark as I shinnied up the next branch just to the right of his. I was nearly even with his feet before something, possibly the shaking of the tree, alerted him to my presence. He looked around but at first said nothing. He had not yet drawn his pistol. As far as any observer would know he was just one among a multitude, there for a luckily elevated glimpse of his Queen.

The cheering was rising in volume and he shouted over it, "You impress me, Doctor."

I had a silly impulse to stop and express my indignation that his men had tried to kill me, but there was no

229

time left for talking even if there'd been a point in further conversation with this man. I continued to inch along the limb, deciding as I went that even if he turned his pistol on me I must at all costs get close enough to propel myself toward him, get a grip on some part of him or his clothing, and drag him from his perch. Only thus could I ensure that he was unable to make the shot. As I scooted awkwardly along the swaying branch, he shouted something else at me, but now the noise was almost unbearable and I could not make it out. From his agitated facial expression I suspect that he was warning me off but in this deafening roar of adoration and patriotism he could have cut loose at me with a pair of Maxims and the crowd below us wouldn't have noticed.

My tale is almost told, and because you already know that the Queen was not harmed that day you must forgive me one brief digression. I have already declared that I have nothing to add to the countless authoritative accounts of the Jubilee Day, but I was not entirely correct. There was this one unforgettable thing that I witnessed—this mighty imponderable thunder of joy. Indeed, many friends who had properly witnessed the entire procession would later comment on this, rather than sunlit London or the historic ceremonies or the brilliant pageantry or even the Queen herself, as the most memorable element the procession: an unimaginably loud and heartfelt outpouring of raw adulatory noise that was neither planned nor fully documented in the official histories of the day. Even in my extreme emergency I could not be unaffected by it. It was as if I could have stepped from my branch and stood buoyed up on that rising roar of jubilation. And for me the most moving feature of it was that even right then in the tree, as the incredible crescendo of cheering washed over me with the force of something visible, every few seconds there arose from beneath the tree the emotional bellow of some leather-lunged old citizen of the Empire: "Go it, old girl!"

But it was only in memory that I had time to reflect and absorb in my mind and heart the power of the greater scene. I was engaged in the greatest life-and-death struggle of my life. And as high-flown and even self-serving as that description of my situation sounds to me now, in seconds the crisis was over, and I must admit that it ended in a way that was very little to my real credit. It ended not in desperate heroics but in clumsiness and an utterly unexpected display of the best in human nature.

It took far less time to happen than it does to tell. As I came almost within reach of Marston—the two of us prone along parallel branches of the tree—I was still separated from him by a good five feet and was a bit below him. I reasoned that he had not already shot me simply because he did not yet need to; he would draw his revolver a second or two earlier than planned, dispose of me, then turn his attention to his real target as she came within range. Even from my lower vantage I could now see that he had at some time clipped for himself an almost panoramic window through the trees down onto the Mall. Some mounted unit or other was straight out from us, but there, coming up from the right, was what must be the Queen's carriage.

In an instant I could see what Marston had long known, that as close and superbly positioned as he was, this was not a simple shot. Journalists reporting on the procession invariably emphasised the grand livery of the eight cream-coloured horses, each pair with its postillion and footmen, and the perfection of every exquisite line and detail of the state carriage. They rhapsodised over the surpassing loveliness of the Princess of Wales and Princess Christian, who were seated forward in the carriage facing back toward the Queen. They even gushed over the proud bearing of the Commander-in-Chief riding just ahead of the carriage and of the Prince of Wales, the Duke of Connaught, and the Duke of Cambridge riding horseback to the carriage's immediate right and left. Above all else they praised the Queen, this unique, diminutive, and quite aged lady in her black silk and white bonnet, shaded cozily under a white parasol and nestled in the midst of this wondrous storybook finery.

An assassin's view was necessarily different, focused on the many obstructions to a clear trajectory. The princesses' hats were nearly as tall and vision-obscuring as the dress shakos worn by many of the troops. Horseback beside the carriage at any given moment might be the prince or a duke. Immediately behind Her Majesty on the carriage's rumble two more functionaries towered over her. In consequence of these various attendants, Marston's only clear opportunity was a few seconds when the carriage came directly opposite his branch. It would not be a long shot but it must be precisely timed.

I could see I was out of time to get any closer and that he must turn and shoot me within a second or two, so I drew both legs up along the sides of my branch, intending to somehow plant one or both feet underneath my body and launch myself in his direction. Just as my feet caught the branch and I began to rise into a crouch, Marston turned toward me, his right hand simultaneously reaching into his coat. As his eyes caught mine, both my feet slid loose and I pitched helplessly into the open air between us.

I will never know and I will always wonder. Was it merely the involuntary reflex of one human being reacting at some elemental level well below conscious thought to the sight of a fellow in jeopardy? Or might it have had to do with our near-fraternal bond as soldiers haunted by the same heartbreaking memories? Or was it something more immediate—perhaps some last-second soul-saving decision on his part? I will never know why, but quick as a thought Marston's right hand whipped back from under his coat and grabbed my flailing right arm. I was too heavy for him, and as he was already a bit off balance from the turn that only a fraction of a second earlier had been positioning him to kill me, he was pulled free of the limb and fell.

I landed hard, breaking Marston's fall almost perfectly as his own considerable bulk drove the breath from me. In an instant every physical outrage that had been visited upon my frame in the past few days returned in full. Leading the charge was my long-suffering shoulder, now in agony at having borne much of the shock when the ground brought my fall to an immediate halt. Where was that handsome, cheering crowd when I could have used a few of them to soften my fall? Where was the sweet oblivion of unconsciousness now that I really needed it?

Marston was up immediately. I was alert enough to feel him loosen my coat and collar, and to hear him authoritatively order the people crowding in to "Give room here! Man's hurt! Ambulance, someone! Ambulance!" Then his hand was inside my coat, where it found and removed the manuscript that I'd folded and stuffed into a pocket that morning. He whispered, "You won't need this now, Doctor, but I may yet," and was gone.

A few seconds later Frances broke through the encircling wall of people. He kneeled and whispered: "You've done it, doctor. She is saved."

Through a haze of pain and relief, all I could manage by way of a feeble response was, "Go it, old girl!" That is the last I remember.

Chapter Twenty-Four
Next to Nonsense

It was my third day in St. George's before I was in any condition to receive, much less appreciate, visitors. Holmes came and went several times by then, though I was so dull from exhaustion and medication that I could hardly converse with him, much less regale him with my experiences or grill him about his. The one time I thought to ask him for the story of the infamous "Persian Yankees" he put me off with "Once you're recovered there will be much more to tell. For now, heal thyself!"

Late that third day he had just left for an early dinner when there came a timid knock at the door and I was overjoyed to see not only Sam Clemens but Jean and Katy Leary. My obvious pleasure and enthusiastic greeting replaced their concerned expressions with broad grins and we were immediately engaged in a disorderly discussion of recent events.

The Clemens girls and their visitors had witnessed the Queen's Procession from Trafalgar Square (the celebrated Samuel Clemens had himself been a major secondary feature of Jubilee Day from his seat in the Strand, apparently not far from the seats that Holmes and I had intended to occupy), and Jean and Katy were eager to share both the highlights and the endless but equally memorable minutiae of the day.

But soon my guests turned to their bigger news, which was their imminent departure. "That thundering land-rush of constables that your friends Lestrade and Gregson unleashed on Tedworth the night before the parade was the final straw. Whatever shred of anonymity we might have maintained to that point evaporated. So," he added with what sounded much more like enthusiasm than regret, "once a few things are taken care of, we're off to Lucerne."

"And then Vienna," added Jean.

"Yes, Vienna too," agreed Clemens, cheerfully.

"So the book is done," I half asked, half declared.

"Yes," he nodded, "For better or worse, it has escaped. And even if it wasn't really the thing behind all this commotion, as I vainly thought it might be, I am even yet vain enough to imagine that it may create some commotion of its own."

"I'm eager to read it," I said. The thought of a few quiet evenings in our rooms in Baker Street reading a new Mark Twain masterpiece brought unexpected tears to my eyes.

"I shall see to it that you have one of the first copies," he said. I suffered only an easily ignored twinge of regret that in my comment I might have seemed to be angling for just that gift, and relished both the prospect of the forthcoming book and the proof of the warm friendship to which it attested.

"You've seen Holmes?" I asked.

"Oh, yes, we've had some good visits," he said.

"So you know what Marston was planning for you, or us, then. That we would serve as his Boswells?"

"Yes, and I must confess it did set me to thinking if I could have done such a thing." At my look of surprise, he went on. "Oh, I don't mean that I would have championed his lunacy. I just wondered how such a crazy tale could be told so that it would do some good. You must have wondered too, Doctor; could it be possible to produce a book about such a man without inadvertently lionizing him?"

"Yes, I have wondered the same thing. No matter how twisted his soul, by the very act of telling his terrible story you also elevate him into history," I said.

"Exactly it," he agreed. "That would never do. But what a story it is, Doctor, what a story. And for all his evil, what a man, too."

"Unforgettable. I'll give him that, if nothing more," I said.

"But speaking of Marston," he said, "the last time we spoke, in Mrs. Wakefield's carriage I guess it was, there was another question about him that I have since got answered," he said, glancing at Katy Leary.

"The note!" I said, turning to her. "Yes, I've thought of that several times when my medications were running a little thin. You must tell me, Miss Leary, your note, the one you handed through the window that night . . ." She was nodding her head and smiling as I spoke so I could tell that I didn't need to finish my question.

I believe Katy Leary had been waiting for just that question; may have come, in fact, in the hope of being asked. She smiled her broad smile and said, "He showed himself in the kitchen, Doctor. You remember he came blowing in like an army with banners, ordering you all around. It was all too fast to suit me, so I attached myself to him like a shadow."

"Yes, I remember that now," I said. "You were right behind him every time he came by the door."

"Mr. Clemens went upstairs and that Marston was talking to you at the door to the sitting room," she said, "Then all at once he tromped off to the kitchen. Constable Stuart was back there that night. I think he'd just been swilling some of the beer but he was sharp enough when Mr. Marston came in and told him that he had to take you two to see Mr. Holmes and that he, Constable Stuart I mean, should just hold on right there until more officers arrived, which was supposed to be any minute."

She stopped for a moment, staring blankly in front of her as if mentally recreating the scene. "Mr. Marston had stopped at one end of that first table, you remember the one, and Constable Stuart was at the far end, near the beer." She rolled her eyes at this and went on. "It was just luck, really. Sarah was just putting away the dishes and things. She'd gone out for something, so there was quite a pile of silver on an old traycloth on the table right in front of him. I'd come around beside him as he was giving the constable his orders, so I noticed that he was fiddling with the silver. Not just picking up this or that the way you might do when you talk, though. He was sorting it, putting things in neat little rows together. Hardly even looking at what he was doing, though; I'm sure he'd barely noticed it himself, like some old habit.

236

"Well, Doctor Watson, you can imagine my reaction to this. This could not be just chance, that both that crazy intruder and this man, who we already had doubts about, could share the same habit. It just wasn't possible. No. They were connected, in some kind of cahoots.

"Well, I'm sorry to say I let on. I was so surprised, I kept watching him for a few seconds. But when he was almost done talking to the constable when he looked down and caught himself. He did a little jump, just a kind of . . . *start*, you know, and dropped a couple spoons back in the pile. That's when he took a quick look my way and caught me looking. I've never seen a man's face look so guilty as his did right then, just for an instant as our eyes met, but then he was back to all business, finishing up his orders to the constable, who seemed not to have noticed anything."

She then spoke more deliberately: "I don't know what he thought I'd noticed. I don't think he expected that I'd just caught him out. He might have just been embarrassed that someone had, you know, caught him at that silly little habit. Anyway, I was sure that I saw more in his look than that.

"He's . . . *underestimated* me all along, of course. Seeing that was just the last straw, after what I'd already made of him and how he wasn't who he pretended to be. How could he be connected with the intruder, whatever his reason, without also being out for some harm to us? And what was this big rush all of the sudden, to get you and Mr. Clemens out of the house? It all stank, if you'll pardon the expression. So with Mrs. Clemens' help—she didn't even require me to explain, bless her—I got the note put together."

"We are deeply in your debt, Miss Leary," I said. "I hardly know how to thank you."

"Mr. Holmes has said the same," she said, beaming, and I could tell that our having said so was all the thanks she required.

Our conversation wandered here and there for another half an hour or so, when the nurse came in and announced that I required some peace and quiet. All three of my guests shook my hand, Sam Clemens last. As the two young women left the room, Clemens continued to grip my hand firmly and said, "I cannot thank you enough, you and Mr. Holmes, for the past few days." He let go of my hand and his own hands fell to his sides as he continued. "You know of my grief. I will never recover from it. Frankly, I have no intention of recovering from it. It will, I fear, be needed to fill some of the void in my life. But you, Doctor, have shaken me loose from all that, just a bit. I feel ready to write again; not just to grind my way through something the way I have been doing the last year, but to write something new."

"I'm thrilled to know that, Mr. Clemens," I said, "Among all the aches and bewilderment of the past few days, it is the most welcome of consolations."

"Oh, don't get your hopes too high," he said with a wan smile. "I'm not making a lot of guarantees about my production any more. It's just how I fill the rest of the void." And at that, Samuel Clemens turned and left the room.

A few evenings later found Holmes and me freshly arrived at Buckingham Palace. I was almost beside myself with anticipation and suffering from a rather bad case of nerves over what was to come. At no time in our recent adventure, even when I considered the possibility that we might be successful in protecting the Queen from harm, had it occurred to me that there would be such a consequence as an audience with Her Majesty—much less that the audience would be for the sole purpose of her thanking us for our service. Dressing for this extraordinary occasion had taken twice as long as usual because I was so distracted that I could barely fumble into my clothes.

Holmes, who was familiar with this great honor from previous audiences, had us there a good hour early. "Sir Arthur is personally introducing us, which means he will be the one to run through the necessaries, you know. Just to make sure we know our protocols and manners."

For obvious reasons this was not to be an audience in the grand style. Fanfare, indeed any public attention to this visit at all, must be avoided. Rather than waiting, as had so many renowned visitors of state, in the great salon surrounded by breathtaking architecture hung with priceless masterworks of art, we had been conducted to a small but perfectly appointed waiting room just off a small audience chamber. Sir Arthur himself did join us and instruct us on the niceties, then left us alone with a promise to come for us within the half hour.

Holmes seemed restless the whole way over in the carriage that was sent for us. I assumed that he too must be dealing with a bit of anxiety over the audience, but as soon as Sir Arthur left us Holmes turned to me and blurted, "Watson, there is something I must tell you. I should have done before now, but the time never seemed quite right."

"Whatever is it, Holmes? You seem distressed," I said.

"I am. Oh, it's nothing you need worry about. Things have worked out for the best. You have acquitted yourself as you always do. You are a pillar."

"You are too kind, Holmes, but then what is it?"

"Even now, I hardly know where to begin. Our very presence here is all the proof you should need of your heroic contribution to Queen and country. And yet all is not as it might seem, and you must know more before we go in there." He nodded toward the door to the audience chamber."

He looked at me in a pained way that I had never seen before, and continued. "As I am sure you have noticed, Watson, my disguises are always downward in the social realm. I mimic a great variety of characters, but they are all, in actuality, characters in the most colourful and even diminutive sense of that word. Never the lord, never the industrial magnate; always the ruffian, always the country parson."

I tried not to let my face reveal that I had never noticed any such thing, though now he mentioned it I knew that it was true, even obvious. He continued, "This is because the least of society are the least noticed. Indeed, some of my portrayals have been aimed precisely at creating the sort of character that most people not only do not notice but wish to avoid; the loud, grating personality, the ragged and foul, the wildly deranged, all tend to push our attention away, leaving me great freedom of movement."

"Yes," I agreed, "I have noticed that about the characters you imitate, but I still have no idea what this has to do with any . . ."

"I'm getting to that now, Watson. You see, this past week I learned a great lesson in the art of disguise. I have been wrong. It is, in fact, even easier to imitate those personages who inhabit the opposite extreme in society."

At the word "personages" I felt a strange chill that I could not explain, but said only, "Yes? And so?"

"I believe this is because when you seek to imitate the very great, you are imitating the familiar. People's expectations will largely be fulfilled by their confident foreknowledge. They already know well who it is they are seeing, and their subconscious minds and memories will simply trim away or smooth out any inconsistencies in those memories. And thus the person who has donned such a fantastically bold disguise has half his work done for him. His audience, no matter how huge and passionately attentive, is in no way prepared for, or even interested in, doubting what they see. Not that my job was easy, by no means. It was the most taxing disguise I have ever undertaken. My back and neck have not yet recovered from those hours of crouching into the unfamiliar posture of a much smaller frame."

At the words "the very great," followed by that about the "huge and passionately attentive" audience, the chill I'd felt grew into shock. I almost shouted "Holmes!" before remembering where I was, but the quieter "Holmes, you don't mean it!" I did utter made up in intensity for what it lacked in volume.

He looked a bit chagrined, but also rather happy about it. "We simply had to, Watson. Even without the Marston situation, by the Sunday night Mycroft was convinced that we were not in control, nor could we become so by Tuesday morning. It was partly the Persians, of course, but there were others we just had no grip on. We could not risk Her Majesty's life on such a bet."

"Say it, Holmes." I spoke quietly but firmly. "I must hear the actual words."

"Yes, that is fair to you, after all you've been through. It was I, not the Queen, in the carriage throughout the Jubilee Procession. We decided it Sunday night after that long meeting, when I was called back into the room. I'm sure you recall."

"I do, and now that you mention it I thought I saw Lord Salisbury in there with you."

"He was."

"Holmes, this is too much. I hardly know where to begin to absorb . . . You could have . . . All those people, and the princesses with you . . ." He watched me sympathetically until I gave up.

"Believe it or not Watson, I understand how you feel." We both sat silently for a moment, and then he said, in an outburst of uncharacteristic exasperation, "You know, this whole infernal affair has been next to nonsense right from the beginning!"

I shook my head and said, "Really, Holmes? That was really you?"

"It was, my dear fellow. And I feel the strangest need to apologise to you for something, but I'm not sure what it would be."

As I seemed to have nothing to add to that, he gave me a friendly pat on my good shoulder and stood up just as the door opened. It was Sir Arthur, come to conduct us into the presence of Her Majesty Victoria, Queen of the United Kingdom and Empress of India. As we rose to follow, Holmes said, "Cheer up, my friend. You did not save the Queen, but I do hope you find it gratifying, as I most assuredly do, that you saved me."

Epilogue

A few days after Sam Clemens and I said our farewells, the mail included a heavy envelope from him containing two entire issues of the *New York Journal*, in which Clemens' fanciful, vastly entertaining, and deeply affectionate version of the Jubilee Procession first appeared. Of course I still have those now-brittle papers, but I treasure even more the same text when it appeared some years later in the form of a warmly inscribed copy of a small book, *Queen Victoria's Jubilee*, privately published in a very small printing and sent me fresh from the press.

As I look back on those events, now many years ago, I still feel a slight pang of regret that except for my one frantic glimpse of the Royal carriage from Marston's tree I saw none of the great procession that so many of us had waited so long to enjoy. In that spirit I will reprint here only a few paragraphs from Sam Clemens' little book. These paragraphs once or twice bring to mind the long, event-filled night that he and I put in prior to what was an almost equally busy day for all of us.

> I got to my seat in the Strand just in time—five minutes past 10—for a glance around before the show began. The houses opposite, as far as the eye could reach, in both directions, suggested boxes in a theatre snugly packed. The gentleman next to me likened the groups to beds of flowers and said he had never seen such a massed and multitudinous array of bright colours and fine clothes.
>
> These displays rose up and up, story by story, all balconies and windows being packed, and also the battlements stretching along the roofs. The sidewalks were filled with standing people but were not uncomfortably crowded. They were fenced from the roadway by red-coated soldiers, a double stripe of vivid colour which extended through the six miles which the procession would traverse.

Five minute later the head of the column came into view, and was presently filing by, led by Captain Ames, the tallest man in the British Army. And then the cheering began. It took me but a little while to determine that this procession could not be described. There was going to be too much of it, and too much variety in it, so I gave up the idea. It was to be a spectacle for the Kodak, not the pen.

Presently the procession was without visible beginning or end, but stretched to the limit of sight in both directions—bodies of soldiery in blue, followed by a block of soldiers in buff, then a block in red, a block in buff, a block in yellow, and so on, an interminable drift of swaying and swinging splotches of strong colour sparkling and flashing with shifty light reflected from bayonets, lanceheads, brazen helmets and burnished breastplates. For varied and beautiful uniforms and unceasing surprises in the way of new and unexpected splendors, it much surpassed any pageant that I have ever seen.

I was not dreaming of so stunning a show. All the nations seemed to be filing by. They all seemed to be represented. It was a sort of allegorical suggestion of the Last Day, and some who live to see that day will probably recall this one if they are not too much disturbed of mind at the time.

There is but one more loose end to attend to, and it involves yet another Mark Twain book. As Holmes and I had time to compare notes in the weeks following those hectic Jubilee days, he told me that during my convalescence, when he spoke to Clemens on several occasions, he had no trouble convincing Clemens that no details of our adventures must be revealed, at least not for many years. "He took that well, I thought," Holmes told me. "I fancy he may even have been a bit relieved to be spared the decision of whether or not to commit some rendition of Marston's story to print."

"I share his uncertainty there," I said. "Setting aside the matters of state security, the scandal that would erupt if your role in the procession were revealed, and the untoward risk of seeming to celebrate Marston's madness, there is still a whopping good tale underneath it all."

"Oh, and that reminds me," said Holmes, "I took the liberty of encouraging him in another literary endeavor. You may recall that he once mentioned to us that he considered writing a parody of your little accounts of my exploits?"

"What I especially recall about it is that you thought such a parody much more a compliment than I did," I said.

"True, but I encouraged him. I couldn't help myself. I think that in the long run you may be pleased."

We left it at that and the subject did not arise again until a Spring morning five years later when a parcel arrived that completely distracted us for a day from whatever it was we were up to right then. It was a small and, again, warmly inscribed book by Mr. Mark Twain titled *A Double-Barreled Detective Story*, and in fact I was expecting it. I had heard from concerned and sympathetic friends that earlier that year the story had begun serialisation in an American periodical.

This was it: the very parody of my books that Clemens told us he had been considering, and that Holmes had encouraged him to write. It was accompanied by a letter that began as follows:

My Dear Dr. Watson:

The first copies of this little book just came today, and even before I got the carton open I knew to whom I should ship the first one. I feel absolutely no need to reassure you that, though the world will see this little volume as a harsh parody (and a lame one, I fear they might add), it is in fact a grateful *pastiche* (though perhaps a lame one of those, too).

As I am sure he must have told you, before my family left London five years ago Mr. Holmes admonished me to share no detail of our adventures, and I must say that when one has been admonished by Mr. Holmes, one stays admonished. It has even occurred to me that letting the world believe this book to be a determined mockery of your stories may be a good way to ensure that no thought of an association (I feel I could say "alliance") among the three of us ever could have existed.

I hope that the two of you will find it pleasant and perhaps entertaining reading, when you get around to it.

Getting around to it immediately, that very afternoon I twice read it through. And though I admit that here and there the obvious absurdly drawn parallels to my little literary flourishes stung a bit, by the time I finished it the second time I was converted to Holmes' perspective and touched by the sincerity of Clemens' gesture. It was indeed a high honor to have a great literary genius of our age devote this much trouble and energy to my work, no matter how embarrassing some of my own literary circle might find the whole thing on my behalf (they seemed almost disappointed that I didn't take it harder, almost impressed that I had the confidence to laugh off so mighty and public a ridicule as it seemed to them to be, and without question jealous of the boost in the sales of my books that such a treatment by such a literary giant would cause).

Holmes read it that evening, with growing joy and even a few outbursts of laughter. For some weeks afterwards, at no particular cue, he would suddenly strike a pose and declaim, "Far in the empty sky a solitary œsaphagus slept on motionless wing!" and we would both laugh for a very long time.

I thus close my tale of the Diamond Jubilee with the remainder of Clemens' thoughtful letter accompanying the book, partly because vanity demands that I do so, but mostly for what these words reveal about the heart of one of the great men of our age.

Doctor, I have not yet forgotten, nor have I forgiven myself for, the hurt look in your face during our first meeting there at your rooms, when I spoke down to you about your books. The worst of that moment was that at the time I did believe what you imagined me to believe. Since that day, beginning even before we parted, I have often regretted my folly in that matter. Recently, under Jean's careful instruction, I have again read all the stories you have written about you and our friend Holmes—read them as only one who has survived one of those astonishing adventures could read them.

I have no doubts now. You and your friend are originals; yes, you as much as he. If I am lucky, people will read Huckleberry Finn as long as they read Sherlock Holmes—and they will read Sherlock Holmes as long as there is even a faint memory of London.

And I'll tell you more than that. All those years to come, Huckleberry Finn and Sherlock Holmes will not merely be read. They will be put to work to accomplish many things that you and I have not imagined, could not have intended, and probably wouldn't even like. I doubt that you will believe this, but that is because you are a normal sane man. From now on, people will talk and argue and philosophise and even write books about what we have said in our books. Imagine that; these people will be thoughtful and erudite, some of them wiser than either of us ever hoped to be. And most of what they say about you or me or Huckleberry Finn or Sherlock Holmes will in fact be mostly about themselves instead.

The entire family, and especially Katy, send their best to the both of you.

Yrs ever
Mark Twain

Acknowledgments

What a treat it is to participate in a small way in the Holmes' tradition. The original stories themselves, the so-called Canon, have become the heart of an immense body of literature—pastiches, parodies, tributes, and a host of studies both light-hearted and scholarly—that testify to the joyous fascination we have with our friends at 221B. I am grateful to many people for their help with *Diamond Jubilee*.

Thanks most of all to my spouse and partner-in-all things, Marsha Karle, with whom I have spent several months exploring England; who listened patiently, enthusiastically, and creatively to my plans for the book; who gave the manuscript its smartest reading; who created the cover art for the original edition; and who is my life.

The staffs of several libraries, including Montana State University, Ohio State University, and University of Colorado were quite helpful with various aspects of the research. In a more diffuse but no less valuable way, repeated rambles in the British Museum, the British Library, the Tate Britain, The Victoria and Albert Museum, The Bodleian Library, The Ashmolean Museum, and a number of other British institutions were directly enriching for this project.

Though they may not have noticed, Rick Balkin, Bob Bender, Ken Cameron, Robert DeMott, Peter Hayes, Andrew Herd, Barbara Herd, Bruce Morton, Dianne Russell, Jeremy Schmidt, Judith Schnell, Kim Allen Scott, and the late Kit Ward provided a great variety of information, advice, and encouragement during the writing of the book.

The staffs of the Hyde Park Hilton, Trafalgar Hilton, and Waldorf Hilton did much to make our various visits to London the delight that we'd always dreamed they would be. London's congenial and eagerly opinionated taxi drivers maintained their famous reputation for expertise about the geography and lore of their magical city.

Anita Fore, Ryan Fox, Valerie Kaplan, Nicole Vazquez, and Michael Gross of the Authors Guild, of which I am a grateful member, were forthright and supportive in their guidance regarding one or the other edition of the book. Members of the Mark Twain Forum, of which I am also a happy member, are always entertaining, and responded promptly to requests for citations and related information.

Emilie Quast at the Wilson Library, University of Minnesota, was helpful with several matters of publishing procedure, as well as putting me on to a publisher for the second edition.

Steve Emecz at MX Publishing in London was kind enough to welcome the book into their amazing catalog of Holmesian adventures, thus giving *Diamond Jubilee* a further and much broadened opportunity for readers of this slightly revised second edition.

Last, Rick Balkin, my friend and literary agent for more than a quarter of a century, has helped me with my work in so many ways that dedicating a book to him seems small thanks, but I am pleased to be able to do at least this much.

About the author

Paul Schullery is the author, co-author, or editor of more than 40 books of history, natural history, essays, and memoirs. He has received the Wallace Stegner Award from the University of Colorado Center of the American West; honorary doctorates of letters from Ohio University and Montana State University; a Panda award for screenwriting from Wildscreen International, Bristol, UK; and other prestigious awards from professional societies and agencies. Paul is married to the artist Marsha Karle, with whom he has collaborated as author and illustrator on several books.

Also from MX Publishing

MX Publishing is the world's largest specialist Sherlock Holmes publisher, with over a hundred titles and fifty authors creating the latest in Sherlock Holmes fiction and non-fiction.

From traditional short stories and novels to travel guides and quiz books, MX Publishing cater for all Holmes fans.

The collection includes leading titles such as _Benedict Cumberbatch In Transition_ and _The Norwood Author_ which won the 2011 Howlett Award (Sherlock Holmes Book of the Year).

MX Publishing also has one of the largest communities of Holmes fans on Facebook with regular contributions from dozens of authors.

www.sherlockholmesbooks.com

Also from MX Publishing

Our bestselling books are our short story collections;

'Lost Stories of Sherlock Holmes' , 'The Outstanding Mysteries of Sherlock Holmes', The Papers of Sherlock Holmes Volume 1 and 2, 'Untold Adventures of Sherlock Holmes' (and the sequel 'Studies in Legacy) and 'Sherlock Holmes in Pursuit', 'The Cotswold Werewolf and Other Stories of Sherlock Holmes' – and many more……

www.sherlockholmesbooks.com

Also from MX Publishing

"Phil Growick's, 'The Secret Journal of Dr Watson', is an adventure which takes place in the latter part of Holmes and Watson's lives. They are entrusted by HM Government (although not officially) and the King no less to undertake a rescue mission to save the Romanovs, Russia's Royal family from a grisly end at the hand of the Bolsheviks. There is a wealth of detail in the story but not so much as would detract us from the enjoyment of the story. Espionage, counter-espionage, the ace of spies himself, double-agents, double-crossers...all these flit across the pages in a realistic and exciting way. All the characters are extremely well-drawn and Mr Growick, most importantly, does not falter with a very good ear for Holmesian dialogue indeed. Highly recommended. A five-star effort."
The Baker Street Society

www.sherlockholmesbooks.com

253

Also from MX Publishing

The American Literati Series

The Final Page of Baker Street
The Baron of Brede Place
Seventeen Minutes To Baker Street

"The really amazing thing about this book is the author's ability to call up the 'essence' of both the Baker Street 'digs' of Holmes and Watson as well as that of the 'mean streets' of Marlowe's Los Angeles. Although none of the action takes place in either place, Holmes and Watson share a sense of camaraderie and self-confidence in facing threats and problems that also pervades many of the later tales in the Canon. Following their conversations and banter is a return to Edwardian England and its certainties and hope for the future. This is definitely the world before The Great War."
Philip K Jones

www.sherlockholmesbooks.com

Also from MX Publishing

The Detective and The Woman Series

 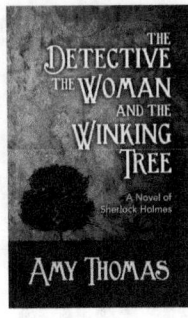 

The Detective and The Woman
The Detective, The Woman and The Winking Tree
The Detective, The Woman and The Silent Hive

"The book is entertaining, puzzling and a lot of fun. I believe the author has hit on the only type of long-term relationship possible for Sherlock Holmes and Irene Adler. The details of the narrative only add force to the romantic defects we expect in both of them and their growth and development are truly marvelous to watch. This is not a love story. Instead, it is a coming-of-age tale starring two of our favorite characters."
Philip K Jones

www.sherlockholmesbooks.com

Also from MX Publishing

The Sherlock Holmes and Enoch Hale Series

The Amateur Executioner
The Poisoned Penman
The Egyptian Curse

"The Amateur Executioner: Enoch Hale Meets Sherlock Holmes", the first collaboration between Dan Andriacco and Kieran McMullen, concerns the possibility of a Fenian attack in London. Hale, a native Bostonian, is a reporter for London's Central News Syndicate - where, in 1920, Horace Harker is still a familiar figure, though far from revered. "The Amateur Executioner" takes us into an ambiguous and murky world where right and wrong aren't always distinguishable. I look forward to reading more about Enoch Hale."
Sherlock Holmes Society of London

www.sherlockholmesbooks.com

Also from MX Publishing

When the papal apartments are burgled in 1901, Sherlock Holmes is summoned to Rome by Pope Leo XII. After learning from the pontiff that several priceless cameos that could prove compromising to the church, and perhaps determine the future of the newly unified Italy, have been stolen, Holmes is asked to recover them. In a parallel story, Michelangelo, the toast of Rome in 1501 after the unveiling of his Pieta, is commissioned by Pope Alexander VI, the last of the Borgia pontiffs, with creating the cameos that will bedevil Holmes and the papacy four centuries later. For fans of Conan Doyle's immortal detective, the game is always afoot. However, the great detective has never encountered an adversary quite like the one with whom he crosses swords in "The Vatican Cameos.."

"An extravagantly imagined and beautifully written Holmes story"
(**Lee Child**, NY Times Bestselling author, Jack Reacher series)

Also from MX Publishing

During the elaborate funeral for Queen Victoria, a group of Irish separatists breaks into Westminster Abbey and steals the Coronation Stone, on which every monarch of England has been crowned since the 14th century. After learning of the theft from Mycroft, Sherlock Holmes is tasked with recovering the stone and returning it to England. In pursuit of the many-named stone, which has a rich and colorful history, Holmes and Watson travel to Ireland in disguise as they try to infiltrate the Irish Republican Brotherhood, the group they believe responsible for the theft. The story features a number of historical characters, including a very young Michael Collins, who would go on to play a prominent role in Irish history; John Theodore Tussaud, the grandson of Madame Tussaud; and George Bradley, the dean of Westminster at the time of the theft. There are also references to a number of other Victorian luminaries, including Joseph Lister and Frederick Treves.

www.ingramcontent.com/pod-product-compliance
Lightning Source LLC
Chambersburg PA
CBHW070857250626
47159CB00003B/1095